Cruel Savior

SINS OF WRATH MC

E.M. GAYLE

GYPSY INK BOOKS

CRUEL
Savior

E . M . G A Y L E
NEW YORK TIMES BESTSELLING AUTHOR

Don't Miss Out!

Would you like to read my New York Times Bestselling book for free and meet another hot alpha?

Visit my website at emgayle.com/newsletter to sign up for my newsletter and claim your free book!

Chapter One

Amanda

I SAT STARING out over the swimming pool, unseeing the crystal-clear blue water or the way the rare winter sunshine reflected across it. I was lost deep in my thoughts of self-pity and worthlessness.

It had been weeks since my return, and I still didn't have a damned clue as to what came next.

"Are you just going to sit there again all day? You do realize your behavior is pretty pathetic, right?"

I didn't bother to look up at my latest stepmother. What was she? The second or the third since I'd left home as a teenager? I couldn't keep track. Hell, why bother?

Only, this one seemed hellbent on getting into my business.

Not that she was wrong. It was pathetic to sit in my father's house day after day and do nothing. Although didn't I deserve some time off after what I'd been through? Where was my pat on the back for a job well done? I shook my head. My thoughts were getting deeper and darker by the day.

No government agency was going to thank me ever again. My role as an undercover operative had come to a whimpered end. My boss, however, had made it a point to remind me on my way out the door, that anyone else would have gone to jail for the shit I pulled.

They didn't know the half of it. Nor did they care to bother finding out. Everything with them was by the book, and I'd pretty much thrown the book in their faces when I got myself trapped in a mafia-controlled snare.

Hell, I might still be there if the man in charge hadn't been killed.

"Mind your own business, uhh—" Fuck. My mind drew a blank. What was her name?

"Theresa," she shrieked. "I've told you like sixteen times. Are you brain damaged or something?"

I blinked, still not bothering to turn in her direction and give her my full attention. I was something.

"Excuse me, Ms. Turner."

We both turned to James, my father's butler. He stood there holding a black cardboard box in his hand. The man was old as dirt and had been with our family for as long as I could remember. His gaze met mine instead of hers, and I recognized his look of sympathy. But why? It's not as if he had any details about what happened to me. No one did. Sure, some of them thought they knew me. But they were wrong.

"A package just came for you."

"Ooh, a package?" Theresa nearly squealed. No doubt she thought whatever inane bullshit she'd ordered from Amazon this time had arrived. However, just before she could grab the box from James, he pulled it away from her.

"I'm sorry," he said. "I meant it's for Ms. Turner, not Mrs. Turner."

I snickered, and my stepmother turned to me with a vicious glare. "Don't be a bitch, A-Man-Da." Before I could decide if I wanted to respond or not, I didn't, she turned back to James and yanked the box from his hand. "What does she care about a package? She hasn't moved from that chair in hours."

James looked at me apologetically and I gave him a slight nod. It didn't matter. I wasn't expecting anything, and if it kept Theresa from bitching at me, she could open the package and have at it.

He turned and disappeared as quietly and as quickly as he'd arrived. I had to admit that I admired that about him. The reason he'd lasted all these years was his ability to blend into the background. My father was rather crotchety about his staff, but James, he seemed to like. Or at least tolerate.

I turned back to the pool and beyond. Here in Washington, it rained more often than it didn't, so it was a necessity to have an indoor pool. However, my father was an outdoorsman at heart, so the room that housed the pool was completely made of glass. It provided the perfect view of his vast property and the snowcapped cascade mountains in the background.

I hated to admit it, but I was willing to tolerate the latest stepmother because of this. My home. As long as I didn't leave the property, I could breathe freely. But beyond the gates that kept us secure, there were constant memories that threatened my sanity.

"Jesus, this package looks soaking wet and banged all to hell. I swear, no one cares about anyone's property but their own. The shipping company could obviously care less about causing any damage."

Theresa rambled, and while I heard her words, I did my best to tune her out.

I'd grown up here on the outskirts of Sultan, Washington. A tiny town that may only be an hour away from Seattle but felt like an entirely different world. Life moved at a different pace here and everyone knew everyone. Which meant nothing was really private here. My father had inherited a fortune from his father after the decades of the lumber boon, and the Turner family had pretty much secured their place as the first family of Sultan.

And while my father ran a decent sized ranch here, the Turner fortune continued to grow mostly because he had a passion for investments. As in, he owned freaking everything. Or at least that's the way it seemed.

From the—

"What the hell? Oh my—" Theresa didn't finish. She started screaming bloody murder. Her ear-piercing screams nearly made me fall off my chair. I had to jump and make sure she wasn't currently being stabbed to death. She wasn't, but there was blood, and lots of it. Her hands were covered, and the terror on her face startled even me.

I ran around the pool and grabbed her by the shoulders, but nothing stopped her screams. "Jesus Christ, Theresa. What is wrong?" Tears streamed down her face and there seemed like no hope of her getting out a coherent sentence. Her breathing had already gone straight into erratic and she was either going to have a heart attack and drop dead or pass out.

I hoped for the latter. The woman was meaner than a snake, but that didn't mean I wanted her to die. Plus, I didn't want to be the one with her if that happened. My father would probably kill me. Or at the very least cut me off again.

I shook her harder. "Look at me, Theresa. Focus. What is wrong? Where are you bleeding?" I tried surveying her body for some sort of injury, but she refused to be still and was stronger than I expected in the throes of panic.

I grabbed her face and turned it until she was forced to meet my gaze. "What the fuck is going on? I can't help you if you don't take a damned breath and tell me what is wrong."

Her screams quieted, but the incoherent whimpers did not.

"Take a breath. A deep one and hold it." She sort of followed my directions, but her eyes were unfocused and wild. Whatever it was, she was scared witless. I turned and surveyed the area around her and that's when I finally noticed the package laying on its side, facing away from me. A black cardboard box.

Something in my gut twisted, and her fear transferred to me. Something in that box that had sent her over the edge. I wanted to know—needed to know, but my instincts screamed that I didn't want to know.

I turned back to her. "I'm going to check it out, okay? Do you think you can stand here quietly while I do?"

She shook her head frantically as her body shook. I'd never seen this woman speechless, and without an insult for me hovering on her lips. It unnerved me to see her reduced to this whimpering mess.

"I have to," I said as gently as I could. "Whatever it is, we'll deal with it." Her eyes widened and her body shook. "I'll deal with it," I promised. Surely whatever it was, I could handle it. I was a trained operative. I'd been undercover and seen and endured the worst of humanity. Of course, she didn't know that.

Nobody did. I'd tried to talk to a therapist, but I'd yet to get the words past my lips. I wanted to pretend everything I'd endured on the Mazzeo compound didn't happen. Or at the very least, it had been worth it, because Frank Mazzeo had lived up to his end of the bargain. My sister remained safe and happy at boarding school without ever realizing how much her life had cost me.

It was worth the price, I reminded myself. I did that on the daily. When I'd been on the job, I'd swept everything under the rug. Since then—not so much.

Enough.

I shook those thoughts from my head. I had a scared woman in my hands who looked like she'd break at any moment. And if that happened, the consequences would fall on my shoulders—again.

Whatever was in that box...

"I'm going to help you into this chair, and then I'm going to investigate. I'll call the butler to bring something to clean you up and a first aid kit. "Can you tell me if you're hurt? Do I need to call for an ambulance?"

That seemed like a dumb question, but I could find no source of blood other than her hands. What the hell had arrived in that package?

I eased Theresa into one of the lounge chairs, and even though she'd officially dissolved into a steady stream of tears, I had to investigate. I had to believe that whatever happened, she'd be all right for a few seconds.

Turning back to the package, I could now see a pool of blood forming underneath the box. It seemed like a lot...

Careful not to touch anything, I stalked closer until the opening came into view. My heart constricted and nearly stopped beating. Maybe it did. My chest constricted so hard nothing would surprise me. It wasn't an animal or a limb or anything that benign.

It was a human head. A male human head. And

despite the blood oozing from the box, I recognized it. Paul Danvers. One of the men who'd worked with me on the Frank Mazzeo task force. I was pretty sure he worked for the FBI.

Fuck.

I bent at the waist and tried to fight off the rising nausea. I'd seen dead bodies. Hell, I'd seen people killed in front of my eyes. But this was a severed head and it had come to my house, addressed to me.

I tried to stand and lost it, throwing up all over the crime scene. Whoever had done this...

My stomach jerked and pulsed until nothing else came along with the heaves. Of course, it was that shining moment both my father and James arrived.

"What the hell is going on? What was all that screaming for?"

Chapter Two

Axel

STANDING IN THE SHADOWS, I watched the man approach our clubhouse. Since he'd made it past security and driven in like he owned the place in his fucking Jaguar, someone must have been expecting him. It wasn't often our club let outsiders in this area. Usually, if the club or its president had some business to conduct with nonmembers, he took care of it at the casino on the backside of the property.

This change in procedure didn't bode well and with fucking Turner being the civilian in question, I didn't think the news would be good. The last time he'd come here, he'd hired us to find his daughter and that had turned into an epic shit show. Especially when it turned out she wasn't missing at all. She'd gone off and gotten herself mixed up with the fucking mafia.

I shook my head and pushed her out of my thoughts. Whatever Turner wanted, JD could take care of it and leave me the hell out of it. The club had enough on our plate at the moment. Since the death of Frank Mazzeo, we'd barely had a day of peace. Not that anyone expected killing the head of the Seattle mafia would halve their operations.

No, crime like theirs went on and someone rose up out of the ranks and took over. Although the new man in charge rarely hid behind the cloak of some corporation now only known as the collective. What the hell did that even mean?

Lame is what I called it. I dropped my cigarette to the dirt and stomped on it with the toe of my riding boots. The soft pelt of the winter rain sounded above me on the metal roof, masking any sounds I made and keeping me hidden from anyone who didn't know where to look.

Turner climbed out of his car and every muscle in my body went rigid. I really had hoped to never see the man again. As unrealistic as that was since he also lived in Sultan, a man could fucking wish, couldn't he?

I was about to reveal myself and stop him from invading our private space when my phone chimed in my pocket. I cursed—silently so as not to give away my position—and pulled the damned thing out of my pocket.

I actually didn't need to see it to know who it was from. I had a specific ring tone for the president.

You need to stop stalking the man and come inside. He has a job for us and we need to hear him out.

Fuuuck me.

That tightening of my gut earlier screwed down harder. If this had anything to do with Mandy, Amanda, Kelly, or whatever she might be calling herself these days, I was out. And I would have no problem letting JD know my position on this. Once had been enough. If she was back in town, she had better keep as far away from me as she could.

She'd fucking walked out of my life without so much as a goodbye. I hated her for that shit. But when her fucking father told me she'd gotten rid of the baby, I hated her with the passion of a thousand suns.

Ten years was not enough time to get over it, and it sure as fuck wasn't long enough to forget.

With anger building inside me, I pushed off the wall and made my way into the clubhouse. I didn't see Turner in the main room. Only a few of my club brothers and some of the women who hung around all the time. I shook my head and made my way to the conference room. He had to be kidding me, right?

I popped the door open with more force than necessary and the door hit the wall with a decent thud. I wouldn't disrespect my president with a raging temper tantrum in front of someone who didn't belong here, but I would make it clear to everyone in the room that this shit was not worth my time.

"Thanks for joining us." JD smirked, the cock of one eyebrow a clear warning that I needed to settle down. Something not likely to happen if this went the way I expected it to go.

"I didn't know we had a meeting."

"Turner has an urgent request for us. I thought you should be here for the whole story, so it didn't have to be repeated secondhand."

I turned to our guest, and at the sight of his scowl in my direction, I had to swallow down the desire to tell him to fuck off and walk out. He didn't like me any more than I liked him, so why he kept coming to the club for help made no damned sense. Except that if you had a situation that needed to be handled outside the law there weren't too many other people to go to.

Finally, he looked away and leaned forward, placing his hands on our sacred table that held our club emblem on it. Something about that only riled me further. He needed to get the fuck on with it.

"We had an incident out at the ranch today, and to put it frankly, it's way more complicated than my personal security team or the Sultan police department can handle."

"And?" I asked, when he paused for too long without elaborating.

"A package was delivered to the house, and my wife had the unpleasant experience of opening it. She nearly lost her mind. It was her screaming that my entire security team responded to, and then they called me. Finding my wife with blood on her hands and arms freaked out our entire staff, and now half of them are scared to come inside the house."

This time, JD beat me to the next question.

"What was in it?"

His face paled and his lips compressed into a grim line as he pulled his phone out of his front jacket pocket and swiped his finger across the screen. "I can show you."

He handed the phone over to JD.

"Holy, fuck. Is that—" JD touched the screen with two fingers and zoomed in on the image. "Who is it?"

I couldn't take it anymore and I stood to round the table.

"A former coworker of my daughter."

I froze mid step, changed course, and retook my seat. Those were not the words I'd wanted to hear. Only my respect for my president kept me from walking straight out the door. JD gave me a warning look and handed over the phone.

Jesus hell. Good thing I had a strong stomach. Based on the conversation thus far, I don't know what I'd expected. But a bloody severed head in a box was definitely not it.

"Who delivered it?" I zoomed into the picture as well, only I wasn't trying to examine the head, I was looking at the surrounding area. There were bloody footprints, possibly some blonde hair stuck in some of the blood. Probably fingerprints mixed in too.

"Camera footage shows a private delivery company

brought it in. Our usual guy, too. Nothing out of the ordinary in that respect."

I glanced up at Turner. "This looks pretty out of the ordinary."

He frowned. "I meant the delivery guy. The head in the box? I don't even know what to say. My wife has been practically catatonic since it happened. My daughter is refusing to talk about it, which is par on course with her behavior since we got her back. She never fucking leaves the house. But is this some kind of death threat?" he asked, his eyes narrowing.

I placed the phone down on the table and slid it a little too hard in the direction of Turner. He caught it, although barely.

"I'm going to take a guess and say this is probably something the FBI should handle. Can't your *daughter* call them and get them to take care of this?" The word daughter barely made it past my lips, and I was well aware it sounded about as eloquent as rocks going through a blender. "If this is her co-worker, they will want to handle this. You probably won't even need to involve the Sultan police."

He shook his head. "After she was shot on the job during her last case, Amanda was put on medical leave and expects to be terminated as soon as that officially ends. Those assholes won't even take any of her calls. Since then, she's all but stopped talking to anyone."

"No one here gives a shit about her employment status." The words slipped out before I could stop them.

I glanced at both Turner and JD to find them both watching me intently.

"I get that you don't appreciate how the last job turned out. However, I did fairly compensate you for all your work. *More* than fairly. No one knew in advance exactly what we were getting into, but that's why people come to you in the first place, isn't it?

"Yes." JD answered gruffly. "But I have to admit, the investigation of this guy's death should be handled by the FBI."

"And it will," Turner responded. "But what I won't get from them is any help protecting my family. And I have a gut feeling that my security team isn't equipped for this kind of trouble either. Hence why I'm darkening your doorstep again. Trust me, I don't want to be here anymore than you want me here."

That last bit had been directed at me. At least we could agree on one thing. "Then maybe you shouldn't have come."

"Let's talk about what you want from us," JD interrupted again. I was going to catch hell later for him having to play referee between me and Turner. It was bullshit for me to hold a grudge against the man simply because he was Amanda's father. But there was a lot of water under that bridge and I couldn't look at him without feeling like I was going to drown in it.

"First, I'd like to keep my family safe. With my own security team looking over their shoulders every second, I don't have a lot of confidence."

"Then hire another one."

He nodded. "I will. But that's going to take time, and they won't know this town. Your club does. Anyone who's been here as long as you all will know when a stranger is in town. Until I have time to get a secondary team in place, I need your help."

"I can certainly handle putting a few extra guns out at your place. And I can have Tel make sure your electronics are up to snuff. There's no one better than him."

"I'd really appreciate that. I think I'm going to have to send my wife off to her family in California until this blows over. But Amanda, on the other hand, she's not handling any of this very well. I'm concerned."

My gut twisted at his assessment of his daughter. Did anyone really know what went on with her? At one time I'd thought I did and she'd proven me wrong in about the worst way possible.

"Are you saying she needs a bodyguard?"

The air in the room felt like it got sucked out by the tension now filling it. I even caught myself holding my breath. I didn't want him to say the words and I didn't want JD looking to me like I wanted to do something about it. He would be wrong. They were all wrong about me. I did not carry a torch for my ex.

A lot had changed in ten years. I wasn't the same kid who'd thought having a baby with my teenage girlfriend was my ticket to proving I would be a better old man than mine. Or that getting her pregnant in the first place was a goddamned turn on. I'd been a foolish fucking idiot.

"I'm saying she needs something. She's planning to

move out of the main house and into the hunting cabin at the mountain edge of our property. I honestly don't know what's going on in her mind these days. But whatever the Feds did to her, it messed her up. Call it fatherly instinct or whatever. But I have a feeling she's going to do something drastic.

Like disappear in the middle of the night without a fucking trace and never come back?

Chapter Three

Axel

"DON'T START." JD was headed down the hall in my direction and I could feel the building vibrating with his irritation. Or maybe that was me. Turner had left after JD reassured him that we could handle whatever he needed until the time came he got his new team in place.

"You're being an asshole. You know as well as I do that Turner is important to this town, and without his assistance, our club would not continue to fly under the radar."

I looked to the sky and mumbled under my breath for some patience. "That's fine. Do whatever needs to be done. Just leave me out of it this time. I've got my hands full anyways."

He shook his head. "No can do. Everyone else is already stretched about as thin as they can be. This Seattle situation has us all on our toes. So, it's going to take the entire club working together to work both cases at the same time."

I'd known that was coming. I'd already worked the logistics in my head as JD finished up with Turner. "Speaking of..." I didn't want to be the one to deliver the latest and greatest, but that was all part of the job. "Another coffee stand went down last night. Molotov cocktail. Just got the news. That makes three in just under two weeks."

"Fuck." JD shoved his hands in his hair. It had more and more gray over the last few months. "We have got to figure out who is targeting us. I tried to write the first two off as coincidence, but three? No fucking way. Any more word on that new club in Seattle?"

I shook my head. "Just that they've been recruiting for a while and they have picked up some heavy artillery when it comes to their new members. Lots of ex-cons with less than honorable backgrounds. Some of them applied with us and were turned down."

"Just fucking great. We need to get some information on all of them that we know of."

"Already on it. Intel is working his magic as we speak. We should have enough information put together before church on Sunday." Yes, it was ironic that motorcycle clubs liked to call their official meetings church, and that we preferred to have them on Sunday afternoons. Not that we gave a damn what anyone thought.

We all needed it. Especially these days. Taking down Frank Mazzeo had been a bitch and a half, and when JD's son got mixed up in Cullotta family business, the club had been pulled into that mess too. Although I had to admit that two recent trips to Vegas had ended up in some good times. While I loved small-town life, and would never give it up, partying in a wild town like Vegas sure had its perks.

Especially the tall blonde ones.

"Perfect. Sounds like we've got our work cut out for us. But about this Turner thing. You have got to quit antagonizing that one. What happened between you and her was a long time ago. It's time to put it behind you."

I was half irritated and half comforted by his words. I had a lot of respect for JD, and in many ways he'd been the father I'd never really had. On the outside, looking in, some people might not think that was a good thing. Our president had a dark history that, at times, still seemed to plague him. But the man had rebuilt this club after tragedy and gave us a very solid purpose.

Yes, we still broke the law. That was never going to change. For one, we ran an illegal casino on our property that could land all of us in prison for a very long time. Except that much of the state's leadership frequented our establishment so it seemed unlikely that would be our downfall. Our propensity to serve justice however, that was a bit trickier.

But it was that work that made it easier to sleep at night.

"I have no desire to revisit the past. I've put it behind me and moved on. But that doesn't mean I want to spend time with her. She helped Mazzeo and jeopardized our entire operation in Vegas. She could have gotten any one of us killed. She got Izzy shot."

"Nevertheless, her father is our silent supporter. Without his assistance, we would not have made as much progress as we have. I will not jeopardize that relationship. Is that going to be a problem?"

He shouldn't have to ask. "Yeah. I'm good. Although, I gotta say, a severed head is some serious business. Not sure how many people out there would cut the head off an FBI agent and have it delivered in broad daylight to a former CIA agent. That sounds like some serious revenge."

"Agreed. Which is why I am assuming Tel is already cross-referencing any cases they worked on together."

I couldn't help but laugh. We knew each other well, and I was proud of our club and how it operated like a well-oiled machine. "Assume away," I laughed again.

"Now we need to make the assignments. Who's available to start tonight?"

Me, Zook and Tel were the only ones not already on duty in one capacity or another. It was supposed to be a long overdue night off, but I'd already bid that sayonara halfway through the meeting with Turner. "I gave a heads up to both Zook and Tel. We'll head over to the Turner ranch and meet with their security team. See what we can do to beef things up."

JD nodded. "That's good. That's good. But..." I clenched for the bomb. "I want you on the girl." He held up his hand before I could get a sound out of my mouth. "I know. I get it. But it's time to put this behind you once and for all. Talk to her if you have to. Just get it done. Tel is going to be too busy with security systems, and I want Zook at his back. That only leaves you, and if I'm honest, you might be the only one who can handle it. Bad blood or not, at least you won't be over there thinking with your dick. Also, this isn't up for debate."

I ground my teeth and forced myself to keep quiet. JD was my president and he'd made his decision. There were times to fight about it, and times to suck it up. "Fine. But I'd like it noted I think this is a bad idea. I'm not going to treat her like some goddamned princess who needs kid gloves. You make it clear with Turner that I'm in charge over there and whatever it takes to get the job done is what will be done."

JD nodded again. "I would expect nothing less. Don't worry, I'll get Turner on board. Just try not to blow shit up, okay? I have a feeling this fight with Seattle is going to spill into Sultan soon, and when it does, we'll need Turner to back us."

On that final note, JD turned and headed out the back door. Presumably to the big cabin out back where he lived. Almost all of us lived on the property. Some years ago, I'd had the idea to populate the property with a nice collection of hand-built tiny houses and mid-sized cabins. Depending on your rank in the club, you were assigned one or the other. It was yours whether you lived in it or not.

The property had once housed a lumber mill and lots of housing for their seasonal employees, so we also had a pretty damn nice bunkhouse for the prospects and guests. Everything was spread out so that no one felt confined or lacked in privacy. I turned in the opposite direction of JD and headed towards my cabin. If I was going to be spending all my time at the Turner ranch until this situation resolved itself, I needed to pack some shit.

I walked through the quiet woods with a light misting rain falling on me, and the fog clinging to the trees around me. The Pacific Northwest had a vibe that I couldn't get enough of. One minute, it might be light and bright, and the next it could be shrouded in a doom and gloom that I enjoyed almost as much as the bike riding weather.

A few minutes later I entered the clearing at my cabin and took a deep, relaxing breath. I loved this place. To most it might seem a little too rustic, but with one bedroom and all the amenities I could possibly want, it suited my lifestyle perfectly. It also gave me quick access to the club and my brothers there.

My cellphone pinged in my pocket and I pulled it out to read the message. Zook and Tel were ready to go and waiting at the front gate. I shoved it back into my jacket and headed into my bedroom. The weight of dread in my gut solidified into a hard, rotten ball.

There was no point in delaying the inevitable. Me and Amanda Turner were about to crash together in the worst possible way.

Chapter Four

Amanda

AFTER HOURS of studying the map of the surrounding area, I was struggling not to pass out from straight up exhaustion. I'd stayed up all night trying to piece together a plan. I'd even tried to call one of my contacts at the Bureau, but my call had been refused. I urged my father to call the police—at least then Danvers' death would get reported appropriately, and dear old Dad wouldn't get charged down the road for obstruction of justice.

My stomach turned again with the memory of my former coworker's head spilling out of a box and onto the patio floor. It didn't help that my ears still rang from all the screaming Theresa did. What a freaking nightmare.

She'd screamed at my father that I had to go, and I honestly didn't blame her. Whoever had killed Danvers had to be some kind of psychopath. I didn't want them near my family any more than she did. However, my father had been adamant that I not leave so we'd compromised and I'd moved out here. First, though, I'd made a big show of packing my bags and dragging them out to my car in case anyone was watching the house.

I didn't want anyone but my father to know exactly where I'd gone. So, after hours of driving to Seattle and to various spots in the city and changing cars in a garage not connected to anyone that could be traced to me or my family, I'd driven the backroads to arrive at my father's hunting cabin on the edge of his property.

Since I'd never been here, I didn't know what to expect, but I should have known it would not be a rustic shack. While it *was* filled with taxidermy from my father's hunting expeditions, the rest of the place was as luxurious as it could get. It may have been smaller in size than the main house, but it rivaled it in every other way.

I'd bypassed the master bedroom completely and chosen one of the oversized guest rooms as my base camp. I had my maps pinned to the wall, and the desk covered with old case files. Case files I technically wasn't supposed to have. They were government property, and I'd been required to hand over all of that information when they placed me on leave. We all knew that was a mere formality. As soon as the medical leave ended, there'd be a misconduct hearing from the Mazzeo case, and afterward I would be dismissed. But my working amidst multiple agencies had created a lot of government red tape so all of that was going to take a little more time.

Until then, I was supposed to maintain a low profile and stay out of government business. The staying out of any legal trouble had not been mentioned, but it went without saying.

Of course, I'd kept copies of my files anyways. After everything I'd been through, I wasn't going to get tangled up in the legal or moral ramifications of my actions. That ship had sailed a long time ago. And as it turned out, it was a damned good thing I'd kept them. After being locked out of all federal networks I wouldn't have had anywhere to start my investigation.

Now, I had a short list of cases that both Danvers and I had worked on that might contain clues. Although none of them immediately stood out as great possibilities when it came to this. The murder of an FBI agent was one thing. The delivery of a severed head took it to another level.

I stood, needing coffee. My brain didn't feel like it was firing on all cylinders, and the lack of sleep was starting to get to me. Although the idea of attempting sleep with nothing more than a security system to rely on for protection wasn't giving me great vibes either. Eventually I would require some rest, but I'd been through enough training to know my limits, and I wasn't there yet.

However, staying caffeinated would be key. Before I could reach for a fresh coffee pod, the alarm system I'd rigged went off.

I ran to the bank of security screens I'd set up on the fireplace mantle and searched them for the intrusion. It didn't take much effort because whoever had come for a visit wasn't doing so in stealth mode. Not only could I see the motorcycle bearing down on the house, but I could also now hear the pipes all the way inside.

My stomach sizzled with nerves at that familiar sound and the memories of the man it came with. Something I had no business even thinking of. That chapter of my life had ended the night I was ripped away from my home and forced to leave everything and everyone I loved. Including him. Now he hated me, and for good reason.

Yet, I couldn't hear that sound without thinking of him. Even back then, before he'd become an official motorcycle club member, that life had been ingrained in him, and by association—me.

I grabbed one of the many guns I had hidden around the property, shoved my feet into some shoes, and headed out the back door. Whoever it was, I would take him by surprise before he could get within fifty feet of the house. Moving as quickly as I could, and using the natural cover of the landscaping to hide my progress, I entered battle mode.

I'd eaten, slept, and breathed the job long enough that it had become my world. I no longer knew anything else.

By the time the motorcycle neared the house, I was in place, easily aimed my weapon, and fired without being seen. The tire exploded, making the bike swerve to the side of the driveway. Somehow, the rider corrected the bike before it crashed, but he did slow and come to a stop only a few feet from my position.

The idiot didn't have a helmet on, but the darkness and shadows obscured my vision, making it impossible to get an ID. However, after a few choice curse words shouted from the rider, I didn't need to see anything to know who had come to visit. All of my muscles clenched, and I found myself fighting the urge to throw up. Suddenly, I felt sixteen all over again.

Axel.

Seriously? Of all the men in the world who could have shown up at my doorstep, why him?

Taking a deep, steadying breath, I lifted the gun and aimed it at him before I emerged from the shadows. "What are you doing here?"

Axel whipped around and faced me, his eyes widening at the sight of the gun leveled in his direction. "What the hell? What is with me and bitches with guns? Do you mind getting that thing out of my face?"

I wasn't about to take that bait and try to figure out what any of that meant. It simply didn't matter. It was hard enough just looking at him up close and personal after all this time.

Dark, unruly hair surrounded his face, reminding me of the silky touch of it on my skin. He never did like to get it cut, and it often went beyond his shoulders before he would do anything with it. Secretly, I'd preferred it like this. It went well with the angular bone structure of his face and the mesmerizing ice blue eyes. Those I felt clear to my soul every time he leveled them on me. Even now with nothing but irritation and contempt filling them, my belly swooped.

My anger sparked over the emotion he still drew from me. I didn't want to feel any of that. Ever. "You shouldn't be here."

"You shouldn't have shot out my tire. What kind of bullshit is that? I came to help you."

"I don't need your help. Never have, never will." I hated the words the minute they were out. They were cold and mean and had come out without my thinking them through. But I wasn't his damsel in distress in need of saving.

"Yeah. You've made that abundantly clear. Repeatedly. Your actions speak loud and clear, sweetheart. However, your father disagrees, and despite whether you deserve it or not, I *am* going to help you because that's what I've been paid to do."

The shame I barely kept contained morphed into anger so white hot I felt the explosion coming. "Paid?" I spat at him. "You're here because you've been paid?" The taste of that felt like poison working a dark path through my blood. Of course that's why he'd come.

"Yes, paid. Why else would I bother?" He echoed my sentiment as if he'd read my mind.

His question dripped with disdain and dug into me with razor-sharp claws. I thought, after everything I'd endured over the years, I was prepared for this meeting. That nothing else could possibly hurt me. I was wrong. I breathed through the pain and forced myself to stay upright. I couldn't let him see how low he'd just cut me. I had to pull it together.

"You wasted your time coming out here. If you want to help someone, go back to the main house. My father thinks he knows how to handle this, but I guarantee he doesn't."

Axel stared at me for a few long seconds before he took a step in my direction, forcing me to step backwards and stiffen my arm still holding the gun.

"Stop right there. I don't want to shoot you, but I will if I feel threatened."

He smirked. "You won't shoot me."

"Don't presume to know what I will or won't do. I will. It's what I've been trained to do."

"Is that what you are now, Mandy? A killer?"

I sucked in a sharp breath. His familiar use of my former nickname made my stomach jolt. He was the last one who'd called me that, and it had been over a decade since I heard it.

"This isn't right. Just go. You don't want to be here anymore than I want you here. That makes for an easy solution." I don't know why I expected him to do anything I asked. I raised my voice. "Go!"

A wicked smile crossed his face, and I knew damn well there wasn't a shred of humor in it. "The days where I take your wants and desires under consideration are long gone—Kelly."

An ugly feeling rose inside me as he practically spat my undercover alias in my face. But it was the contempt he delivered with a smile that sealed the deal. "This is your last warning. Leave, or I will make you leave in an ambulance."

He held out his arms and all but dared me to shoot him. As my finger itched at the trigger, he had no idea how close he was to getting exactly what he dared from me. I wanted to pull the trigger almost as much as I didn't. Logic when it came to him was nonexistent, and if there was anything I needed right now, it was logic.

"That's what I thought," he said, dropping his arms. "You shouldn't play with guns if you aren't going to take them seriously."

I looked down the sight of the gun and squeezed the trigger, my body absorbing the blowback, so I could keep the gun level and in place for another shot if necessary.

Axel grabbed his ear. "Jesus fucking Christ. You crazy bitch." He pulled his hand back with a spot of blood where the bullet had scratched him. "You almost fucking killed me."

"If I wanted you dead, you'd be dead." My heart beat slow and steady as he freaked out. He had no idea that there wasn't anyone currently in the CIA who was a better shot. How could he? I'd been recruited for covert operations. Hell, technically, I didn't need this gun to kill him. There were dozens of ways to get the job done without an official weapon.

"What if I'd fucking moved? A few inches, and that

bullet would have landed in my skull. What the fuck is wrong with you?"

That was a good question. However, I did relent and lower my weapon. I'd proven my point. I would shoot him if I had to. That's simply who I was now and he'd better get used to it.

Chapter Five

Axel

THIS BITCH WAS CRAZY. I'd seen that look in more than one person's eyes over the years and—what was that old song? —oh yeah—her give a damn was busted.

I had half a mind to give her what she wanted and leave. Anger seethed through me that she'd almost killed *me*. If nothing else, it cemented how little she thought of me. Not that her feelings had been in question.

Her message ten years ago had been delivered with a precision that I wasn't ever going to forget. I would, however, put it back behind me where it had been safely tucked for a very long time.

"Look. I don't know what kind of bullshit is going

through that head of yours right now, and I really don't care. However, my club has made a commitment to your father and this case, and I will see that through, because that's what I do. I honor my commitments.

I let that insult land. She was a smart girl. She knew what I meant. Although girl was not the word any normal human being would use to describe Amanda Turner. In ten years she'd changed in more ways than one, and the girl had been replaced by a woman. As a teenager, she'd been the prettiest girl in school hands down, but now—

It didn't seem possible that someone this beautiful on the outside could be so ugly on the inside. Unfortunately, that was exactly what made her so dangerous.

Everything about her seemed designed to mislead. From the long blonde hair currently caught up in some kind of sexy messy bun on the top of her head to the curves of her body that refused to be hidden in her fucking Lulu Lemons and a ragged-looking Jason Aldean t-shirt. Guess she also still had a thing for country music.

Not that it. Fucking. *Mattered*.

It pissed him off further that he kept having to remind himself of that. She wasn't the point. Finding a killer—that was the point.

"You're not going to go away unless my father says so, are you?"

I shook my head.

"And if I don't cooperate with you, you are going to get in my way every step of the way, aren't you?"

I decided to humor this train of thought she had going if it ended where I thought it might. I'd rather her agree to cooperate with me rather than me looking over my shoulder for her and that gun.

"Probably," I answered. "Although keeping you alive isn't normally considered getting in the way."

She snorted at him. It was such a loud, un-lady-like sound, I almost cracked a smile.

"I don't need you, or anyone else, to keep me alive. I can take care of myself."

I was beginning to understand that quite well, but I was never going to admit it. I was having a hard time seeing beyond the memory of the sixteen-year-old cheerleader. What exactly had happened to her?

I shook my head. Again. It. Didn't. Fucking. *Matter*.

I was going to have to keep that mantra on a continual loop in my head until it got through to my stubborn brain. I would not be fooled again by a beautiful face, or eyes that looked sad. As far as I was concerned, she'd made her bed, and it was time to lie in it.

God, I hated that fucking saying. How many times had my father uttered those words in a drunken slur?

I was not him.

"Fine. You don't need anyone's help. Message received. That doesn't change the fact I'm here until this situation is resolved. So, I guess you can keep working alone, in which case I'll be here in the background doing the same thing. Or maybe we cooperate, and together we can get this figured out in half the time. Which means I'm out of here sooner rather than later."

She looked ready to tell me where to go.

I was ready to argue with her until I wore her into the ground. I wasn't particularly patient, but I was persistent. And I didn't like to lose. Ever. I had my next line of reasoning ready to go when she opened her mouth and said the last thing I expected.

"Whatever. Do what you want. Except let's get one thing straight, right now. You are not staying in the house. There's a gym out back. You can stay in there."

Say what now? "Excuse me?"

"I said, okay. I'm too tired to keep standing here arguing and I can see it's going to get us nowhere. And since I'm not in the right mood for a standoff, I will concede to us working together. Under conditions, of course."

"Which are?"

"I already stated one. You don't stay in the house."

"Okay." That suited me fine. More space between us the better. "Is there a second?"

She plopped her hands on her hips. "Hell, yes. Second, no personal questions. I'll talk about the case all you want, but if you start getting personal, you're out of here."

"You're pretty fucking bossy."

She glared. "And that brings me to condition number three. I am in charge of this investigation. This is my fucking case, and I've agreed to let you assist. Do not even think about taking charge."

Someone needed a goddamned spanking. And a lesson or two in humility. I was getting paid to do a job. However, for the sake of argument, I could let her have a little moment and let her be in charge. Temporarily.

"Anything else?"

She smiled, but it rang hollow. Her eyes remained as cool as ever, reminding me once again of who I was dealing with. Amanda Turner, a woman without feelings.

"I like my coffee black, with a dollop of cream, no sugar. Do you think you can handle that?"

I didn't bother to give her a response. She could take her coffee and shove it up her...

"I've already created a profile and a list of potential suspects," she said, interrupting my thoughts. "One of the cases you are going to be quite familiar with. Are you ready for that?" She turned on her heel, punched in a code at the front door and disappeared inside, leaving me standing there like a jackass with no choice but to follow her. I grated my teeth together hoping I wasn't about to make the worst possible mistake of my life and followed her inside.

One glance around and I wanted to roll my eyes. While I'd expected no less, because Turner liked to flaunt his wealth at every chance, of course his cabin was the equivalent of a fucking mansion. As far as I was concerned, it was an insult to cabins. Cabins were supposed to be small and make you feel comfortable, not make you stiff and afraid to touch any damned thing.

"This is a bit much."

She stopped and looked back at me. "What? The cabin?"

"It's not a fucking cabin. I thought your father was a hunter. This does not look like a place you bring a kill to so you can clean it up."

She shrugged. "My father doesn't clean anything. That's not his style. He has someone else handle that, and by the time they make it here, they look like that." She pointed to one of the many animal heads hanging on the wall.

"You all are so privileged it hurts. I'm not sure I realized exactly how much until now."

"You can paint me with the same brush as my father if you want. But I haven't lived here in a long time, and this is no longer my reality."

I let it drop despite the many questions that went through my mind. All I saw was a rich, spoiled princess with too much time, money, and guns. If it wasn't for her father and his influence, she would probably be rotting in a jail somewhere.

"Since I didn't expect anyone would be joining me out here, I set up everything in here." She led the way into a bedroom.

I gaped at what she'd done. There were maps on the walls. Photographs were pinned to several corkboards, along with sheets next to each photograph that I couldn't read this far away, and a giant whiteboard she'd obviously been using to brainstorm her random thoughts. I wanted to start organizing it all into a system to identify any patterns.

But first things first. "What are the maps?" I moved closer. "This one is Sultan and its surrounding areas. But what's this one?" The largest of the three had many topographical details and obviously encompassed a great amount of land mass around Sultan and extended to the base of the mountains. If I was reading it correctly, this property went on for miles."

"That's the Turner Ranch."

I jerked around and met her nonchalant gaze. "Are you fucking kidding me?" When she didn't answer me right away, I moved closer to the maps to see. It took me about two seconds to realize she'd gone way too far. JD was going to have a conniption. A low rumbling sound built in my chest before I turned and dragged her close. "Why in the *fuck* are you surveilling my club?"

Chapter Six

Amanda

I SHUDDERED under the hard grip Axel had on my arm. I'd known this was going to be a problem. Which was why I'd figured I'd get it over with, first. The Sins of Wrath was nothing if not big on their privacy. And these weren't ordinary maps.

"Amanda." He growled, a clear threat in his tone now. "What the fuck is going on?"

"It's not what you think. I'm studying every possible route in and out of this area, and to be thorough, I have to look over every inch of land. That includes yours."

"But that's not a public fucking map. It's not even still images from a satellite. That's fucking drone footage of someone seriously invading our privacy. Is that what you're doing out here in the first place?"

The anger in his voice and the dark expression on his face gave me pause. I'd known he would be pissed about this, but I hadn't bargained for this kind of reaction. How did I know this wasn't about to turn ugly? I didn't know him. Not really. Axel ten years ago was a far cry from the man standing here still holding onto me so hard I'd likely bruise by tomorrow.

"Let me go," I hissed, looking pointedly where he'd grabbed me. His gaze followed mine, and as if he hadn't realized how far he'd gone, he dropped his hand like I'd burned him.

I rubbed the skin and put some distance between us. I wasn't too worried about what he might do. I could defend myself, after all. But that didn't mean I liked dealing with him like this.

"You need to start talking before I lose my shit," he warned, his face still clouded with darkness.

"You need to chill or get the fuck out of my house. I let you in because I could see you weren't going to go away. However, if I don't give you permission to touch me, then you don't ever fucking touch me. Got it?" My voice had risen to a near hysterical level, but he was just going to have to deal. I didn't *need* him to conduct this investigation.

We stared at each other for too long, both pretty much daring each other to make the next move. Of all the times I'd dreamt of a reunion with Axel, not one had ever gone quite like this. Although I had known it wouldn't be pretty. Leaving him behind the day after I'd told him about the baby was one of the worst things I'd had to endure, and considering my line of work, that was seriously saying something.

When his expression suddenly changed and he looked away, I couldn't help but think maybe we were both messed up from the past. It made me want to ask him questions, but I had no right to dig up the past now. What would be the point of putting us both through that again when nothing could ever change?

And whatever had gone on in his life since then was none of my business.

"I didn't mean to hurt you." The look of regret on his face matched the feeling that seized in my chest. My life had been built on the back of one regret after another, until the word had come to mean very little. But just as quickly as the expression had appeared, it disappeared. "But you do need to explain what is going on. Why are you spying on the club?"

"I'm not, I swear. I did, however, think it was prudent to be sure your property couldn't be used by whoever is responsible for what happened to Danvers."

"It can't be. Our place is secure."

I wanted to point out that while that might be the case, I'd had no problem getting that drone footage the Bureau obtained when they thought the club could be interfering in one of their investigations. My boss on the task force, Agent Reed, had shut down the operation as soon as he got wind of it.

He might be loyal to the Bureau, but not at the expense of his motorcycle club family.

That had been my first real connection to home in so

long, it had scared me. Not because I thought Agent Reed would hold it against me, but because for the first time in too many years it had made me feel something other than hate and fear.

I nodded. "Yeah, I don't think whoever is responsible for this is using your property, but the club could be tied into it, whether they know it or not."

"I'm pretty sure I'd know if we were involved in something this insane."

I walked over to the desk and rifled through the files until I found the one I was looking for. Turning back, I handed it to him. Bringing this case to his attention might not bode well, but being thorough was more important than any sensitive feelings. "This is one of the few cases Danvers and I worked on together."

He opened the file. "Frank Mazzeo," he curled his lip when he said the name. "He's dead. What the hell does he have to do with this?" He studied a few of the pages before he continued. "If you think someone from his organization is out for revenge, that would be a stretch. No one cares that Frank is gone. Hell, whoever is in charge now is probably grateful we got him out of the way so they could take over. He was singlehandedly ruining a lucrative business..."

He paused, staring down at the page before he finally looked up again and caught my gaze. I wished I had braced myself for what came next.

"Besides, why would they want revenge against you? You were his little bitch, making sure he could slide in and out of the law without anyone touching him. Because of you Izzy almost died. Hell, I'm surprised you aren't on your knees in front of his successor right now begging for whatever scrap he might give you. Or did he tell you to fuck off too?"

The air in my lungs froze at the pure venom laced into those words. I tried to take a breath and felt like I would choke if I did. My head spun as my mind rushed back to all the things I'd done because of Frank. Axel thought he knew, but nobody really did. Not the full extent of it. They couldn't.

Bile rose in my throat.

He continued to rifle through the file and photos. His demeanor as lax and casual as if he'd not just taken a knife to my heart and shredded it to ribbons.

"I don't see anything here that jumps out as cause for the kind of death Danvers endured. Is this all of it?"

As far as he was concerned. I'd whitewashed the case file a long time ago. There were a couple of agents at the CIA who knew some of the details surrounding my time with the Mazzeo organization, but not one knew everything other than me. That knowledge allowed me to take in a thread of air and answer him.

"Yes." I took another small breath and forced my voice into an even tone. "And I would normally agree that that case is the least likely to give me trouble now. But none of the others are obvious choices, either."

He closed the file on Frank and looked up at me, his eyes as ice cold as his words. "Where are those? I'd like to look through them all. You never know what a second set of eyes could find."

I pointed to the remaining case files piled on the desk. "Have at it. I need coffee, and since I was in the middle of making some when you arrived, I'm going back to the kitchen." And if I didn't get away from him now, I couldn't guarantee I wouldn't break.

He nodded without saying anything else. I'd basically been dismissed. Axel outside his club seemed like a lone wolf, but I'd kept up with them over the years, and he worked as well with a team as he did on his own. But he was the kind of man who chose who he worked with, and not the other way around.

I paused. If JD had forced him into this assignment, it would explain the hostility. Not that he needed an excuse. I wasn't naive or narcissistic enough to not realize that what happened that night so long ago, tore two lives apart. But after... our lives went in very different directions. So why take this job if he hated me so much?

These were thoughts and questions I had no intention of voicing out loud. Not only would I not like the answers, but it would also force both of us to look at a past we were better off not touching. Too much time had passed. We were different people.

He was a rockstar badass motorcycle man with a passion for righting wrongs, no matter what it took or what laws he broke to get it done.

I was... well...

Who the hell was I supposed to be?

I left him standing in the bedroom and went to the kitchen. Only then did I finally get a good breath into my lungs. Seeing him was harder than I thought possible, but working with him? God, that was going to be unbearable.

What did that say about me?

Chapter Seven

Axel

I TOOK MORE time than I needed to go through all of Mandy's case files, and it still didn't feel like enough. She'd gone to retrieve coffee and never returned. So, I'd moved on to the rest of the information she had posted around the room.

The room she was also using as a bedroom, if her smart watch and a book on the nightstand meant anything. Not to mention the small suitcase on the stool at the end of the bed. I picked up the book and flipped it open to read the dust jacket. The fact she was reading a book about high profile serial killers didn't surprise me a bit.

She'd certainly changed from the easy-going teenager I remembered who had nothing more important on her mind than dance routines and spending time on the back of my bike.

These little jolts of memories were not what I wanted to focus on. I didn't need any information on her personal life to make sure she stayed safe from a killer. I placed the book back on the table and moved back to the whiteboard with her scribbled notes.

I liked her brainstorming methods, though. She'd thrown a lot of ideas into the mix whether they were viable or not. It was a method that JD liked to use when he had a problem he thought seemed impossible to solve. No idea was too crazy, and all were at least worth considering. Because, nothing was impossible, and more often than not, the solution was right in front of your face...you just had to see it.

I grabbed the file on Mazzeo again. It was an insane coincidence that both she and Danvers worked on the case the MC was involved in as well, and now Danvers had been killed, his head delivered to her door and I stood here representing the MC.

A chill swept over me. I didn't believe in coincidences.

But who in that organization would give a shit about Frank's death? Izzy was out of the question. She was as close to lily-white as a mobster's daughter could be. In her short time with the MC, I'd learned more than enough about her to know she hated Frank Mazzeo as much as the rest of us had. That old bastard had arranged his only daughter to marry a psychopath who raped women for fun, and then sold them to the highest bidder.

If Houston hadn't killed him, any one of us certainly would have. Both men had gotten exactly what they deserved.

After what she'd been through, Izzy deserved a life free of her father's past, but she'd taken the money she got from Frank and used it to fund an organization that rescued women from sexual slavery and then helped them get back into society and on their feet again.

Not in a million years would she have anything to do with this.

But... That insane nagging at the back of my skull told me something wasn't right. I was missing something right in front of my face. I just had to figure out what it was. It looked like I'd be making a call to Houston to discuss it. In the meantime, I wanted to check my contacts again in Seattle and see if there was any news about the new conglomerate taking over the criminal space that Frank had once occupied.

The mafia wasn't known for keeping their leadership a secret, and they'd want to come in with a strong show of force.

"What do you think?"

Her voice behind me slid down my spine and caused a slight shiver. Having her this close irritated the fuck out of me. Especially since I wanted to get through this with no reaction at all. And yet...

I opened the file and pushed those thoughts away. I had more important things to worry about. This case had a lot of moving parts and a lot of details I needed to digest before I could decide what direction to go next. Although I was going to bring Tel in here and let him do his thing with this information. Between her brain and his tech skills, they might get a better picture of what they were up against.

"I think there's a lot of information here we need to go through."

"That's true. That was a big part of the job that hardly anyone ever talks about. Sure, running after bad guys with guns and going undercover sounds sexy, but most cases are solved like this. Staring at the facts until they make some kind of sense. It's all about getting into their heads, which isn't exactly a pretty place to go."

I turned and faced her, focusing on the beginning part of what she'd pointed out. "Was? Am I to take it that you no longer work for the government? Because you having all of this," he waved around the room, "tells a different story. What's the deal?"

"Technically, I'm still on medical leave. But that's just a temporary measure while they file their formal complaints against me with HR and push the paper-work through and I'm terminated permanently. They already took my ID and my government issued weapon. I'm done. There is no way back in. Hell, they won't even take my calls."

I could hear the sorrow of loss in her voice, but I couldn't quite muster up the same feeling in myself. When you get down in the shit with pigs like Frank, you don't come out clean. "I guess you play with fire, you get burned."

Her eyes narrowed, but her mouth stayed shut. I didn't know what that look meant, but whatever regrets she might have, those were her demons, not mine.

It was a good thing she didn't work for the Feds because we were already riding a line on this as it was. This case stunk to high heaven and if the government caught a whiff of it, we ran the risk of getting caught in the crosshairs.

"So, what was your plan? Or what was next on the agenda? You've gathered this information, you've brainstormed some scenarios, now what?"

"Usually field work. Hitting up contacts, using CIs to pick up new rumors on the street. Checking alibis for any suspects we might be looking at. That kind of thing. Except, I have a hunch that none of that is going to work in this case. This whole thing feels extremely personal and private. But I've read those case files backwards and forward, and I don't know what I'm missing. Nothing seems to fit."

I nodded, my mind circling back to Frank for a moment before shaking free. I had to keep an open mind to all the possibilities, not just focus on the man I hated the most. But that left me little else to do except think about the obvious. While she seemed to be lost in thoughts of this case, I took stock of *her*. I'd learned a long time ago, the longer you ignored the elephant in the room, the bigger it got. And in this case, I wanted to keep my perspective clear and my head on straight.

Not the easiest thing to do as she stood there chewing on her bottom lip, staring off into space, reminding me of another time and place. The messy blonde bun aside, she didn't look that much different than she did back then. A little curvier, but that was an improvement if anything.

Basically, she was even more beautiful than I remembered. And while looking at her now had made my dick twitch in her direction, I wasn't ruled by my dick, anymore. My heart, on the other hand, had a lot to say right now, and that, I would listen to. Specifically, the fact she'd shredded it and it had been a bitch to stitch back together again.

I closed my eyes and willed the memories to stop. They had no place here. The only reason we were in the same room again was because I had a job to do and it was critical that I kept focus on that. Thinking about how soft her lips might be pressed against my skin, or what her hips would feel like clenched in my hands was a sure-fire path to destruction.

"How about we go over each of these files together?" I asked. "I'd like to hear your thoughts on each and come up with my own as we pick them apart."

She blinked at me, looking at me as if she too had been so lost in thought she almost forgot I was there.

"Uhm—okay."

"We should probably get some food. Your stomach is growling," I pointed out. "When was the last time you ate?"

She shrugged. "I probably ate something yesterday.

I've been a little busy. Besides, this is my true life blood," she said, lifting her cup to indicate her coffee.

"Don't get me wrong. I live and die by my coffee in the morning as well, but that's no substitute for food. What do you feel like? Pizza? Mexican? Chinese? Burgers? That's about all we can get delivered in Sultan. No one around here has embraced the Door Dash concept yet. Not that we have many other choices."

"Some things change and some don't," she said, sounding wistful before seemingly pulling herself together again to continue. "Unfortunately, no one is going to deliver this far out, and we don't want anyone to know where we are. So, if we want to eat, we're going to have to make it. Lucky for you, I stocked up on cold cuts and chopped veggies to nibble on. My father also keeps the pantry and freezer stocked out here year-round, so tomorrow we can cook if we have to."

He wrinkled his nose. "Cold cuts and chopped veggies? Do I look like a rabbit to you?"

A half smile lifted up one corner of her mouth. The first I'd seen from her in a decade, and as much as I hated to admit it, it looked really good on her.

"No, you definitely don't look like a rabbit. A bull maybe. Those are pretty stubborn and force their way into places they aren't wanted, right?"

I snorted. "If you say so." I brushed past her and headed into the kitchen. If I stood here much longer, staring at her lips, I was going to do or say something stupid.

The kitchen out here was bigger than the industrial

one we had in the clubhouse, and it was decked out with what I expected would impress even a top chef. "What else do you have in here? Surely something to cook right now."

She followed me towards the fridge and stopped to prop her hip on the island and watch. "I could put together a charcuterie board. It's all finger food, but it would be pretty hearty with the selection of meats and cheeses I have."

"Mmm, I don't know what the hell a charcutafuckall is." I hummed, opening the fridge to take stock. "Cheese, though? Now you're talking more my speed." I quickly took in what was available and noted she had not lied about our limited choices. There were stacks of little bags from the deli that looked to be filled with a variety of meats and at least—I counted the bags—eight varieties of cheese. That was about four more than I usually considered.

Fortunately, there was a large, cooked rotisserie chicken as well. Now that, I could work with. I grabbed all the cheeses, the chicken, and a few of the peppers she had probably planned to chop and nibble on. I placed everything on the counter and went in search of a pantry. "What about bread? Any tortillas?"

"Of course. Top shelf of that cabinet." She pointed to the big one opposite of where I'd been looking, moved around the island and took a seat on one of the many leather chairs placed there. "What are you going to do?"

She looked skeptical and a little worried.

"Hopefully, Mexican depending on how well Turner

stocks this place with spices and such." I grabbed a package of tortillas and added it to the mix before searching the rest of the pantry. "Aha," I withdrew a large can of enchilada sauce from the very back of the cabinet and held it up like a prize.

I thought I heard a laugh from her spot at the island, but by the time I turned to look at her, she'd gone back to looking serious.

"I take it we're having enchiladas."

"I assume you still like them. Mexican used to be your favorite." I froze, the minute the words came out, realizing too late what I'd said. Fuck. Apparently, not bringing the past into the present was going to be harder than I'd thought.

"Enchiladas are fine." She stood, looking as panicked as I felt. "I'm going to go move all the case files while you do whatever it is you are going to do."

I snorted. "Cook, you mean?"

"Sure. Although I would be fine with just a sand-wich. It's not necessary for you to cook for me."

"I'm not doing it for you," I said.

Her eyes widened, and that pang of regret went off in my gut again. Fuck if she didn't make me feel bad for —what? There was nothing to feel guilty about. Ever. If she didn't like it when I spoke the truth that was also her problem. She was all grown up and could figure out all on her own how to deal with my being here.

I had a job to do. And. *Nothing*. Else. Matters.

Reminder number nineteen. Check.

Chapter Eight

Amanda

BY THE TIME I finished carrying all of the files into the dining room, and then dragged the white board across the cabin, the scents of Axel's cooking had filled the rooms. My mouth salivated and hunger tugged at my gut. I'd lied about eating the day before. It had been at least two days, and likely would have been longer if not for him.

I'd grabbed food because I knew it was a necessity, but there was also a case of protein bars in the cabinet that would have sufficed. But now he was cooking for us...

I'm not doing it for you.

Those words had sliced deep. He'd made it crystal

clear more than once that he didn't want to be here. But I could read between the lines. He hated me.

As the tears I would never let fall burned at the back of my eyes, I pushed harder to get the whiteboard in place. Now more than ever, I needed to put all of my effort into the job. Except the sight of Axel, sleeves pushed up, leaning over the stove, made my heart skip a beat.

He was so much bigger than he'd been as a teenager. There was a lot more muscle, that was for sure. He'd removed his leather jacket and the heather-gray shirt with three-quarter sleeves beneath it clung to his body in a way that highlighted every cut plane.

There were also a lot more tattoos. I remembered his first. We'd been together at the tattoo shop, him getting the handlebars of his bike inked on his upper arm with a view of the mountains in the background, as if he was riding towards them. He'd said at the time that riding meant the ultimate freedom to him and that it was always going to be a part of him.

I'd had the silly teenage notion that we would get matching tattoos, but I wasn't a biker and had no intention of being anything other than a passenger on his. So, I'd opted for a small red heart with a thorned rose sticking out of one side. Since I was deathly afraid of getting caught, I'd had it placed on my hip, well inside my panty line.

Over the years I'd thought about getting it removed since seeing it every day reminded me of him, but I'd decided against it. I wanted to remember. If for no other reason than to remind myself that nothing would ever last forever. Teenage crush or not, he'd left a mark on me, and so far, it was the only one worth having.

"What's that look for? What's wrong?" Axel's question caught me off guard.

"What?" I shook my head. "Nothing."

His frown made it clear he didn't believe me, but he chose to drop it. "After we eat, I have a few questions about these cases. If we go over them, maybe we can knock something loose."

"Sure," I mumbled, turning my back to forget about looking at him by arranging all of the paperwork and information into organized stacks.

"Food's ready. Come and get it while it's hot."

I took a deep breath to steady my racing heart. Having him here was going to be a lot harder than I thought. Especially if he did things like cook dinner.

I'm not doing this for you.

His words had been deliberately harsh and I'd be best to remember he meant them. This wasn't a reunion, or a blast from the past. We had a dangerous case to solve before it got worse.

Feeling a little steadier with those serious thoughts on my mind, I made my way back to the kitchen island and accepted the plate he held out to me. My stomach instantly growled again. "It smells really good."

"I get that from the noises you're making."

My face flamed hot. Stomach or not, him noticing little things about me made me uncomfortable. I didn't want to be under a microscope. It took a lot of effort on my part not to fill my plate and go eat alone in my room. The idea of sharing a meal with him was not my idea of fun. He would keep asking questions and it was only a matter of time before he crossed the line and wanted personal answers.

I ignored his comments and dished up a small serving. I was not going to run and hide. I reminded myself that this was my house (sort of), and I didn't have to answer anything I didn't want to. He couldn't intimidate me. Before I took my seat, I grabbed a bottle of water, the napkins, and some silverware and moved to the farthest seat from his.

He glanced at me and I quickly looked away. I opted to focus on my food, but one bite in, and I moaned my appreciation. "This is really good."

"It's okay, being that it came from a can. I prefer homemade sauce, but this will definitely do in a pinch."

I thought he was undervaluing his skills. I'd watched him wield the array of spices like a pro and this no longer resembled bland can sauce. However, I wasn't going to argue the point. If he could do this with boring pantry ingredients, I couldn't imagine how it would be with fresh.

"Do you cook a lot?" I asked.

"Not often. Since so many of us live on the compound, we usually have the prospects cook for us. It's a prerequisite for them now."

"To cook or live on the compound?" I didn't have to ask what a prospect was because Axel had been one when we were dating. Although his probationary period to become a full-fledged member of the motor-cycle club had been coming to an end. He'd likely patched in right after I left.

"Both. Everyone has to start out living there these days. Prospecting is more than a full-time job and they're expected to be available for anything at any time."

"That sounds harsh," I said before taking another delicious bite of food. This time I managed to contain my moan, but it was no less delightful. I shuddered to think what this man was now capable of if this was just a hint of what he could do. How many other skills had he mastered since we were teens?

He shrugged. "It is and it isn't. It definitely is a huge time commitment, but every time we allow someone we don't know inside and out on the compound we are taking a big risk. By each man sacrificing most of his time to the club, it allows us to not only get to know him and what he can do but gives us a little bit of a safety net that he isn't going to cause us trouble because he's under a lot of supervision."

I paused, fork halfway to my mouth. "That sounds incredibly paranoid. Even the training I got from the federal government didn't require round the clock supervision."

"I don't know what to tell you. We've tested out different methods and styles of training over the years and this is the best for the club."

For the club. There were three little words that could consume a person's life. It seemed for these men, everything led back to that. I would know because Sins of Wrath was not the only motorcycle club I'd dealt with in my life. The government had used my experience in convenient ways.

I grabbed my glass of water and drank down several swallows. This, sitting here and talking to him like it was nothing, was a lot harder than I'd expected and I'd known it wouldn't be easy. Luckily, Axel must have understood the tension as he finished his meal without any more conversation. When I was done, I got up and put my dirty dishes in the dishwasher and cleaned up the kitchen, wrapping up the leftovers before placing them in the fridge.

"Those will be even better the second day," he said, his voice suddenly right behind me.

When I turned back around, I nearly jumped to find him so close. "Then we shouldn't let them go to waste." I hated that I sounded so breathless, but I couldn't quite catch my breath.

"Did I scare you, Mandy?"

I shook my head, unable to verbally respond with the sound of my nickname from his lips drowning in my mind. This close, I could smell him, and that combination of pine, motor oil and the musk from his soap was an immediate time warp to the past.

I closed my eyes and forced a breath deep into my lungs. I'd forgotten that smell and how it affected me. Until right now.

My chest squeezed. He did scare me. In so many

ways, and I hadn't realized how much until now. This was bad. So so bad.

"No, I'm fine," I lied, scooting around the island to put some much-needed space between us. I never should have let him in. Just because my father hired him didn't mean I had to cooperate. He could have stayed outside. Slept in the barn. There was a decent apartment out there that would keep him a nice distance from me.

You wanted this.

The little bitchy voice inside my head taunted me. There was no denying I'd made this too easy for him. Now I was backed into a corner and had no choice but to continue down this path with him. Dammit!

"I bet you're regretting letting me in right about now."

My head swiveled around so fast I nearly got whiplash. How was he practically reading my mind? "I would say that's ridiculous, but I think I was pretty clear that I didn't think it was a great idea. Why? Are you having second thoughts? You don't have to take this job. My dad's just covering all his bases. If Theresa hadn't opened that package for me none of this would be happening."

"Why's that?" He took several steps in my direction. "Would you have tried to hide a severed head?"

"From my family? Of course. I still believe my best course of action is to lead whoever this is away from here. I don't need my family getting caught in the crosshairs. They may not like me very much right now, but that doesn't mean I want anything to happen to them."

"You wanted to run—again?" Something very dark and very dangerous crossed over his face. I wasn't sure quite how to decipher it.

"I'd do whatever it takes to keep them safe. Sometimes leaving my loved ones behind is the only choice."

He glared down at me, the planes of his face rigid in anger. I could feel it boiling just under his skin. It even made the hairs at the back of my neck stand on end. What were we even talking about? Was this still about the case?

"Go then," he said, marching across the cabin to the front door and yanking it open. "If your best plan is to run. Do it. Get out of town before it's too late. But this time, don't come back."

I stood transfixed, unclear on how to respond. Although a big part of me wanted to grab my shit and hightail it out of here. I didn't need his help and I sure as hell didn't need his shitty attitude. The longer I stood there the more my muscles twitched. Would running actually accomplish my goals? Would it be enough to draw a killer away from my family?

"Can you really blame me for wanting to keep my family safe?"

"I can blame you for whatever the hell I want. When it comes to you, nothing makes sense. It never did, and it probably never will."

Okay we definitely weren't talking about the current case. I needed to tread carefully here. But maybe he did deserve some answers. I'd honestly thought he didn't care. Especially after all this time.

Had I been wrong? My head spun. I needed to sit down. Maybe drink some water.

"Shut the door, Axel." I took a slow breath in and out of my lungs to keep myself calm. "I'm not going anywhere. Not right now and not without a plan."

Chapter Nine

Axel

THE ANGER inside of me was growing with every passing second, becoming a living breathing thing. It was taking every ounce of effort not to grab her by the shoulders and shake some sense into her. Why did she need to run? What had gone so wrong that it had become her go to in life? I couldn't understand. And I was sick of people running away.

She came from a rich family with a father who seemed to adore her. She'd had a boyfriend, who'd been less than thrilled initially about a pregnancy, but had planned to stay by her side no matter what. Sure the town had turned on her a little when one of her friends spilled the beans about her situation, but this was a small town. No secrets remained secret forever. It was impossible. They thrived on gossip, but not much lingered for more than a few weeks. The busybodies in town would move onto the next thing as quickly as some people changed their shoes.

"You might as well ask what you need to ask. I can see that you're going to let whatever this is fester. I get that you're pissed. Things didn't end well. But we were teenagers. What did you expect?"

"I expected my girlfriend to talk to me like the adult she proclaimed to be."

"But I wasn't an adult."

"You were adult enough to get pregnant. If you can fuck, then you can certainly talk. Don't try to hide behind the teenager bullshit. We had serious issues to deal with, and you took matters into your own hands without even giving me the time of day. One day we were talking about our future, and the next you were gone. Poof." The angry energy sparked in the room between us. Mostly from me, because once I'd opened my mouth, I couldn't seem to shut it. "Would it have killed you to tell me the truth before it was too late?"

"Talking would have changed nothing. My father was horrified and embarrassed by my pregnancy. Once the stories picked up steam, I had no choice. I was a minor." Her voice had risen in volume, but it remained stone cold.

"We always have choices. Some are just harder than others. Just because you keep jumping to the wrong side of a good choice, doesn't make you helpless. It makes you pathetic."

Her mouth dropped open and the shock was written all over her face. I'd hit below the belt and didn't regret it a bit. I still couldn't fathom why she did the things she did. And those were just the things I knew. I could only imagine how much more was unknown. My stomach turned vile at the idea, and I was beginning to regret those enchiladas. Becoming a CIA agent was one thing, but turning dirty, with someone like Frank Mazzeo? It disgusted me.

"Fuck you and the piece of shit motorcycle you rode in on. You don't know shit about me and the choices I've had to make." She slammed the stool at the island against the wood and stalked toward the bedroom. It would have been amusing to watch if I wasn't so damned angry. This assignment was bullshit. When she disappeared out of sight and slammed that door hard enough to rattle the pictures on the wall, it took all of my control not to let my rage get the best of me and go after her.

The anger on her face was one thing, but there had been more. For a moment, when my words came spewing out, I'd caught more hurt than anything else cross her beautiful face. It had punched me in the gut and made me feel guilty. Not that I had anything to be guilty over. I wasn't the one who got dumped via messenger and then found out she'd gotten rid of the baby. What the fuck did she expect? Roses and sunshine? Fuck that. *FUCK. THAT.*

I picked up a vase from a nearby end table, hurled it

at the wall, and watched it shatter into thousands of tiny pieces.

"I hope you know you're going to pay for that," she yelled through the closed door.

"Take it out of my fucking bill," I yelled back, uncaring whether it was a thirty-dollar piece of glass or three thousand. I needed to get out of here as soon as possible. After I checked in with the guys at the main house security, I would place a call to JD.

And say what exactly? That I was a little bitch and couldn't handle the job? I paced across the room a few times, trying to work out some of the excess energy that had built inside me before finally giving up and flopping into one of the deep leather armchairs. I pulled out my phone and sent a text to Tel to call me when he got a chance. I wanted to fill him in on the information out here as well as get an update on the main house.

The muscles in my arms and neck were tense and I needed to do something to relieve them. This is when a good fight came in handy. I was going to miss the ring at the compound for just this thing. The prospects, in particular, liked to volunteer for fight duty and I was more than eager to teach them a thing or two. I glanced around. It would be a bad idea to leave her alone to investigate the gym she'd mentioned. She'd just have to go with me. Which meant I would have to inform Miss High-and-Mighty of my needs when she decided to come back down from her throne of self-righteousness.

At that time I could retrieve my bag that was still out on my bike which needed its tire fixed anyways.

After receiving a thumbs up from Tel, I shoved my phone back into my pocket and stood. I'd seen a massive garage off to the side of the house before I'd gotten my bike tire shot out. There might be some supplies out there to help me fix it.

I glanced at the closed bedroom door and debated telling Mandy where I was headed. Since it was doubtful she'd care or want to know at this point, I passed by without knocking. Later, we'd come to a truce for the sake of the case. Once we'd both cooled off and level heads prevailed.

I yanked open the door and something white at my foot caught my eye. I looked down to find an envelope with the name Agent Kelly Smith scrawled in small, blocky, handwritten letters. What the hell? So much for keeping this place and her location a secret. If she was having official packages delivered, we might as well take out a billboard on main street giving everyone fucking directions.

Jesus Christ. I scooped up the envelope and headed back into the house. So much for cooler, level heads...

I banged on the door harder than necessary and gave no fucks about it. In fact, the muffled squeak I heard behind it made a smile twist at my lips. That's right, little dove. The big bad wolf has come to your door and he's about to get some fucking answers.

"Go away."

"There's a fucking delivery here for you. What the hell, Mandy? Why in the fuck would you give anyone this location? If you need anything, we have people that can bring it here without announcing that you're here."

"What are you—" She jerked the door open and saw the slim envelope dangling from my fingertips. "I didn't tell anyone I was here. You wouldn't have even found me if my father hadn't told you where to go."

Fat chance. She woefully underestimated my abilities if she believed that. "Well, someone knows something," I said, as the hairs on the back of my neck began to prickle. She reached for the envelope and I swiped it out of her reach. "You really aren't expecting this?"

"No, dumbass. I'm not."

I threw her a dark look. She had no idea how close she was to getting turned over my knee. I knew exactly what to do with a brat. "I'd be careful what you call me. If you think because we have history I'll let you get away with that kind of disrespect, you'd be wrong. No one talks to me like that."

She opened her mouth to say something smart probably and caught herself. Whatever had been on her mind suddenly seemed less important as she turned white as a sheet.

"What's wrong? You can dish it out, but you can't take it back?"

She shook her head. "Uhh—no. The envelope. I recognize that handwriting."

I turned it over and examined it again. "From where?" The raising of the hair on my neck had just turned into a full-blown itch. Somehow, I knew the answer before she actually said it.

"On the box that was delivered to the house. The one with the..."

She didn't need to finish that sentence. I dropped the envelope and rushed the front door, pulling my gun from my side holster as I moved. "Stay here," I said before I hit all the light switches and plunged us into total darkness.

"I'll check the cameras." She crossed the room behind me as I methodically went window to window checking to make sure all were locked and we weren't in here with an intruder. I wasn't about to get caught off guard again.

"This house is too fucking big," I grumbled under my breath. "It's a security nightmare to begin with.

"I've got something," she whisper yelled as if anyone within one hundred feet hadn't heard her. "Twenty minutes ago. Fuck. Whoever he is, he knows where most of my cameras are. I've barely caught more than a glimpse. A shadow basically."

I returned to the living room and crossed to her side to see for myself. "He probably doesn't care about them. He was in and out so fast, and he took care to keep everything covered, including his face and hands." Dude had fucking gloves and a face mask. Asshole. "I thought there were proximity alarms? Your father said this property was fully secure."

"The property is too big and too open. Those kinds of alarms work better inside of a fenced property."

"This is bullshit. What's in the envelope?" I turned

and searched the room, until I spied it in the chair she'd dropped it in. "Here."

She took it from me and ripped into it.

"Shouldn't we dust it for fingerprints or something?"

"You saw the gloves, right? And I'd bet big money whoever delivered it wasn't the actual killer. I doubt he takes chances like that."

"You a profiler too?"

"Not technically, but I've worked enough cases over the years to get a sense. We aren't dealing with a garden variety serial killer. This is someone with some serious anger issues who wants revenge. More than likely daddy issues too."

"You guessed all of that from a box with a head in it?"

She rolled her eyes at him, but before she could come back with a quip, she pulled out a stack of eight by ten photos with a red circle on the first one. "Oh my God."

While she once again went white as a sheet, I grabbed the stack of photos from her before they fell to the floor. The top one was of her lying in bed reading a book. The bed here in this house. For a second, I thought the photographer had been inside the house because it was a high-quality clear image. But I caught a spot in the corner that looked like a glare from glass. "He wasn't in the house."

I thumbed through the rest of the photos to find a variety of pictures of Mandy in different areas of the house, outside on the property, and even in her car when she'd first arrived.

"He's been here the whole time..." She didn't look okay. Her skin had gone from pale to ashen.

I dropped the photos and pulled her into my arms. She burrowed her face deep into my chest and I held her as tight as I could without crushing her. "We're leaving."

"What?" The question was muffled because she was still clinging to me like a stage three clinger. Not that I blamed her. Not much scared me in this world, but the idea of a stone-cold killer being that close to her... "Where?"

"My place."

Chapter Ten

Amanda

I'M NOT sure how it happened, but it felt like one minute, I was standing in my father's cabin staring at a photo of me in bed reading, and the next, I was on the passenger side of Axel's truck on our way across Sultan to the Sins of Wrath motorcycle compound.

Where exactly had my life gone wrong? Was this even real?

Several men I didn't know, but identified as prospects to the club, had shown up at the cabin within an hour of us receiving that envelope. They'd brought Axel his truck and helped him load his motorcycle into the back of a second truck. Promises were made it would be fixed upon return. I'd barely had time to object or gather what I'd need before we were on our way.

While I felt safer with Axel at my side than I did alone, I still felt vulnerable being out in the open like this. Whoever our killer was, he had eyes on me contin- uously. Now that I knew that, I couldn't seem to shake the feeling.

"I'm not sure this is the best course of action," I stated quietly. "We are putting others at risk."

He gave me a side-eye with a side of smirk. "This is part of the job. While we do try to keep things away from the compound, it's not always possible. And trust me, our compound is far more secure than your father's property. No one is going to get close without all of us knowing."

"Unless they have drones."

"What?" The angry frown stamped on his face hadn't gone away in quite some time.

"You said no one can get close, but we both know that a drone can get eyes in almost all situations."

"Oh, I already filled in Tel and JD about your little drone stunt. Tel will be making changes to our security to account for that before the sun comes up. No one appreciates that shit."

"Why do you call him Tel? Is that short for something?"

"Intel. That was his job in the military and the man is quite literally a genius, especially when it comes to computers. He's way too smart to be hanging with us, but he got burned by the government and I guess this is his way of fighting back against the system."

"They seem to do that a lot, but their loss is your gain."

"Damn right." His grip tightened on the steering wheel as we fell into silence once again.

I wasn't in the mood for small talk, but the silence didn't bode well for me either. That left me nothing to do but think, and to think meant all I saw were those damned pictures. This wasn't the first time I'd been stalked by someone I burned during an arrest, but it was the first since everything that went down with the Mazzeo operation. I was due to talk to my government appointed therapist again, but I still didn't want to reveal anything. I wasn't in denial, but I did want to put it behind me.

All that mattered to me was that the two principals in that investigation were dead. What I'd had to endure to get the job done didn't matter. If they'd survived, maybe I would feel differently, but as it was, that case was closed. Until this.

Lost in thought, I didn't realize how close we were to the compound until Axel slowed at the gate until it opened enough for us to get through. He didn't stop to talk to anyone, but the burly tattooed bald man at the manned hut tipped his chin up when Axel flicked him a little finger wave. Guys played it so cool when they greeted each other. Especially these ones.

MC men were an interesting breed. Strong loner types, but fiercely loyal to each other and whatever oath the club followed. They often didn't have a lot of family outside the club, instead the club became their family. Six months ago the FBI would have been ecstatic to see me this close to the Wrath.

They were outlaws on the short list of clubs that often got looked at and getting someone on the inside had been on the dream list for quite some time. But now they didn't give a shit. Not about me. They'd cut me out like I'd been nothing more than a common criminal.

Because I was.

Like it or not. I'd given in to the impossible pressure of Frank Mazzeo and the destruction he had been capable of, and that had made me one of the bad guys. I had plenty of blood on my hands and no one was going to forget it, least of all me. Gah. I wanted to throw my hands up in the air and scream. I hated that being involved in a new case kept me thinking about the recent past. I was never going to be ready for the future if I couldn't let the past go. I needed to look forward.

I took a deep breath and looked over at Axel. I could still smell him and it was definitely messing with my head.

We drove past the main clubhouse, but in the dark, I couldn't make out much beyond the fact the building still looked the same. Because of Houston, Axel's best friend at the time, we'd all spent a fair amount of time out here as kids even though, at the time, Axel had not been part of the club. That part came with being best friends with the club president's son. Because of that, we'd had a certain amount of leeway on the property.

Coming here as a teenager had been a thrill. An act of rebellion against my father, who despite his standing in the community, was kind of an asshole. Everyone seemed to love him, but I was pretty sure what they really loved was his money. And while money couldn't buy respect, it did buy him a lot of power in the community and a new wife every few years. I'd like to think my mother had been an exception, but I kind of doubted it. A drunk driver had killed her only three years into the marriage and already the strain had begun to show.

I had only been three at the time so I shouldn't have remembered much, but I did. While I couldn't picture what my mother looked like outside of a picture, I did remember hiding in the kitchen cupboard when the two of them fought.

After her death, it was our nanny that held us together, not him. It definitely wasn't the string of step-mothers. After a decade away, so much continued just as it had before.

This club, for example. While it looked the same, I knew it had grown. Only how much I wasn't sure.

However, when we drove past the main building, many newer ones came into focus. While I'd seen them on the drone footage, those grainy images had not done them justice. There were cute wooden cottages dotting all across the property, as well as a handful of larger cabins beyond the trees. And then there was the big building in the back that I couldn't see at the moment, but it was where the FBI suggested most of their illegal activity took place. The tree coverage over that area was intense and no drone could get a good look.

It wasn't anything more than a plausible guess because nothing—outside that one building they couldn't get access to—indicated anything but businesses that were run legitimately and above board. They paid taxes, they employed staff, they even gave back to the community more than any other company in the county.

When the truck finally halted and Axel threw it into park, we were in front of yet another cabin. This one medium in size with a wide front porch and lots of woodwork that made the entire structure blend with nature.

"Where are we?" I didn't want to sound stupid, but I had no clue how things worked inside the club. For all I knew this was a bunkhouse and I was about to be faced with a group of big, tattooed men who might not be too happy to see me.

"This is my place," He offered, pushing open his door and grabbing several bags from the seat behind him. "We'll be staying here for the time being."

My hand froze on the door handle as I let that soak in. Since I didn't know what I was supposed to say, I pushed my own door open and climbed out of his oversized truck. Axel certainly had an affinity for his vehicles. The custom Harley he rode was one of the most beautiful bikes I'd ever seen. I especially liked the matte black color scheme. With the lack of shiny chrome, the entire machine blended seamlessly together. It had made him a much harder target when I'd taken aim on him earlier.

How had that only been hours ago? It felt like days. Suddenly, the late hour and my lack of sleep chose that moment to catch up with me as I stifled a yawn before grabbing the duffel I'd packed. He marched up the walkway, while I trudged behind him, each step getting heavier and heavier. I don't know if it was the fatigue or the knowledge that I was about to walk into his personal space that was weighing me down.

Together at my father's cabin was one thing. There was nothing there to reveal much about either of us. But this was an entirely different situation. He opened the unlocked door and when he turned to hold the door open for me, I gave him a look.

"Locking a door out here isn't necessary. I trust my club brothers implicitly and I wasn't kidding about the security. The entire property is a mapped out set of laser security that will alert our team to even the slightest movement when enabled."

"Is it enabled now?"

"Yeah, it is. I saw the lights when we drove in. And no, no one else can see those lights and disable them. If you don't know where to look, you'll never find them."

I was skeptical that some lights could be that well-hidden, but I trusted the club was serious about their security. Motorcycle Clubs like theirs were not immune to enemies and they had to plan for all contingencies.

I stepped inside, and a moment later, he flicked the lights on, illuminating the space. I'm not sure if I was surprised or just grateful, but the place looked pretty awesome and cozy as hell. The main area was one big room, but each area was well defined by furniture in the living area and an island and cabinets in the kitchen.

I dropped my bag next to the door and made my way to the couch. All I wanted to do was close my eyes for just a few minutes. Maybe a quick catnap, and then we could get back to working on the case. With him watching us, there really wasn't any time to waste.

"Why don't you go ahead in the bedroom," he said, just as I collapsed on my side on the couch. I think he said something else, but I couldn't make it out and it was the last thing I heard before everything went black.

Chapter Eleven

Axel

BY THE NEXT morning at dawn, I was too antsy to stay in bed any longer. Sleep had been fitful at best. I'd hoped to give Mandy more time to rest before she heard me moving around, but I couldn't sit still any longer. We'd both been dead on our feet last night, but her more so than me. I'd considered carrying her into the bedroom, so she could have the bed, but I was afraid to wake her.

She was strung tight, that much was obvious. The dark circles under her eyes spoke volumes as did the lack of fight she'd put up last night when I'd made the unilateral decision to move her to the compound. Between the lack of sleep and real food, life was taking its toll on her. I padded into the bathroom, quickly going through my morning routine as quietly as I could.

However, by the time I was dressed in a pair of ratty jeans and a warm sweatshirt, I couldn't stay in here any longer. There were too many things to handle. JD had gotten a quick rundown on what had happened, but there were more details to hash out. Only, when I exited the bedroom, I hadn't planned on finding Mandy sprawled on the couch, the blanket I'd placed over her tossed to the ground and the long-sleeved t-shirt she'd slept in riding just under her breasts exposing her smooth, flat stomach and the barely-there thong panties bisecting her perfect ass.

Fuck my life.

Under normal circumstances I would have sent a silent thank you out into the world to the designer of those panties, but these were not normal circumstances, and looking at that ass wasn't good for my mental health.

Look away.

Yeah, that was a realistic thought. Not.

Look the fuck away.

It didn't even matter that I hated the fact she could spark my interest after everything. I still couldn't tear my gaze from the view.

Not when everything in me inexplicably wanted to round that couch, spread her thighs wide and get lost between those long, sexy legs of hers. They were even more perfect than I remembered. And I was already imagining the little birthmark mole on her right thigh just below the apex of where her legs met her pussy. I wanted to bite her there.

Fuck. Fuck. Fuck.

My dick went instantly hard and I pressed against it, hoping I could get it under control. As if that was going to happen. I suddenly had a one-track mind, and it wasn't in my fucking head.

As if fate had finally taken pity on me, someone stomped onto my porch and pounded against my front door. I glanced from the door back to Mandy as she began to stir.

"Wake the fuck up, and go in the bedroom. And for fuck's sake, put some decent clothes on," I managed through gritted teeth. It was bad enough I'd had to see her like this, I sure as hell didn't want anyone else to.

Something in my voice must have alerted her awake. Her eyes popped open and she looked down at herself. "Oh shit." She scrambled for the blanket and wrapped it around her lower body before she sprinted for the open bathroom. I scowled after her, because she'd done a half ass job of covering up.

Forcing my attention away from her, I headed to the door and yanked it open.

"Figured we should talk. I brought breakfast. Sasha wakes up before the sun to make these," JD grumbled as he pushed past me and into my place. "You better have some fucking coffee though."

"Are those her orange cinnamon rolls?" I grabbed the foil wrapped plate out of his hand, sniffing at the edge of it as I headed into the kitchen. "And yes, I have coffee. Just give me a second to make some. And why are you fucking bitching? She get too tired from baking to hoover your dick?"

"Fuck you. The last thing I need this morning is you worrying about my dick."

I snorted. JD had been a lot testier lately than usual and I had a feeling something was going to have to give between those two. She was way too sweet to be content as just a club girl. "Fine. I'll get your coffee old man. Then we can talk."

"Where is she?"

I tipped my head in the direction of the bedroom, refusing to elaborate. When his eyebrows climbed into his hairline, I ignored it. He could think whatever the hell he wanted. When it came to women, I answered to no one.

"I woke her ass up and told her to get off my couch. I suspect she'll make an appearance soon." I grabbed the coffee canister I kept fully stocked and went about setting the coffee to brew. I needed the caffeine. Especially since my day had already gone to shit.

"Always the host with the most. I'm surprised you didn't dump her in Izzy's old cabin." He hit one of the island stools and copped a squat directly in front of the plate of rolls I'd set there. He could grumble about Sasha all he wanted, but not a one of us could turn down her cooking. Especially not those beauties.

"Thought about it. But it was late and we were both too tired to do anything more than pass out. Besides, I think she was more freaked out by those pictures than she actually admitted, and leaving her alone didn't set right."

JD nodded. He'd just read between the lines no matter what I said. Thank fuck he'd not seen those panties. And why the fuck was I still thinking about them? FUCK.

"I'd like to see the shit you brought. If this guy is bold enough to risk himself around the club, then we may have a bigger problem than we thought."

"No shit." I poured the first cup of steaming coffee and slid the mug across the island in front of JD. "Her initial assessment is that he's not just a serial killer, and I tend to agree. This isn't just some sick fuck out to get off. Whoever he is, he's pissed and wants to fucking scare her."

"And is she? Scared I mean." He sipped at the black coffee without so much as letting it cool. The way he drank his coffee black and scorching, it was a wonder he had a single tastebud left.

"No, she isn't." We both looked up at the sound of Mandy's voice. She must have taken a quick shower because her hair was wet and she'd changed into different clothes.

"Mandy," JD beamed, a smile growing wide across his face. "Look at you, girl. You are a sight for sore eyes."

She smiled back at him, and I stood there stupefied as she walked over to him and he stood to hug her. "Oh please. I am not a sight for anything. You could park your motorcycle in these eye bags I've got going on.

Ooh, what's that?" she asked, eyeing the plate of pastries.

"One of our club girls made them. She is a wizard in the kitchen."

"That's not all she's a wizard with," I mumbled under my breath.

"What was that?" Mandy asked as she picked up one of the sweet rolls and took a big bite. I stared, immediately forgetting the question she asked. I was too caught up in the sight of her sugar-coated lips to focus on anything else. It gave me ideas I had no business having, but the image of where else I wanted to see those lips had already invaded. And when her tongue peeked out to lap up the sugar?

Fuck my life.

I clenched my fists and reminded myself that I wasn't a teenager anymore. My dick didn't get to control my actions. Especially not with her.

"Pussy." JD barked under a cough, forcing me to look away. I met his hardened gaze with my own pissed off version and flipped him off.

"Don't we have serious shit to do this morning? I thought we were going to talk about the case?" My surly attitude hit its intended target. Mandy's momentary cheerful mood disappeared as fast as it had shown up. She dropped the pastry on one of my paper plates and grabbed a napkin to wipe away the sugar she'd seemed to be enjoying just moments ago.

The word dickhead filtered through my mind, which I decided to embrace, rather than take as some sort of sign to stop. The smartest thing we could do was to get down to business.

"By all means. Get on with it, boy." What normally would have been an endearment from JD definitely didn't come out that way today. I'm not sure why he seemed so annoyed with me, but I was going to ignore it—for now.

"I have all the case files and the pictures from last night if you want to see those."

"Yeah, might as well. Axel gave me a rundown on what happened, but it doesn't hurt to look."

"Got it," she said, leaving the island to retrieve her bag as well as a pad of notebook paper and a pen. "I'm going to take notes in case anything we say now jogs something loose later. I'm more of a visual learner than anything else, so seeing it in writing or in a picture really helps."

"Makes sense." JD turned his full attention to Mandy, and for the next thirty minutes, she went over every detail of the case while I grabbed a second cup of coffee and slid one to her as well, fixed the way she'd described yesterday.

"Thank you," she said, her demeanor as rigid as ever, except for her eyes. They were definitely softer than they had been yesterday.

"Are we absolutely one hundred percent sure that this couldn't have something to do with Mazzeo?" JD asked.

"That was my thought exactly. I don't believe in any coincidences, and this one has way too many. I'm going to put in a call to Houston and see if there's anything he can contribute. But my understanding is that both Izzy and Frank were only children, and his parents are long gone. That doesn't leave anyone behind to seek revenge."

"What about business associates?" Mandy asked. "Surely, one of those could take up the torch a son might have."

"You would know his business associates better than us," I bit, teeth and all.

"I was surprised to hear that you were helping Frank." JD's words caused Mandy to flinch, and instead of finally feeling vindicated, I wanted to stand up for her. Because there had to be some reason she would help a piece of shit like him.

"It's not as cut and dried as you might think, but that's a long story for another time. Suffice it to say, no one in his organization cared enough about him to go to these lengths. Although someone had to take over the business. The mafia would never allow the business to go fallow without someone new to take over."

"They haven't," I said. "We've already started to see trouble brewing out of Seattle. It sounds like his organization has been taken over by a secret cabal type of thing. Whoever's in charge now are keeping their individual identities a secret."

"Seriously? Wow. That's fascinating." She sipped more of her coffee.

"Is it? I pretty much think it's a pain in the ass. Ours, specifically. They seem to be aligning themselves with a rival MC out of Seattle that has been nothing but a colossal headache since they hit the scene. If they are going to be the muscle for the new mafia of Seattle, we're all going to have a lot of new problems down the pike."

"Let's not get ahead of ourselves," JD offered. "Why don't you go make that call to Houston, while I go through these files again. There must be a clue here somewhere. Otherwise, we are going to be stuck waiting for him to make another move, and that is not my preferred choice."

"Agreed," I said, slipping my phone out of my pocket and disappearing into my bedroom. Not only would a call to Houston give me something to focus on, but it would also give me some much-needed head-space away from her.

Chapter Twelve

Amanda

"WE SHOULD PROBABLY TALK."

Those were about the last words I wanted to hear from anyone, let alone the president of the Sins of Wrath motorcycle club. I'd thought Axel leaving the room would give me a chance to breathe and pull myself together. His biting words were wreaking havoc on my emotions this morning and I needed to pull myself together.

"Yeah. There's a lot of details to go over. Although I don't know if it's going to help. I feel like I'm at a dead end. I was going to ask if your guy Tel could help me access some security cameras outside my own network... I hoped I wasn't reaching too far asking to help me hack into the county system and any other private businesses in the area who might have cameras. But someone, somewhere, had to have picked up something. In this day and age, no one could get around without being filmed one way or another.

"Sure. Tel can do that in his sleep, but that's not what I meant. I'm talking about Axel—and you."

"There is no Axel and me. That is ancient history. We were just kids. Neither one of us is looking to re-hash any of that."

"You sure about that? From what I can see, he's still looking at you for answers. He might not ask the questions, but trust me, they're there. And they aren't ever going away if you don't answer them."

"Why? He already hates me. What good is it going to do to talk it out? Nothing is going to change what happened. It's done. Why not leave it buried in the past where it belongs?"

"But is it buried?" he asked. "That boy is the best damn VP a man like me could ask for, but when it comes to you, he still wears his heart on his sleeve. Or the pieces that are left anyways. He deserves to know the truth."

I narrowed my eyes at that. It sounded like he might know more than he should, but how could that be? Just like Axel, I'd chosen to bottle it all up and bury it. It was the best way then and it was the best way now for me to keep moving forward.

"What truth? I hope you don't think anyone lied to him about what happened. I'm not holding out some secret love child on him. She died. I know it's probably my fault, but I don't know what I could have done to stop it." I looked away from him then because I could feel the unshed tears burning at the backs of my eyes and watching his face would only make it worse. I wouldn't spill another tear but that didn't mean it didn't hurt.

A big rough hand reached out and covered mine. "I know, baby girl. But that's not what he knows."

I turned back to him. "What does that mean? What does he know?"

"Talk to him."

I wanted to scream bloody murder right then, release all my pent-up frustration, but the lump in my throat prevented me from responding. Leaving was not my choice. Taken, was more like it.

"And what about Frank? Why did you help him?"

My blood turned to ice at those questions. I could have answered, maybe even garnered some sympathy. But that's not what I wanted people to think of when they looked at me. I'd rather they hate me than pity me.

"That's what I thought." He suddenly grabbed my hand and yanked me in his direction, his hard grip so unrelenting I had no choice to move as he wanted, and no hope of breaking free until he was ready to release me.

I don't know what I thought was going to happen. Maybe he was going to hurt me for causing his club so much trouble. I should have known. God, I was an idiot. I should have known.

He shoved at the sleeve of my shirt until he'd revealed my right forearm.

"And what about these?" He jerked my hand again until we were both staring at the series of scars that bisected my wrists and halfway up my arm. "How did you get these?" It was then I realized his anger wasn't exactly directed at me, but was about me, maybe even on my behalf.

"I had a rough job. Lots of accidents happen," I whispered, jerking my hand again that he finally set free.

"Don't try to bullshit me. I know better than that. Speak the truth."

I shook my head, unable to form the words.

"Then tell him—or I will. I'd normally stay out of this kind of business, but his anger with you makes him vulnerable."

"Then quit the job. My father can hire someone else to bolster security. I'll recommend someone."

He shot me a dark look. "There is no one better for this job. You know it, and so does he."

That need to scream in frustration rose sharply again. "Jesus Christ. Then why the hell did you put him on this job? Don't you have others who can babysit me?"

"If I thought all you needed was a babysitter? Sure. But this case is too dangerous for that, and I'm not risking any of my guys more than I have to. You need a partner."

"Axel is *not* my partner." I practically spat back. "He can barely tolerate me."

JD stood from his chair and leaned in. "Then fix it. Stop fucking around. Don't play any more games, and just fucking fix it."

I was ready to tell the old man to shove his demands where the sun didn't shine when he disappeared through the front door, leaving me to stand there staring after him.

"What happened?" Axel came up behind me, and I shrugged. "I heard you arguing with him. What was that about?"

"He wants us to kiss and make up."

"Excuse me?"

I turned and faced him. "He wants us to talk about what happened all those years ago. He even implied that you misunderstood what happened. Is that true?"

A cold, dark look crossed his face. Honestly, I'd thought I'd seen his worst long before now, but I was wrong. The hate filled expression now aimed in my direction threatened me in a way that made every single thing I'd endured to this moment mere child's play. I half expected him to wrap his hands around my neck and squeeze until I could no longer breathe.

JD was right about one thing. My being here with him put him at risk, but in more ways than one. Not only was there a chance he could end up collateral damage in this case, but he was also in danger from himself. He could snap. And when that happened...well, he might not come back from that.

"I'm not doing this with you," he growled, sounding more animal than human.

"I tried to tell him. He seems to think we must be partners to work this case. I disagreed." I could feel the fire I was playing with licking at my skin. And yet, I couldn't stop. I needed that hate from him more than I needed air. It was the only thing I could feel anymore.

"We aren't partners," he said through gritted teeth.

"My words exactly. He even implied that you might not believe what you were told about our baby. What the hell is that supposed to mean? Do you think I secretly had her and didn't tell you? I would never do that to you. She died, Axel."

"Stop." His tone deepened to a threat I could clearly hear. Whatever it was JD thought he needed to hear, he clearly didn't. Did I get smart and let it go? Of course, I didn't, because I'm a fucking idiot when it comes to Axel. Always was and always would be.

"She's gone." I wish I could have cried then. Maybe it would have made a difference. But I couldn't and we'd never know.

"I said,"—he grabbed me by the shoulders and marched me backwards until my back and head slammed into the door. It didn't hurt like you would think, but it did stun me."Stop! I can't hear another word from you. It was enough to hear it from your father. Now you're telling me it was a little girl? What the fuck made you so fucking cruel?"

The anguish in his voice ripped something inside me. "I'm so sorry. I didn't mean to—"

He cut me off by covering my mouth with his hand.

"Fuck you, Amanda. One more word about it and I

won't be responsible for what I do. So just stop. *Now.* Because I will never—*never* forgive you for killing our baby. Legally, that might have been your right, but I deserved to hear that decision from you *before,* and not after the fact, and not from your fucking father. "

Chapter Thirteen

Amanda

Ten years ago

"GET IN."

I stopped in the middle of the sidewalk and blinked at the car in front of me.

Oh boy. This couldn't be good. What was my father doing in this area of town? I was only half a block away from the Sins of Wrath compound, where I was supposed to meet Axel in five minutes.

With one last look in the direction I'd been headed, I reached for the rear door handle and pulled it open. I slid inside and closed the door behind me. My father didn't exactly approve of me hanging out with Axel, let alone me being out here with what he called ruffians.

Kind of a weird word to use when referring to the club of outlaws. My father knew as well as I did that a lot of illegal shit went down with them.

Houston's father was even currently on trial for accidentally killing his wife.

I spared a glance at my father who remained facing forward as the driver pulled away from the curb. The only sign of emotion was the tight set of my father's jaw.

Yeah, this definitely wasn't going to go well.

The ride home went by in silence as I considered pulling out my phone and sending Axel a text. He'd been expecting me so we could talk about the baby. Only today had gone to shit from the beginning.

Now I was going to have to tell my father the truth before he learned from someone else. We lived in a small town where scandalous news traveled like wildfire.

We turned through the gates of our ranch, but instead of continuing to the house like I expected, the car rushed to the helipad my father often used.

"Are you going somewhere?" I asked, assuming my father had a business trip to take.

He didn't answer right away, and I frowned. This silence wasn't like him. If he was unhappy about something he rarely held back. A man of silence he was not.

The car slid to a stop in front of the hangar, and fifty feet or so away, his personal helicopter was gearing up for an obvious take off.

The driver hopped out of the car, went to the rear

hatch and retrieved what I assume was my father's luggage. But when he approached the pad, I recognized two of the suitcases as mine.

"What's going on?" I stared out the window as my stomach twisted with nerves.

"You're going away."

"What? Why? I—I can't." I couldn't contain the panic rising in me.

"You can and you will. I heard the news about your pregnancy today. Do you have any idea how horrifying that was to hear on the street? My own teenage daughter, who I didn't even know was dating anyone, had spread her legs for a criminal."

"What? No! It's not like that. He's not like that. We're in love."

He laughed. "Don't be naive. Those men don't love. They kill. They rape. And they deal drugs. The only thing that motivates them is money. I won't allow my daughter to go down that path."

"Axel isn't like that." Tears streamed down my face as I stared at the stubborn expression on his face. He'd already made up his mind, and there would be no changing it, and he'd made sure I couldn't escape whatever fate he had in store for me.

My father knew me too well. If he'd given me any warning I would have immediately run to Axel.

I still had my phone, though. I could get a message to him.

As if he'd read my mind, my father held out his hand. "Phone," he demanded.

"Why? If I'm leaving, I will need to let people know. You don't want anyone to come looking for me, right?"

He laughed. "That won't be an issue. Where you're going, there won't be a chance in hell anyone could find you. Phone!" he ordered again, raising his voice.

Something snapped inside me as I slapped my phone into his outstretched hand. "My baby needs a father. I will hate you for this."

"Your baby is a mistake. I'd rather you hate me than lose you to a gang of low life criminals. That is not your destiny. It is not what I have worked my entire life for you to accept. It is not the life my grandchild deserves either."

"You can't control me forever. One day soon, I will leave."

"Someday that will be true. And I hope by then you'll have learned to do the right thing. Forget about that boy, because I promise you, he will forget about you."

As I exited the car and turned toward the waiting helicopter, I held my head high. Whatever he did, wherever he made me go, it wouldn't matter. I would have Axel's baby inside me and that he could never take away.

Present day

· · ·

I sat on the floor with the feel of Axel's fingers still digging into my cheeks. He'd delivered a verbal blow far deadlier than anything he could have done physically, and hours later, I still couldn't move. He'd stormed from the cabin and had yet to return. I wasn't sure he ever would. If I was smart, I'd get the hell out of there and be gone before he came back.

I didn't doubt his threats. If I brought it up again, he would do something drastic. But I was so damned confused and I needed answers. He'd made it sound like—

I needed to make a call. Where was my phone? I dragged myself to my hands and knees and crawled to the couch where I'd spent the night. I shoved my hands between the cushions and felt my way around. I pulled a few quarters and remote control out, but no sign of my stupid phone.

It had to be here. I yanked the cushions to the ground. Nothing. I shoved my hand under the couch and felt around, even going so far as to bend and twist so I could see under there. Still nothing. Where the hell was it? I didn't have it with me at the island so it couldn't be there. Maybe I'd taken it into the bathroom and forgot I had it?

I was about to haul myself to my feet when I spied it on the end table, next to a glass of water and my smart watch. For a second I hesitated, thinking about how thoughtful he'd been, first by covering me with a blanket and then going so far as to laying out my things so they would be available to me when I woke. My eyes burned, and for a moment, I thought I might finally crack. When the tears failed to materialize, I grabbed my phone and punched in the number I knew by heart.

"Amanda? Are you all right? I heard about what happened last night. Please tell me you are somewhere safe?" The concern in his voice washed over me, and as usual, it added to my confused feelings where my father was concerned. I knew he loved me, but his actions were often so contradictory. Love one minute, indifference the next. I thought I'd gotten used to it, but now I wasn't so sure.

"What did you say to Axel?" I asked, my voice thick with anger and pain.

"What do you mean? I haven't spoken to him. All of my communication comes through his boss."

"Not about this. Fuck! I'm not talking about that right now."

"You need to calm down and watch your language with me, Amanda. I understand that you're scared about this nightmare, but that's no reason to behave this way, especially when you're the one that brought this to my door."

His admonishment sent me over the edge I thought I'd already gone over. "Just shut the fuck up, *Dad*, and answer the question!"

He sputtered on the other end of the line. "I haven't talked to him directly in ten years, so whatever you think I did, it's absurd." I could hear the lie in his voice from the moment it left his lips. While I needed answers from him, I wasn't sure he would give them to me so I took a different approach and went for the jugular.

"Did you tell Axel I had an abortion?"

The commotion at his end went completely silent. So quiet, I pulled the phone away from my ear to see if he'd hung up, but according to the screen we were still connected.

"Amanda," he started. "You were sixteen. You had no business getting hitched to that man for a lifetime—"

A surge of anger whipped through me in a violent rage. I couldn't listen. I knew the truth. "You bastard!" I yelled, throwing the phone as hard as I could at the cabin wall. It crashed to the floor, a few pieces breaking off. Oh my God. I couldn't breathe. I was back on my hands and knees trying to pull in a breath and my lungs wouldn't allow it.

"What was that? Amanda?"

Oh my God, I couldn't even destroy my phone so as to not listen to his voice while I tried to stop a panic attack. Hate. Hate. Hate. This was total bullshit. As if that wasn't enough, the front door popped open and a familiar pair of boots appeared in my narrowed vision.

"Amanda? Are you still listening? I did what I thought was best and at the time that meant getting him out of your life."

"Dad. Stop talking. Just stop talking and hang up. You've done enough damage. Goodbye." It was difficult to push words out in between wheezes, but I was determined to make him stop.

"What difference does it make anyway? Whether

you had an abortion or a miscarriage the result is the same. The problem was gone. That's all he needed to know."

"Dad!" I screamed, scrambling for the phone. Axel, however, beat me to it, his boot stomping down what was left of my phone, turning it into a mangled mess, effectively silencing my father.

Finally. I slumped against the wall and pulled my legs up into my chest. It was too much. All of it. I sure as hell hoped this was rock bottom because I couldn't take a single thing more.

Not. A. Single. Thing.

"Mandy."

I don't know why now, but that one word from him broke the fucking dam. Tears streamed down my face, into my mouth, down my neck. For years, I'd waited for this. A woman who couldn't cry for the death of her unborn child, or the loss of the only man she loved had to be broken beyond repair. And when the tears didn't come during the weeks of torture at the hands of Frank Mazzeo and his business partner Marco, I'd given in to the notion that I was beyond saving *or* redemption. I would never be normal.

I wasn't sure what difference it made at this point, but apparently Axel had heard my father's words. I felt his arms wrap around me and I slapped them away.

"No!" I screamed in between wails. "Don't touch me." He said something, but his words were beyond my hearing. I was consumed with a lifetime of sorrow and it had to get out. I didn't want a witness let alone any help. I fought harder, suddenly fueled with pain. My fist connected with something and he cursed.

"Let me—"

"No! Get out!" I flailed and fought, even biting at him when he got too close. "Get out."

"Okay. I'm going. But I'm not leaving. I'll be right outside."

"Go!" I screamed, nothing coherent beyond the feeling of my soul being ripped from my body. The door finally closed behind Axel and I collapsed against it, sliding to the floor. I thought the day I'd lost my baby would be the worst of my life. I'd been wrong...

Chapter Fourteen

Axel

I STOOD at my front door only inches from her wails. Over and over, they stabbed into me.

What I'd heard over that phone had nearly stopped my heart. What the hell was going on?

I was going to kill her father for this. With my bare fucking hands so I could watch the life drain from him slowly.

Motherfucker could burn in hell.

"You need to give her time." JD said from behind me. His knack for being in the wrong place at the right time still unnerved me. Especially when it came to this. I wasn't sure if talking to him about this would make one damned difference.

"I fucked up."

"We all do when it comes to people we care about. Why don't we take a walk?"

I shook my head. "I can't leave her. She's falling apart and she won't let me in."

"That's because she wouldn't want you to witness all of this. She's an independent woman used to relying on only herself. Seriously son. Give her some space. Your time to talk it out will come soon enough. For now, she needs to deal with this alone. We need to talk anyway. Did you talk to Houston? I need an update."

"I left him a message. Told him what was going on and what information we were looking for. I guess he'll call me back—eventually."

JD nodded. "He'll call if he has some news. Until then, we need to look at the other possibilities."

"Sure. But all the files are in there."

JD smiled. "You think so? You should know better than that."

It took me a second, but my brain finally caught up to what he'd said. "Tel got something? Already?"

"Is that even a question?" He slapped me on the back and walked me off the porch. "I'll send Patty over to check on her. She'll watch over your girl."

Calling her my girl felt like a stretch. But my brain was fucking scrambled and I wasn't sure about anything at the moment. I did agree, however, that we both needed some space and having Patty nearby seemed smart.

Patty wasn't just an old lady to one of our longest standing members who'd been around from the beginning with JD and Houston's dad, she was a licensed psychologist who specialized in abuse cases. This was not the first time we needed her services and it likely wouldn't be the last.

We walked in silence to the clubhouse, my stomach still churning from the shock of Turner's revelations, and Mandy's subsequent breakdown. I wasn't sure I'd be much help tonight, but at least there was liquor in the clubhouse. I was ready for a shot or ten.

And the sooner I got through this, the sooner I'd get back to her. The amount of space I could give her had a limit and it was already counting down.

Walking into the building, I was surprised to see so many members in attendance. "What's going on?" I asked. "Why is everyone here?"

"I called everyone in. We need all hands on deck right now. We've got multiple problems, and I believe they are about to intersect."

"What does that mean?"

Before JD could answer, their arrival was met with the shouts and greetings of their club brothers that hadn't had a chance to gather as a group like this in far too many weeks.

"Axel, brother." Cash, one of the biggest brothers at six foot six, and at least two hundred and fifty pounds, greeted him with an arm shake and a display of strength that he returned enthusiastically.

"Good to see you," I said. "When did you return?"

Cash laughed and handed him an oversized mug of freshly pulled beer. "Only last night. And it's fucking good to be here."

"Breakfast of champions?" I asked, laughing as Cash finished off his own glass.

"Damn right. It sounds like we might not have another chance to drink together for a while. Word is we're going hunting for a killer."

I spied the bloodthirsty look in Cash's eyes, understanding that feeling well. There was a man out there, possibly closer than was comfortable, looking to kill Mandy, and I planned to do anything it took to keep that from happening. I didn't care who I had to hurt, or how many laws I had to break to get it done, but get it done I would.

I tapped my glass to Cash's. "Every man needs a hunt now and then. I don't know about you, but I'm looking forward to it."

"Looking forward to what?" Zook joined the conversation. He'd just come from his shift at Turner's place so he knew better than most of them what we would be up against.

"The hunt!" Cash laughed.

Zook gave me a side eye, while neither of us laughed. Cash hadn't been involved thus far so his exuberance couldn't be faulted. He'd not seen the evidence of what had been done to Mandy's coworker, or the pictures that had arrived at her doorstep.

And only JD and I knew about the rest.

Not to mention he was a crazy fuck when it came to danger. He wasn't stupid or reckless, but he always ran towards danger versus avoiding it. However, when the time came to fight their way out of a situation, having Cash on their side always presented an advantage.

It was important to remember that.

I finished my beer, thought about a shot of whiskey to follow up and changed my mind. Today promised to be a long day, and I preferred to face it with a clear mind and an angry heart. I refused to dull the pain when I needed clarity.

"I gathered us here, so we could talk about what's coming." JD interrupted his thoughts and ended the jovial conversation with Cash and Zook. "We don't have all the details, but Tel has found a connection between what's going on in Seattle and what's going on here in our own town."

I sucked in a breath, shocked that JD hadn't told me this in advance. "What the hell?"

"I know. I know. I just found out."

"We need to bring Amanda in on this."

JD threw me a narrowed look. We both knew that couldn't happen right now, but we'd need to bring her into the loop as soon as possible. I may not know everything about her, but I did know she was capable of being a part of this fight. Would insist on it.

As much as I may prefer to keep her safe on the sidelines, it was never going to happen.

"We'll talk to her when she's ready. For now, we are going to work the information."

"Which is?"

"Tel was able to trace the order for the box delivery to Turner's house to a shell company in Seattle. We thought it was a dead end, but when he was investigating some of the payments going in and out of the new MC out of Seattle, he noticed similarities."

"What?" several of the members all echoed together.

"Are you certain?" I asked.

JD and Tel were both nodding.

"So, this new group that seems to be moving in and absorbing Frank's operation is associated with whomever killed the FBI agent and is currently trying to track Mandy?" I repeated the obvious because I couldn't seem to wrap my head around it. "How is that even possible? Every sign of this murder and the associated threats comes across as personal. Why would some conglomerate care about avenging Frank's death? That doesn't make any sense. If they aren't family..."

We were missing something. There had to be a connection beyond this. "We need to know who's behind the corporation."

"Agreed. However, they've buttoned up their operation pretty tight. I'm honestly surprised we found this. I think someone screwed up when they sent that box. Maybe they didn't understand what they were dealing with."

"You think it was the MC?"

"There's a better than decent chance. Their president isn't as much of an idiot as we wish he was though. He's former Army Intelligence. Tel broke that file too.

Got himself into trouble overseas and court marshaled. He had connections though and a very high-priced lawyer got him out of a less than honorable discharge with minimal time in a military brig. But mistakes can happen."

Cash whistled beside me. "That's a lot to unpack."

"Right?!" I said. "It sounds like whoever is behind this corporation has been busy making plans for quite some time. Like since maybe before Frank's death. Is that possible?"

"Anything is possible. I'm not ruling out anything at this point. Frank was a mean bastard, but he had more tricks up his sleeve than a shittastic magician. I wouldn't put it past him to have planned for what happened after his death. Most of those mafia types do. Although usually, there is a hierarchy in their organization that is followed unless someone fights to usurp the heir. And we had enough people on the inside of his organization that should have known if that was the case. Especially if there was someone being groomed to take his place."

I pressed my thumbs to my temples and rubbed the headache that now pounded there. I didn't need any more evidence to know that we were in this much deeper than we'd known. I should have been surprised that these two cases might be connected, but I wasn't. It seemed to be the way these things tended to go.

As we all moved to the conference room where we held Church, Tel began laying out all the facts and figures he'd uncovered.

I wasn't going to lie, while the information was critical in connecting the dots, it was far from sexy. I wanted to hear about guns, drugs, and violence. Those were the kinds of crime I wanted to sink my teeth in. Money-laundering, embezzlement, and mail fraud were not my specialties.

By the time Tel finished spelling it out hours later, I had to admit it all looked kind of iffy and coincidental. But again, I didn't believe in coincidences. All this information was more than enough for me to jump onboard the Mazzeo train. We thought our mix-up in the Seattle mafia had ended with Frank's death and Izzy's refusal to touch anything to do with his business.

Apparently, that was not the case.

I rubbed the back of my neck and stretched my head from side to side. "I need to get back to Amanda," I said to JD. "It's been too long."

Both of them looked at the time on their cellphones. "Yeah. I think we're about done here. Tel has all of his surveillance set up, and to be honest, we're gonna need this guy to make another move."

"I hope you aren't suggesting we use Mandy as bait."

From the look on JD's face that's exactly what he was suggesting.

"She's safe here. As long as she doesn't wander off, there shouldn't be anything to worry about. If this fucker comes here looking for her, then so be it. Saves us some time of hunting him. But we're also going to have a crew on both the Turner house and his hunting cabin. He's not getting close again without us knowing."

"That's assuming he plans to be the one making the moves. If he's part of that corporate mafia group, then he's got countless thugs at his disposal."

JD shrugged. "Don't matter either way. We're ready. If he sends someone to do his dirty work, we'll nab him and get the information we need any way we have to."

Fuck. This situation was getting dark. JD had just implied that we'd be using the basement again. How long had it been since we'd had to torture anyone?

"I've got to go." I palmed my phone as I stood and then shoved it into my pocket. I had a woman I desperately wanted to talk to waiting at my place, and we were long overdue for a conversation.

"Check in later, so we can figure out our next steps," JD said, before turning his attention back to the rest of the men gathered around the table.

I smiled at his dismissal. He likely wouldn't admit it, but our president seemed to have a soft spot for matchmaking. This wasn't the first time he'd made overt nudges.

I headed out of the clubhouse in the direction of home when my phone vibrated in my pocket. I pulled it out and stared down at the screen. Shit.

Houston calling.

As much as I needed to talk to him, taking this call now would take too long. I was seconds away from my cabin and I couldn't risk derailing that plan. I touched the dismiss button and made a mental note to call him back as soon as I could.

With my stomach clenched and braced for anything, I opened my front door and walked in. Only I found… What the hell?

Chapter Fifteen

Amanda

TWENTY MINUTES after Axel had finally left, the tears had dried up and the dry sobs began. To make matters worse, a strange woman I didn't know from Adam showed up at the door. My first assumption—that she was there to see Axel—had been incorrect.

She was there to see me.

"What do you mean JD sent you? For what? Does he need something?"

"Not at all. He figured you might need someone to talk to, and I tend to be pretty good at that."

I stared at her for a long time trying to figure out her deal, when it finally dawned on me. "Oh my God, are you some kind of therapist? Did he send you to talk me down from an apparent breakdown?" I was proud that my words were clear and the hiccups were gone, but that didn't mean I could hide the swollen eyes or splotchy skin.

But that was beside the point. How dare he!

"Yes, I am a psychologist, but more importantly, I belong to the club. That means not only do you have complete confidentiality in anything we talk about, but you can talk freely about club business that you normally couldn't share."

I don't know why, but her words annoyed me more than they comforted me. Did they really expect me to just welcome a stranger into my personal business and reveal all of my secrets? Maybe on a cold day in hell.

"I'm afraid they've wasted your time. I'm not in the market for a confidant."

The woman laughed. "That's a new one. I don't think anyone has ever called me that, and I've pretty much been called everything else you can think of."

I tightened my grip on the door, trying to remain calm. "I was trying to be kind."

"Oh really?" She looked skeptical. "Why would you be kind? I mean who would blame you if you were pissed that a strange woman showed up at your door expecting you to bare your soul to her?"

"Then why come?"

"Because I can't resist. If someone is hurting, and I'm in a position to help, that's what I want to do."

"Well, I definitely don't need a fixer. I can fix my own problems."

"Most people can. Although a lot don't realize they

can for a while. That's where I come in. I offer a little clarity."

"Oh, my clarity is just fine. For example, I'm perfectly clear on the fact that the men in this town think they have all the answers."

She snorted. "Good God, isn't that the truth. And yet we still love them anyways."

She could speak for herself. If there was anything of mine that was broken, it was definitely my capacity to love. Plus, I was pretty certain no one would mistake my anger for love. That would be insane. Okay, so maybe I had a lot of thoughts I *could* share, but that didn't mean I *wanted* to share them.

"Can I at least come in, so when JD asks how it went, I can say I tried? We don't have to talk about anything you don't want to. In fact, we can just gossip about the boys of the club if you want. You must have some questions."

It felt like a definite ploy. But I'd dealt with my fair share of psychotherapists over the years and I was pretty sure I could handle one more. I'd become quite adept at keeping them out of my head without being too obvious when I had to. But in this case, there was no reason to pretend. Nothing in my life hinged on whether this woman wrote a positive report and gave me a clean bill of mental health.

"I guess." I stepped back and allowed her entry, and then closed the door behind her. "It wouldn't hurt to get a rundown on the who's who around here. I didn't know the club members all that well ten years ago, since Axel wasn't quite a prospect yet, but there are a lot of new faces."

"That there are," she said taking a seat at the kitchen island instead of one of the comfier chairs in the living area. "I also haven't been in here since Axel took the place over." She turned and surveyed the spacious living area. "Not bad for a bachelor."

While I agreed, I opted to keep my comment to myself. But with her at the island, I felt like I needed to do something to keep myself busy. "Can I get you something to drink? I was just thinking about baking some cookies, if Axel has the ingredients..."

"Some water would be good. And if he doesn't, we can get one of the prospects to bring us whatever you need. The kitchen at the clubhouse is kept fully stocked."

"Okay," I said absently, already searching the cabinets for what I would need. While my first thought had been to make chocolate chip, I found no chocolate anywhere. That felt downright criminal. Who doesn't keep a stash just in case? If I had to stay here long, I would have to remedy that. Not that I intended to be here long at all. Hell, for all I knew, I'd be out on my ass when he returned. His expression when I'd ordered him out mid breakdown had not been good.

I pushed that memory out of my head for now. I'd deal with that when the time came.

While he had no chocolate, I did however, find everything I needed to make oatmeal cookies, including the raisins. I wondered if that was his favorite. I couldn't remember him ever mentioning anything like that when we were younger, but he was eighteen at the time. All I remember him being focused on back then was drinking, fucking, and riding his motorcycle. Not necessarily in that order, but pretty damned close.

Before I could stop it, a memory of Axel naked popped into my head. He'd been like a God to me back then. A sex God with his lean muscles, smooth skin, and a big—

Fuck.

I glanced over at Patty sitting there staring at me. "Everything okay?" she asked, an all too knowing look on her face.

"Yeah," I said, blinking a couple of times to get that picture of Axel out of my head and me focused again on the task of baking cookies. I had to do something to keep my mind occupied or I'd go crazy. And with Patty here, this wasn't the time to delve back into the case, although that couldn't wait much longer. Based on the timeline of the two deliveries, it wouldn't be long before the killer struck again.

"Did you find what you needed for the cookies, or should I text down to the clubhouse?" She wiggled her phone in her hand as if she was ready to order whatever I wanted right then.

"He doesn't have any chocolate for chocolate chip cookies, but he does have everything for oatmeal raisin. I'll just make those. They are my second favorite."

She smiled. "You sure? I know for a fact they have lots of chocolate in the main kitchen. Lots of the guys have some serious sweet tooths. You wouldn't neces-sarily think they would, considering how they look, but ever since they put that boxing ring in, most of them don't have any issue burning off extra calories. Which is totally unfair, by the way. I so much as look at a cookie and I gain a pound. It's total bullshit."

I could relate. To both. Before I started working out, I struggled to keep my weight from creeping up. Nowa-days though, it was a lot easier. I also didn't indulge in cookies very often. Today, however, I was going to eat my feelings and enjoy every minute of it.

"Yeah, I'm good. I don't really need the cookies either, but staying cooped up in this cabin has me needing to do something, and this is the only thing I could think of besides cleaning. And since this place doesn't look like it needs a cleaning, cooking it is."

She laughed. "Don't be too impressed with Axel's cleanliness. That is also done by either a prospect or one of the club ladies. JD likes the men to keep their focus on their jobs, so there are perks, like this cabin and the others as part of their membership. He's former Army you know. He's a man who thrives on order and broth-erhood. He likes rules too, but this isn't the military, so he keeps those to a minimum. Instead, he offers perks that the guys enjoy and keep the club running smoothly."

"I hope the prospects and the ladies get paid for all of their hard work. I remember when it used to be a privilege to even be allowed to hang around. I always hated that. I often thought those women might have suffered from low self-esteem to put up with that. If JD is still pulling that shit, I'm going to have a problem."

Patty laughed again. "You're quite a pistol. I like that. And don't worry. Those days are long gone. Although I was one of those women back in the day. But I was so head over heels in love I didn't even care. Being able to contribute to their wellbeing played to my strengths, and I took a lot of pride in that. But after JD's co-president went to jail, things around here changed quickly. JD made a lot of changes and lost half his club over it. But they rebuilt and came back stronger than ever. One of these days, Axel will be the president and he'll probably make changes too. It's what they do."

I tried to imagine JD stepping aside and Axel moving up to take his place. I could see it. Although not any time soon. JD wasn't that old and Axel didn't seem settled enough to take on the entire club. Just like me, he needed more time.

"I was gone by the time Houston lost his dad, but I was here when he lost his mom. It was kind of surprising that he left the club after that, but not really, you know?"

She nodded. "Yep. It was definitely not a great time."

"And JD never settled down with anyone after that?"

Her face fell. "He lost the love of his life the day she got killed. As unconventional and unhealthy as that relationship was, she was still everything to him. I don't think he'll ever take on an old lady unless he truly forgives himself for what happened."

"I'm surprised you are telling me all of this. I'm an outsider. Wouldn't JD frown on that?"

"Are you, though? Do you really think you'd be here in the club VP's home if you were truly an outsider? I've seen them take on a lot of cases, and not once has Axel brought anyone here. Even Izzy, who I think Axel had quite a crush on, stayed in one of the guest cabins on her own."

I shrugged that off. "He just wants to keep me close so he has access to my data. You know that whole saying about keeping your friends close and your enemies closer? That's all this is."

She frowned, and I could see she thought I was full of shit if I believed the words coming out of my mouth. But I refused to believe in anything else. I'd gone well past the point of hope years ago, and I wasn't about to fall into that trap again.

"If you say so." To which I had no answer.

After that we went back to small talk as I mixed up a big bowl of cookie dough and began getting them ready for the oven. By the time the first tray went into the oven, I'd learned more about the club than I thought I ever would. There weren't a lot of the OG members left, which meant most of them had no idea who I was or probably what I'd been to Axel. Patty had informed me that like me, he did not like to talk about the past.

"But you still know, right?" I asked. "About me?" I couldn't help it. Despite my attempt to keep my mouth shut about the past, I couldn't resist the question.

"That you were his high school girlfriend before he

became an official prospect? Yeah. I remember you coming to the compound a time or two with Houston and Axel back in the day. Those two were inseparable back then, and it seemed you showed up in the mix more often than not. For a while I wasn't sure which of them you wanted the most."

"Really?" I'd always been head over heels for Axel from the first time I'd seen him. I didn't care if no one else believed in love at first sight or young love. Back then I did, and it was as real as any other emotion I'd experienced. "Houston was fun," I blushed, hoping she didn't know exactly what I'd meant. "But it was always Axel for me."

"And now?" she prodded.

I could have shut her down. It was easy enough to see where she was going, but something in me had softened towards this woman and I believed she truly meant no harm or had any sort of secret agenda. Over the last hour I'd gotten a pretty good read on her and it wasn't deceitful.

"There hasn't been anyone since then who's meant as much, if that's what you're asking." I pulled some cookie dough off of the beater and stuck my finger in my mouth. "But that doesn't mean I'm looking for anything from him now, either. Things didn't end well the first time around. That doesn't make me want to repeat it."

"That's not exactly what I asked. But I can read between the lines. You still care about him."

I shrugged, hoping she would take that as noncommittal as I meant it. "I would have been fine if our lives hadn't intersected again. Especially under these circumstances. With a killer after me, I don't want him getting accidentally caught in the crosshairs."

"And that's it. You just don't want him to get hurt?"

"If you're hoping for a grand confession of unrequited love, you're going to be disappointed. I know what we had died. It's okay—now. It doesn't always take a therapist to heal. Sometimes it just takes time and a realistic belief that mistakes were made and sometimes that's how it goes. It doesn't always have to be this big tragic thing."

"Except you did suffer a tragedy, didn't you?"

A fresh wave of anger sparked in me. It was one thing for JD to send her here to talk to me and to try and get me to talk, it was another for him to fill her in on any specific details. That was no one's business, least of all his.

"I think you should leave."

"Amanda, don't. I didn't mean to upset you. I only sensed—"

"Bullshit," I'd quickly gone past anger and straight into rage. "You came here because JD told you about me and my baby. Well, you can march back to him and tell him to keep his nosy ass out of my business. I'm his client, not some charity case who needs to be fixed."

I don't know why I was so mad now. I'd known immediately why she was here and who had sent her.

"I'm sorry." She grabbed her purse from the floor at her feet and walked a few steps backward, her eyes wide, but still soft with pity. I fucking hated pity. It was the one thing I could never handle.

"Don't do that. Do not give me your pitying look. I do not need your pity or anyone else's."

"Pity is not the same as concern. You should know that."

I probably did, but my heart had hardened and my mind was made up. Maybe later, when I'd calmed down again, I could look at this conversation through a rational lens. But for now, I could not.

"There are just some things I'm not ready to talk about with a stranger. Or anyone else for that matter. And definitely not JD. Anything concerning me, outside of this current case, is none of his business. I'd appreciate if you'd pass that along."

"If you'd like. If you change your mind though—"

"I won't. I'm really tired of people butting into my personal business. But I'll tell you what, if I ever need to talk to anyone, I'll talk to Axel. He's the only one who deserves those details. Not JD. Not my father. Not you. Axel. He's all that matters."

Chapter Sixteen

Axel

I STOOD JUST inside my open door and stared at the insanity before me. Every single surface I could lay my eyes on was covered in a sheet of cookies. Dozens of them. Everywhere.

"Uhm—Mandy?" I was almost hesitant to call for her because this didn't seem normal and I didn't know what I was about to find.

Her head poked around the corner from the laundry room, but before either of us could say anything the timer on my oven went off. "Oh shoot. Hang on."

She opened the oven and then must have realized she already had her hands full with a tray. "Crap. Can you clear me a spot right there?" She pointed at the island. "Those should be cool enough to just stack on top of each other."

As if I'd walked into the Twilight Zone, I did as she asked and made room on one corner of the counter, which she immediately filled with the tray in her hand. She then returned to the oven, grabbed the next tray out and then frantically turned from corner to corner looking for somewhere to set it down.

"It looks like you're out of space."

She smirked. "Thanks, Captain Obvious. How about you help me move some of these around and keep the snark to yourself."

The odd smile on her face made me realize she was poking fun and I wondered even further what alternate reality I had just walked into that had turned Amanda Turner into Suzie Homemaker baking cookies in one of my t-shirts and a pink pair of criminally too-short shorts that she had better never ever leave the house in.

I decided not to question her as long as she had a hot cookie sheet in her hand, plus I was dying to try one of these. I had already made out chocolate chip, chocolate chocolate chip, and dear God—oatmeal raisin. And since I'd passed on food all day at the clubhouse, I was suddenly starving.

"I'm going to eat one of these," I warned her a second before I snagged my first one and popped the whole thing in my mouth in case she said no.

"Good. That's what I made them for. Those anyways. The rest we are probably going to have to take to the clubhouse, so I don't attempt to eat them all."

After taking a moment to savor the heavenly experience going on in my mouth, I accepted the glass of milk she handed me to wash it down. "Wow. Those are good."

"I kind of guessed they might be your favorite since you had all the ingredients for them in your cabinet. Not a bad choice actually. They are my second favorite."

He laughed. "Let me guess. Your favorite is chocolate chip."

She smirked. "How'd you guess?"

She was smiling amidst dozens and dozens of cookies and I didn't know what to think. This woman was nothing at all like the one who'd pushed me out just this morning. That one had been falling to pieces, and this one …. I guess baking her stress away wasn't the worst thing she could have done. Although standing there looking at her bare legs gave me different ideas on what we could have done with all of that excess energy.

I tried to stop that runaway train, but it was impossible. This Mandy reminded me so much of the one I remembered. She even had her hair up in a ponytail, no make-up on, the booty shorts that reminded me of the cheer shorts she'd worn so often. My cock was hard, and there wasn't a thing I could do to stop it.

"How long have you been at this?" I asked, reaching up to brush a spot of flour from her cheek. She sucked in her breath when our skin connected, and my brain short-circuited, forgetting all about the question I'd asked or all the others I had from this morning. All that mattered was the rise and fall of her tits as she tried to take in a breath. And her warm breath fanning across my skin.

"I don't know. I didn't keep track. Maybe a few hours or so." Considering there were enough cookies to feed a small army, I imagined she'd been baking for a lot longer than she realized.

"Do you feel better?"

She nodded, her eyes dilating. "I had to do something, and I wasn't sure if going out for a run right now was the smartest thing to do. I'm still not clear on security."

"I'm glad you stayed inside. Security here is state of the art, but I don't like seeing you at any risk, no matter how small."

"Oh," she squeaked when I brushed a lock of hair that had gotten loose behind her ear.

"I have to ask, Mandy," my own breath increased as I backed her slowly against a vacant wall.

"Ask me what?"

"Why did you leave?"

Her mouth opened and closed as if she wasn't sure how to answer that, even though we both knew exactly what I was asking and how important the answer might be.

"I didn't leave." She hesitated, her breathing growing ragged as I stroked my thumb along the column on her neck. When my fingers reached her jawline, she turned and nipped them with her teeth.

My nostrils flared at the sudden rush of arousal she

inspired shot through me. But I still needed an answer that made sense.

"I'm going to need you to elaborate because one minute, we were planning our future, and the next, you were gone. Just tell me the truth." My voice came out raw and broken as the memory of that day filled my head. The pain of betrayal...

"I wouldn't lie to you. I may be a lot of things, but a liar isn't one of them."

I narrowed my eyes. "Isn't that exactly what the government trained you to do though? Lie."

"What I do professionally and personally are two very different things. Was I good at my job? Yes. Do I regret the lies I told on the job? Not really. I always had the greater good in mind in everything I did. My only regret is how it ended."

Some of the arousal between us waned as anger blossomed once again. "Stop avoiding the question and just answer. I'm not sure we can continue to work together until we clear this up. What I overheard on that phone was both enlightening and confusing. So, before I go off halfcocked and do something I regret, answer. The. Fucking. Question."

"I did," she said, shoving ineffectually against my chest. I had her pinned and right where I wanted her.

"You can't push me away that easily this time. Until I get a real answer, neither one of us is going anywhere."

"You are such a stubborn ass. For someone who does the kinds of things you do, living in the gray areas of life, you sure as hell only see black and white when it suits you."

Her voice rose, and I hoped we were getting somewhere.

"I didn't leave. It really is that fucking simple. I was taken."

Those three words pierced my chest with the force of a lethal dagger. They could not mean what I thought. "What the hell do you mean, you were taken?" I pushed that question through clenched teeth as I tried to hold onto my sanity.

"I was on my way to meet you as we'd planned. But I obviously didn't make it. Less than a half a block from this place my father's SUV intercepted me. I knew I was in trouble, so I went with him. How the hell was I supposed to know he wasn't taking me home? Do you have any idea how many times I have berated myself for believing in that man? But I was a kid, and he was well within his rights to take me wherever he chose."

My eyes were wide, as the distress she must have felt that day came through now in her voice. Also in the tremble of her body against mine. I was perilously close to losing my shit. If I thought I wanted to kill Turner before, there was no doubt I would now.

"Why didn't you run? If you were that close, I could have helped you."

She shook her head. "Like I said, I had no idea about his plans. I had no way of knowing he'd already heard about the baby and was halfway to crazy town because of it."

"Halfway?" I snarled.

"You're wrong about me though. I did fight back. More than once. I didn't make it easy for his security team to get me on that helicopter. I fought them every step of the way. I knew—KNEW that if he got me away from Sultan, I would never see you again.

"I guess it wasn't enough." My stomach pitched thinking about my teenaged version of Mandy trying to escape the clutches of her own father. The one person who she should have been able to trust more than anyone on this earth.

"You have no idea. Things got crazy as they did their best to get me strapped into that helicopter. Whether they intended to be so rough about it, I wasn't sure. But somewhere in the middle of it I got slapped and punched a few times, which in turn made me fight even harder. I even got loose a couple of times and had I been a little stronger and a little faster, I might have escaped."

"Mandy." I touched her lips, unsure if I could hear anymore and remain upright.

She twisted her head out of my touch. "No. You asked for the truth, you're going to get it. All of it." She gulped for air until she was able to get enough air in her lungs to continue. "My father was getting mad that they couldn't keep me pinned. Even when two of them grabbed me at the same time, I fought like a fucking banshee. I had never been so scared in my life. Or certain that I had to stop them. That's when it happened." She bowed her head. "The true beginning of the end. I don't know if my father told them to do it, or if they were just desperate to stop me, it doesn't really matter now. But one of them kicked me as hard as he could, that blow landing in the middle of my body."

I ripped myself away from her, unable to hear anymore I needed to hurt someone so bad, but there was no one there who deserved it. So, I grabbed the closest thing, a tray of cookies and threw it across the room as hard as I could. And then another. And then another. I was shaking so hard I had to grab the island to steady myself.

I don't know if she thought I needed to hear the rest of the story right then like the ripping off of a band aid, but she continued. And as much as I wanted to stop the words from being spoken, I *had* to hear them.

"By the time the helicopter took off I was in agony in every way. My body hurt from the fight, my heart hurt knowing I might never see you again, and the fear for our baby consumed everything else. I lost all concept of time and location on that flight. It could have been an hour or four for all I knew. I put my head in between my knees to stave of the nausea rolling through me and I prayed to God the entire time, making every bargain in the book if he would only save our baby."

I wanted to say something to comfort her, but I could think of nothing. There were no words that could make any of that better. Especially now.

"By some miracle I didn't lose her that day. I thought my prayers had been answered and I was prepared to do whatever it took to follow through on the promises I'd made. I went quietly into the institution my father had chosen for me, even going so far as signing the papers that I was there because I wanted to be. My father had to sign, too, but I agreed to it all. They promised state of the art medical care and security to keep me safe."

"Jesus fucking Christ," I spat. "Did he put you in a mental institution?"

She nodded. "Yes, he did, and he left me there for three years. But that first night, I didn't care. Our baby was safe, and it was all that mattered."

I heard the butt coming before she said another word. "You don't have to tell me the rest. I can guess. I've been around enough pregnant old ladies to know that miscarriages happen."

"Do they? Because I didn't think so. Not when two nights later I found blood on my sheets. I also sure as hell didn't think so when the doctor told me that blow to my stomach had probably contributed to the loss. Nor did I think so when I couldn't sleep at night because every time I closed my eyes and relaxed I heard the words baby killer running through my mind."

"That's bullshit," I exploded. "You did nothing wrong."

"Really? Because nine hours ago you said the same thing." Her words were cold and steady as they hacked me into pieces.

"That's because I'm a fucking idiot. I've lived by a lie for ten fucking years. If anyone should be persecuted for anything it should be me. What the fuck is wrong with *me*?"

"You were taken in by a man who has spent his whole life lying to everyone. You. Me. His wives. My sister. Everyone. I wouldn't beat yourself up too bad about it. We were all in one way or another his victims. He never gave a shit about anyone except himself."

"If that's so, why in the hell did he hire us last year to find you? What exactly happened? How did you get out? *When* did you get out?"

Chapter Seventeen

Amanda

I STARED BACK at Axel thinking he looked every bit
as strung out as I felt after this. I'd known this morning
that this conversation would happen when he returned
and as much as I'd done to prepare for it. It wasn't
enough.

Old wounds were opened and growing larger by the
second. It was time to rein it in before we both hit the
point of no return. I pulled on the old training to
remind myself that the past was over and had no business here anymore. This was the present.

Only he still wanted more answers and there was
only so much I thought he could handle.

"Six months after my eighteenth birthday I was

given a choice. Stay at the institute until I turned twenty-one or I could go to the college of my father's choosing. I could not return home and I could not have any communication from my past."

"That's asinine. You were an adult. He had no power over you."

I choke laughed. "I thought that too. But after two years of being locked up and my eighteenth birthday coming and going without even a hint of release, I took the deal that got me out of there. I ended up at a pretty decent college in the Northeast and I decided to embrace getting an education."

"You should have called me. We could have helped you."

She shook her head. "By the time I felt comfortable in my own skin again, not to mention safe enough on my own, it had been years. We weren't the same people anymore, especially me. I couldn't go back. I just couldn't. I had to move forward. If you can't understand that, then just know that I did what was best for me at the time."

I stopped and waited to see what he would say. I was expecting something cold or cruel, but he remained silent. After a few untenable minutes of waiting, I let out a loud breath and turned away from him.

"Why would you come back now? You're fucking living in his house again after he destroyed everything. What kind of bullshit is that?"

Now he was getting into territory that I didn't want to explore. Not with him. "I don't want to talk about this anymore. I did what I had to do and coming back here was the only choice I had. That's all you need to know."

"I'm not sure what you expect me to say. I'm fucking livid and frustrated that I don't have anyone to take it out on. I'll tell you this, though. Your father is going to pay for this shit."

"Don't. I can't afford for you to fuck this up. I need his resources. At least for now."

"The money? That's what's important?"

"Money makes the world go round. You know that. If I have to swallow my pride to get a job done, then that's what I'll do. I don't care. He can't hurt me. Not anymore."

He shook his head. "What job are you trying to get done?"

I had no intention of answering that question. Everything I had done to this point had been tainted by my sins and the sins of others. Everywhere I went trouble followed, and it was up to me alone to break that cycle. I wasn't a villain, but neither was I a hero. I'd already accepted that.

"Right now, we have a killer to catch. That should be our focus. The rest we have to put behind us. Just let it go."

"I've known the truth for all of five minutes. I'm not going to just let it go. If you think I would then you really don't know me. Which brings us full circle again." He was on the move, and by the sound of his voice he was getting closer.

"I'm sorry you had to find out this way. I thought you would be told about the miscarriage and that would be that."

"It was never going to be that simple, Mandy. Not with us. I remember having a feeling when your father came to me that it couldn't possibly end like that. And while the years went by and that feeling faded, it was still there, until our lives intersected in Vegas."

"That wasn't supposed to happen."

"But it did. And now we're here, another case bringing us together again. It seems that the universe needed us together at least one last time."

"That's a little too woo woo don't you think?"

"I already told you I don't believe in coincidences." He said that from only inches away. I could tell because I felt the warmth of his breath threading through my hair. I really didn't want to think about how he made me feel when he stood too close.

I didn't need to see him to feel the effect of looking at his handsome face. Ten years apart and I could still picture everything about him. Particularly his blue eyes that seemed to shimmer when he laughed and turned dark when he got intense. Looking into those right now would be dangerous.

My focus needed to stay on the job of rebuilding the walls this morning's breakdown had crumbled. I was afraid if he looked at me now, he would see past the facade to the hurt underneath. The man had a knack for seeing in me what no one else should.

"Look at me, Mandy." His continued use of my nickname was bad enough. Especially when it was delivered in that smoky timbre of his that rubbed along my spine like a caress.

"I don't want to."

A quiet rumble of laughter rolled over me, making it even harder to resist. I was relieved that he could still laugh. I didn't want the news he took in today to turn him into something darker. He didn't deserve that. Not after everything he and JD had done to pull their club out of the depths of wretchedness.

"I didn't ask what you wanted." He gently wrapped his fingers around my shoulder and turned me until I faced him. "But I need to see you, angel."

My breath hitched. I couldn't remember the last time I'd heard him call me that. But I remembered well how it made my belly swoop and my body tingle. "What is it about you that pulls me in so easily?"

One of his eyebrows shot up. "You think this is easy? If so, I shudder to think what you consider hard. I feel like I'm working my ass off to get through these walls you keep throwing up. You gonna stop now?"

It was my turn to laugh. "Not likely. Those walls keep me safe."

"*I* keep you safe. I know I did a shit job of that ten years ago, but we didn't know what we were up against back then. Now we do."

"That's noble of you, but it isn't necessary. Taking care of me isn't your job. Not anymore. Your contract is with my father. You and the club should be taking care of him."

"I'm going to pretend you didn't just say that to me," he seethed. "Because there's no way in hell I'm lifting a finger for that asshole unless it's to slit his fucking throat."

"Look, Axel, I'm not trying to piss you off. I'm trying to do the right thing. I don't belong in this town anymore. I should have never come here, but I legit had nowhere else to go."

"Why's that?"

"Because after the case with Frank Mazzeo, the government burned me. Do you know what that means?"

He furrowed his brow. "Basically, but maybe you should explain it to me."

"Basically, they completely disavow knowledge of you, and they freeze or take assets, leaving an agent with nothing more than the clothes on their back."

"That's what happened to you? For working with Frank?"

I gnashed my teeth at his words and the tone in which they were delivered. He clearly didn't approve. Not that I blamed him. He didn't know the whole story. However, we'd been through enough for a lifetime today, and I had no plans to reveal anything more. Enough was enough.

"I really can't talk about it. All you need to know is that I came back here because I literally had no other choice. Even a job won't be easy to get. I now techni-cally have no work history. I was recruited out of college and the US Government is the only employer I have ever had."

"How the hell am I supposed to accept that. I was there remember? I need an explanation for why you'd risk anyone's life for that piece of shit."

I cringed.

"Haven't we been through enough today? Let it go, Axel. Please. I have enough trouble on my plate without adding to it."

He looked hesitant, like he couldn't decide what to do. But for me, there was only one choice. Walk away.

"I should go. I knew this wouldn't work."

I started to walk by him, attempting to skirt around him without touching, but he had other plans in mind. When I got next to him, he grabbed my arm and tugged me against his side.

"You're not leaving. It's too dangerous."

"But I— "

"If you leave, then I leave, as does the rest of the club. Which puts everyone at more risk. Either way, we aren't letting you face this alone. We've already made a promise and we will see it through."

I winced at the multiple implications in that statement. If he didn't think I could see anything through, then he didn't know me at all.

I also didn't want to put anyone in the club at more risk than necessary.

"What do you think we should do?" I asked.

"For starters? Tel is waiting to fill you in on everything he's found. He's followed a money trail that seems to connect our killer with the current Mazzeo operation."

"Wait. What?" I shook my head to try and clear the sudden buzzing in my mind. "What Mazzeo operation? I thought that ended with Frank."

Chapter Eighteen

Axel

HOURS LATER, I felt like both our heads were going to explode from an overload of information. Mandy had insisted on hearing every single detail from Tel and many of them more than once. Clearly, her and Tel were in their element, while I was itching for some action.

I didn't want to just sit around and study spreadsheets and maps. As much as I knew having all of this data at our fingertips better prepared us for a confrontation, it was driving me up the wall.

Although I had to admit she had impressed me every step of the way. Her methodical and thorough approach to the information she was presented meant she didn't miss anything.

Something akin to pride washed over me as I watched her work.

"I can't believe all the information you've discovered." She sat back in the chair, slapping the papers down on the desk, obviously impressed. "There's no way our agency could have pulled this information together so quickly."

"That's the difference between operating under the radar and operating within the letter of the law," Tel offered. "I didn't exactly have to get a warrant or worry about whether any of it would be admissible in court."

"That's true. I definitely see the appeal. It's a refreshing change to get things done without all the red tape. Although, some government agencies also operate a little in the gray area too. Especially when it comes to certain types of terrorism."

"Yeah, spooks have all the fun," I joked.

Tel laughed, but Mandy didn't. Instead, she looked uncomfortable. Luckily, I was saved by Bone from any further awkwardness.

"I've got food. I figure you all have to be starving by now." He turned to Mandy and asked, "Tuna melt or chicken?" He held up both plates for her to pick one.

"Definitely tuna melt," she answered, taking that plate out of his hand while he handed me the other.

"Thank Christ. If she picked chicken, I would have been forced to choke down that shit."

"I know right?" Bone laughed too.

Her mouth dropped open and I laughed.

"If you don't like tuna, and he knew you didn't like tuna, why in the world would he give me a choice?"

"Because I'm a gentleman, and the right thing to do was ask what you wanted."

Both Tel and I snickered at him calling himself a gentleman. Bone was our newest full patched member, and he was anything but a gentleman. He was a fucking monster who just happened to know how to cook, which we took great advantage of when he was a prospect. And now that he was a brother, he just kept cooking because it had become routine.

"What about me?" Tel asked. "I'm the one doing most of the work tonight. You don't think I need to eat?"

"Don't be a pussy about it, dude. Your chicken is in the kitchen waiting on you. I'm not a fucking waitress, and I'm not about to carry more than two plates at a time."

Tel grumbled but jumped to his feet and followed Bone back to the kitchen. Everyone knew due to his weird social skills that he preferred to take his meals alone. He'd probably take it to his room and return later when he'd finished. The man was the most extroverted introvert I'd ever met.

He also wasn't much of a talker, and yet, he and Mandy had put their heads together and chatted nonstop about all the data he had coming in.

"You guys have the strangest dynamic. Half the time I can't tell if you hate each other or love each other."

"Love's a strong word for the brothers. *And* that's a

chick word. Although we do share a bond, it's steeped in brotherhood, trust and loyalty. We're our own family of sorts and that makes us solid."

"Don't most people love their family?" she asked.

"That's not a good question for me. Love was a four-letter word in my house growing up. No one ever spoke it. Not out loud anyways. Annoyed and angry were the only consistent words I remember hearing."

"I know I'm sorry. I didn't mean— "

"Don't apologize," I cut her off. "It's not necessary. I'm sure a lot of families share love, I just don't have that experience."

"We're quite the pair, aren't we?" she asked, her sandwich frozen in midair halfway to her mouth. "Although I have to admit that I thought for years that my dad did love me. When I was young, we were really close. I don't understand what happened to change him so much."

"I'd venture to say your mom's sudden death played into that." I almost choked on those words as they came out. Shit. I should not have brought that up. "Not that I'm defending the bastard or anything. I very much hate him and I'm busy plotting his death."

"I know," she said quietly. "He deserves your hatred. I get it. But I'm not on board with death. I'm more of an eye for an eye gal myself." Some of the light in her left when she took a deep breath and exhaled it nice and slow before she continued. "I don't know how much he actually loved, her but you're right, my mom's death changed him. It messed him up and left him with a way too young me to deal with. It's not an excuse though, just speculation. I'm not sure there's any excuse for all the bullshit he's done."

Since I had a mouthful of chicken, I hummed my agreement. But honestly, I was more focused on the way Mandy said fuck.

While I happened to think it was about the most perfect word in the English language, and appropriate in nearly every situation, it was not every day I heard it from her. Actually, never when she was younger, and it still sounded a little awkward. I liked it. And every time she said it, it made me think of sex.

I wanted to fuck her. When I hated her, I still dreamt of fucking her again. There was a lot to be said about a good hate fuck that you walked away from afterwards.

Only I didn't hate her. Not anymore.

Today, everything I'd believed for a decade was turned on its head, and a lot of emotions had flowed between us.

I couldn't help but wonder if I could actually fuck her out of my system.

"Why are you looking at me like that? Did I say something wrong?"

"Like what?" I asked, setting my food aside because my appetite had suddenly gone in a different direction.

Her eyes widened as if she could read my intent. "I don't know. Like you want to hurt me or something."

"Or something," I answered as I stretched forward, grabbed the edge of her chair, and rolled it in my direction.

"What does that mean?" Her voice rose and sounded slightly panicked.

"I find the woman you've become both fascinating and infuriating. It's an odd juxtaposition. But watching you work, your mind work, it's brilliant. I can't believe how much you've changed."

"Two years of college and years of training go a long way."

I took the plate out of her hand and set it on the nearby desk.

"Hey, I was eating that."

"I'll make you a new one after."

Her mouth opened and closed with indecision again. I enjoyed seeing her get so flustered.

"After what?"

I pulled her out of her chair and into my arms. I wasn't sure how she would react when she learned my intentions, but there wasn't much I could do to hold back anymore. Despite everything, I craved her. She'd made some pretty big mistakes in her life, but I couldn't judge. When she'd first left, I'd thrown myself into the club, first as a prospect, and then a couple of years later as a full-fledged member. Wrath had not been as clean then as they were now. There was still a lot of drugs, guns and violence.

Under certain conditions I didn't hesitate to take the law into my hands. My past was riddled with the blood of those I'd tortured to save others as well as the dead bodies of those that had committed such crimes they didn't deserve to live.

So when I reached up and touched her face, I knew my hands were no cleaner than hers. In fact, I would bet that they were much dirtier.

I still didn't know for sure if Turner was one of those men or not, but I didn't have a good feeling and I usually went with my gut.

"What are you thinking about?" She raised her hand high and rubbed her fingers across my forehead. "When you get upset or unhappy it shows here. These lines get pronounced."

I closed my eyes against the warmth of her touch and savored the intimacy of this. I wasn't a cuddler or even much of a kisser.

When I wanted a woman, I generally got in, got us both off, and then got the hell out. I was creative enough for most not to notice, but I generally didn't want a lot of touch.

Mandy's touch, though. Fuck. I was going to drown in it. I was already imagining her soft fingers all over my body. My shoulders when she held on as I fucked into her…

My chest when I took her breath away…

And my dick. God damn that was going to be the best moment. When she wrapped that delicate hand around my shaft and pumped it…

My eyes blinked open, her soft face only inches from mine. Her lips slightly parted.

Her breathing sounded as ragged as mine.

"You're not saying I look old, are you? We're practically the same age."

She chewed a moment on her bottom lip as I leaned a little closer.

"No. Just for a minute there you seemed stressed, but it's gone now."

"What do you see now?" I asked, determined to make her say whatever she was thinking.

"I'm not sure."

A smile twitched at my lips. "Liar. You just don't want to say it."

"I assume nothing, especially when it comes to you," she whispered, her lips trembling.

That quake of her body was impossible to resist, I leaned forward and nipped at the bottom lip drawing me in. Her mouth opened on a small gasp, her nostrils flared, and her eyes went wide with arousal.

That was all I needed to continue as I gently pressed my lips to hers. That sweet, almost chaste first touch exploded across my senses and broke the rougher, needier part of me free. I pulled back for a second to stare into her wide eyes before I swooped in for something far more savage. This kiss was all tongue and teeth as I bent her over the arm I'd wrapped around her back and poured every bit of me into it.

To most I came across as hot headed, argumentative and a bit of a perfectionist. But I was actually more self-controlled than I appeared. I liked to fight and I liked to fuck, but I chose my partners for both quite carefully. I argued with JD a lot because that was my job. I refused to believe that a president of an MC needed a yes man.

Except with Mandy, it seemed everything I thought I

knew about myself got set on fire and burned to ash—
including my common sense. When she kissed me back
with as much strength as she possessed, I could still feel
the gift of her vulnerability, and I wanted to both
protect it and obliterate it.

If I was going to lose myself in this woman, I needed
her to be right there with me.

"Give in to whatever your body demands. It's okay
to let go. Neither of us is perfect, and that's okay," I
murmured against her wet lips as my free hand slid
into the silky soft curls of her hair. God, that touch
alone was almost as powerful as her mouth. It was
instantly obvious I'd crossed the threshold of a slippery
slope, but I couldn't seem to care.

Not with the heat of her body pressed to mine and
her tongue dueling wildly with my own. If ever a
woman tasted like fire, this one did, and I was going to
get burned to ash. Fuck.

"I can't stop kissing you." I gave her no chance to
speak, diving right back into the inferno that would
claim my soul if I let it. Ha. What a joke. As if I had a
choice when it came to her. This woman had somehow
imprinted on my teenage soul and I had no idea how
get rid of her mark.

She wrapped her hands around my neck and
gripped the edges of my hair tightly in her fist. *Yes*.
If I wanted control with her, I would have to fight
for it, and I loved a good fight. All I had to do was
find an opening and take the upper hand. The
motion of her heaving chest caught my attention and

I released her hair and slid my hand down the side of her neck.

It would be so easy to wrap my fingers there and absorb the feel of her pulse against my flesh. Her already fast heartbeat would go wild against the mild threat, knowing that it could change at any moment. It would be fascinating to watch. Next time. I thought as I continued my path down her neck to the space between her breasts beckoning me.

The feel of my rough palms against her soft flesh nearly had my eyes rolling to the back of my head. It was a sensation I would never forget. But it still wasn't enough. I momentarily left her mouth so I could trail mine down the same path my hand had just traveled. I nipped and licked at her skin, all while imagining what this would be like if she were naked and we were completely alone.

It wouldn't take anyone by surprise to find a brother having sex with a woman in the clubhouse, but I was feeling possessive about Mandy and didn't want anyone else watching. She wasn't a club girl and never would be. Not as long as I drew breath.

"Mandy," I rasped against her skin at the same time I pressed a little harder into her lithe body. I hadn't planned to line my cock up perfectly against her pussy, but I wasn't sorry that I did. Especially not when a rough shudder rocked through her, and a whispered cry slid from her lips. It was taking all of my control not to peel her clothes off and shove inside her. I doubted she was ready for that, but I believed she might soon be.

Until then, I would steal a kiss here and there. Even cop a feel when I could. Whatever it took to break down her defenses a little bit more. This Mandy wouldn't say no and I couldn't get enough of her.

"Axel." She grabbed my arms and tried to steady herself in the face of the arousal causing her body to tremble.

"Soon, baby. I promise. When we're alone. For now, though, just let me kiss you some more."

She moaned in response as I brushed the collar of her shirt aside and pressed my lips to the tender skin at the top of her breast. I even flicked my tongue a time or two until she practically squirmed in my arms. She was so responsive.

A noise sounded from the doorway a moment before Tel's voice broke through the haze of lust surrounding us.

"Oh shit. Sorry. I—uhh—just let me know when— "

I grunted mid-kiss and he got the message that I was telling him to shut the fuck up. He shuffled out of the room and the space got quiet again, but the spell was broken.

I gripped her tighter, pressing her body full against mine for one last minute, soaking in every taste, scent, and sound she made. Her barely there whimpers were my favorite and I ate them up like fucking candy.

By the time I broke free from the mind-numbing pit of arousal and took a step back, I was on the verge of banging her right here on this desk. However, now was not the right time. Nor was it the right place. I wanted to be alone with her, not in the middle of the clubhouse surrounded by other men.

I pressed my forehead to hers. "We should get back to work. I think Tel has more to show you."

She nodded, squirming free while righting her shirt. "It's for the best."

I wasn't sure I liked the way that sounded. Fuck the best. With her I wanted nothing more than her wet and wanting, and damned if I wasn't going to find a way to get it.

Chapter Nineteen

Amanda

WAKING up alone in Axel's big bed was not ideal. Not when everything around me smelled like the man I seriously couldn't get out of my head.

After what happened in the clubhouse I had expected more when we returned to his home. Being dismissed and sent off to bed like a child had burned more than it should have. I was supposed to be grateful that he'd realized that what we both needed was our own space.

And yet...I still wasn't satisfied. We were on the precipice of a breakthrough, and we needed to work together. On the other hand, it had given me some time to process my thoughts.

Although it should have been me on the couch not him. But he'd insisted and practically shoved me into his room. Since I'd been exhausted, I figured it wasn't worth the fight. Now I was annoyed and ready to give him a piece of my mind.

Plus I needed coffee.

For that alone I'd drag my ass out of this bed and investigate the situation in the kitchen. After Axel turned his anger on my cookies the day before, neither of us had returned to clean up the mess. I guessed if I wanted his coffee, then the least I could do was see what could be done to recover his kitchen.

I hastily threw on the clothes from the day before, making a mental note to find the bag I'd packed, and slowly opened the bedroom door hoping it made no noise. With Axel sleeping on the couch, it was going to be a challenge not to wake him, but I couldn't stay cooped up in here waiting for him to stir.

Only when I got the door open and glanced at the couch, it was empty and there were no signs anyone had even slept there.

"Morning, sleepyhead."

I swung my head around to find him seated at the island, sipping on what looked like coffee, and a smile playing at his lips.

"How long have you been up?" I may have grumbled the words, but I had zeroed in on caffeine and it was my primary focus.

"Long enough." He indicated a tray of cookies in front of him. "I was able to salvage some of your cookies." The smile on his face distracted me. Was he being funny? It was hard to tell, when the way he'd said it made my mind race off into a much dirtier place. I glanced around the room and gasped. It had taken me a minute to notice, but the place gleamed. It was freaking spotless.

"What did you do?"

His smile dropped, and his eyes filled with remorse. "I ruined all your hard work. The least I could do was clean up the mess."

I forced my brain to engage my legs and carried myself to the coffee maker and poured myself a cup before I responded. I really needed caffeine. "I was going to take care of it."

He made a sound that came out like a cross between a hum and a grunt. That sound vibrated across my senses, tickling the fine hairs on the back of my neck, and weakening me once again. Honestly, I'd had trouble sleeping because I couldn't stop thinking about that kiss...

As if that wasn't enough to make me crazy, I was now faced with this insanely domestic scene after he'd done something so extraordinarily ordinary as clean up the mess we'd both made. It was an unfair glimpse into the world that might have been if the world had not torn us apart.

"Do we have a plan for today?" I asked, trying to shove down the feelings that made me weak in the face of them and focus on something else. Like the killer we needed to catch.

"You and Tel are going to continue digging for clues, while I go and have a chat with your father. I have more than a few choice words for that asshole."

"What?!" Panic seized my chest. That was not what I'd been expecting either. "No, you can *not* do that." I shook my head and placed my mug on the island a little too hard, making some of the coffee slosh over the side.

"I can and I will. If he interfered in our lives like he did ten years ago, can you imagine what he's done since? The club has trusted him for far too long. I think it's time to question what his real intentions are. Especially when it comes to our club. He's hired us so many times over the years to do his dirty work, and as long as it met our case criteria, we allowed it. Everything about him makes me sick."

"And you think he might have been lying to you all along? About what? Why? As long as you and I were apart, he didn't care what you did." My heart froze for a split second as I realized what I'd almost let slip. And the only thing I could thing to do to cover it was to forge ahead . "You need to think about this more before you confront him. It's never a good idea to go into an interview halfcocked. In fact, you shouldn't go in until you're certain you know the answers. Someone like my father would know that, and I can guarantee he will be prepared for whatever you try to throw at him. He is a master manipulator who will find a way to turn anything you have to say back against you."

"Is that the CIA agent talking? And are you actually

suggesting I just forget what he's responsible for? Because that's bullshit, and you know it."

"Are we going to fight about this every day?" I couldn't seem to stop even though I knew I was teetering on dangerous ground. "Are we going to relive that pain every time we see each other? I need to know now because I'm tired of ripping open those wounds. I've been through that enough." I braced my hands on the island and took a deep breath before continuing. "This isn't working. I'm going to ask JD for a room in the clubhouse. I can't stay here."

"That's not going to happen." His words were calm, but I could feel the intensity behind them. The tension and barely leashed violence practically vibrated off of him.

"Why? Because you say so?" I don't know why he thought he could just order me around. It was total bullshit. "God, you are so infuriating."

"Welcome to the club, baby. And to answer your question, no, not because I say so. Because it's not allowed. No one who's not a part of the club is allowed to stay in the clubhouse without supervision. That's a rule JD will never break. Not even for you or *your* father."

His hatred towards my father was as palpable as the emotions I'd harbored against him for years as well. I hated that for him as much as I did for myself. Especially since he'd lived with a lie this entire time. "That anger you feel for him is the same as I had for years. Trust me, I get it. It festered until I figured out how to use it. Eventually, it spurred me towards freedom and allowed me to become who I am today. Without it, I'm not sure I would have survived much of what I've gone through. But it is poison, Axel. If you don't let it go, it could eventually destroy you."

"Like it destroyed you? If the anger you had created the woman in front of me, what is that supposed to say? You didn't escape. Not really. If you did, you would not have turned against the government and partnered with a mafia douchebag, you wouldn't have been disavowed by them, losing everything in the process, and probably wouldn't have a psycho killer after you right now. So yeah, what the *fuck* does that say?"

I flinched against his cruel words. Just because they were mostly true, didn't make them less hurtful. I should have let them go. But he'd ripped open one too many wounds in the span of a minute, and I was on overload. I reached forward and slapped him across the face. The loud crack of my hand hitting his flesh startled me as much as it did him.

"Fuck you, Axel." I shoved my coffee cup across the island in his direction and turned toward the bedroom to retrieve my meager belongings. Fuck him and the dark steel horse he rode in on. Whatever fleeting thought I'd had about telling him the whole story, evaporated in an instant. I didn't need him for any of this. We weren't light and bright teenagers with our entire futures in front of us anymore, and we'd both seen our fair share of shit in this world, but that gave him no excuse to strike me down at every turn.

But in the back of my head, the little devil that sat on my shoulder laughed because that's exactly what my silence gave him.

"You're not leaving." He grabbed my arm and whirled me around almost before I realized he was there.

"I'll damn well do whatever the hell I want."

He leaned close to my face, and I remained still and unflinching. Although it was hard. Damned hard. I wanted nothing more than to lash out at him—again. I was sick and tired of feeling like shit.

"Normally, I would agree. I'm not fucking trying to control you. But I'm not letting you run around on the loose while a fucking psycho stalks you." He took a breath and clenched his jaw a moment before he continued. "If he gets his hands on you, I will fucking die, but not until I've killed him and every fucking person he is associated with. The blood will run, and run deep. No one will be safe. Do you hear me? No one."

A chill ran down my spine at his words, but I could say nothing. Not when something in my brain was going haywire. What else could explain the elation I felt at the idea of him exploding into violence over me—for me. Or the zing running through my blood for no other reason than I was suddenly turned on more than I had ever been. The hard grip he maintained on my bicep burned, not from pain but excitement. He—

What was wrong with me? I tried to shake my head clear, but the emotions between us were too strong. We were being pulled together like a cosmic magnetic force.

He took a step closer and his harsh breath fanned across the shell of my ear, eliciting a shiver from me. But it was when his teeth scraped across the tendon that ran from my neck to my shoulder that I nearly lost it. Arousal spiked and I knew when this was over, I would need new panties. The air in my lungs froze as I waited for him to bite me. He'd already drawn blood figuratively, why not literally?

I heard him chuckle, and I wondered, did he know?

"God dammit, Mandy. You want this don't you? Your desire is thick like mine. It seeps from your skin laced with pheromones that make me ache to be inside you."

My breathing hitched again, my throat constricted. I couldn't answer him even if he wanted me to.

"You want my dick in your cunt right now so bad you can practically taste it."

Fuck. I did. I really really did. But could I say it? Was it in me to give him that kind of permission? To take whatever he wanted, however he wanted. The words were hovering on my lips. I had to be nuts.

"Do it," I whispered, my voice more guttural than sexy.

"Fuck." He sounded a little regretful, but he turned me towards the couch and pushed me against the back of it. "Say no right now or forever hold your fucking peace, baby. Because in two seconds, I'm going to be so far into this there will be no turning back."

"Do it," I repeated, my voice a little stronger and steeped in desperation.

There was so much pent-up emotion and frustration between us, we were both going to implode if we didn't see this through. And apparently, he didn't need to be told twice.

I gasped when he fisted his hand into my hair and pulled my head back to his. "Every time you prance around in my house in these fucking shorts, I want to rip into them. I mean, half your ass hangs out of them. I swear if you ever walk around in front of anyone wearing these fuckers, I will blister your ass until you can't sit down. Then I'll fuck you blind."

His possessive words slammed into me as the pain in my head morphed into something far stronger. Desire like I had never felt in my life. As soon as he touched me, I was going to go off like a damned rocket. This Axel was so different from the one I remembered and the change excited me.

My heart raced as I waited impatiently for what he would do next. I didn't wait long. He pulled my hair to the side and exposed my neck again before he buried his face between my shoulder and neck. There, he was all teeth and tongue along my feverish skin. The fact he seemed to like using his teeth on me shoved me to the brink of wild.

My nipples were hard points against the shirt I still wore, and even that touch against them was almost too much. When he bit at my neck, I felt the sensation everywhere. My skin tingled with it.

"Please, Axel." On one hand I wasn't sure what I was asking for and on the other I knew that I needed so much more from him. If we were going to do this then I wanted it all. Especially if this was the only chance I would get with him. Just one more time. That's all I needed. One more time.

Or so I told myself—even if I didn't quite believe it.

"You don't have to beg. Nothing is going to change my mind now." He tugged a little bit harder on my hair until my head fell back against his chest. "Although I have to admit, hearing those words from your lush lips makes my dick harder than I expected."

I couldn't decide if his words were tinged with anger or desire or whether it fully mattered which. Maybe both. Sometimes those two things weren't as different as might be expected. They were strong emotions that could illicit the same reactions. "Then show me," I told him, my harsh tone no more than a whisper.

"Show you, huh?" He chuckled, his voice sounding very close to my ear. "Will you still be so eager for this when I put you on your knees and make you take my cock down your throat?"

I shivered again. If he thought he would scare me like that, he couldn't be more wrong. I would gladly get on my knees to pleasure him, and when he lost control to that pleasure? Now, that would be a true highlight for me.

Another growl rumbled in his chest as he sucked on my neck and fisted his hand in my hair tighter. For now,

I was more than happy to relinquish control to him. The man had a skilled mouth and I couldn't wait to see what he did with it.

And it was official. I would definitely, one hundred percent need new panties after this.

Chapter Twenty

Axel

I WAS on the verge of losing my mind. That's what she did to me. I thought for a moment she might fight me on this, and I'd be forced to let her go. But I'd been wrong. ALL wrong. She needed this as much as I did.

"You are going to kill me. I know this—and yet—I won't stop. Turn and kiss me. I need your mouth." This beautiful convergence between us made me want to possess her all the more so when she did as I demanded and turned her head, I took her mouth with a savage kiss meant to claim as much as give pleasure.

She was mine.

I wasn't sure what I was supposed to do with that thought yet. It wasn't smart or logical. But it was the truth. I'd made a huge mistake. I'd lived years under a false preconception that had robbed me of so much. Now she was here, and we could barely stay in the same room together without fighting. And now this. No matter how this whole thing turned out, I didn't think the possession I felt would ever change.

My dark thoughts continued to swirl in my mind as our tongues dueled in a fight that mimicked real life. If she thought this would dissuade me from doing it again, she was sadly mistaken. If this is how a fight could end between us, our relationship would likely be built on the need to clash.

That thought made me pull away, but only long enough to press her back forward more across the couch giving me better access to the lower half of her body. Her mewl could have been a protest or a plead for more. I would never know because it was closely followed by a gasp when I shoved my hand between her legs and rubbed across her covered pussy.

I could feel the dampness through her shorts, and a wicked sense of satisfaction rolled violently through my body. What had started in anger and frustration had officially morphed into this storm of desperation that couldn't be denied.

I rubbed harder, only giving her a small taste of what was to come before I dropped to my knees and forced her legs farther apart with my shoulder.

"What are you doing?" she gasped again, her breath one big heavy pant.

"Don't play dumb, sweetheart. You know exactly what I'm about to do to you," I responded, reaching for the waistband of the tiny offensive shorts and shoving them down her legs. Her panties went with them, leaving her completely bare to me. As it should be, I thought, another growl rumbling through my chest.

"I don't—"

"Mandy, we already discussed this was happening. And after such a long wait, I intend to savor every beautiful inch of you including this gorgeous ass," I said, rubbing one perfect round cheek while imagining what it would look like pinked up after a good hard spanking. "And this exquisite pussy that looks as juicy and ripe as a fresh piece of fruit. I cannot wait to get a taste." To emphasize my intentions, I leaned forward and bit into the fleshy cheek of her ass hard enough to leave a little mark. I was so going to enjoy this.

I then spread her cheeks and rubbed my finger back and forth across her tight little hole, imagining how incredible my dick would look sinking into it. I would, no doubt, die of strangulation, but it would be so worth it.

"I don't—don't do that anymore," she gasped out as another finger slid across the damp lips of her beautiful almost bare pussy. I had to admit that I enjoyed the fact it wasn't clean-shaven. When I ate her, I was going to enjoy that tease of hair tickling through my beard.

"Why the fuck not?" I bumped gently against her clit and she gasped, raising onto her tippy toes. If that was supposed to get me to stop, it had the opposite effect. If anything, it pushed her backside closer to my face and my eager tongue.

She didn't answer or protest so I took that as my cue to continue. I would watch her closely, making sure to keep her interested if not comfortable. This wasn't about comfort. This was about getting her out of her head, pushing her limits, and pleasing us both.

"I am really going to enjoy watching you lose control." That was the only warning I gave her before I leaned in and swiped my tongue through the glistening folds before sealing my mouth temporarily over her clit. Her entire body jerked and my mind raced with satisfaction.

While delving deeper into my nirvana, I palmed her right ass cheek and squeezed. The whistle of air sucked through her teeth made me smile like the devil I was. I was rough and unforgiving, but I balanced it with pleasure by lapping at the savory satin between her legs. Something we both could revel in.

"Fuck. I could do this all day. I thought I remembered what this was like, but it's a thousand times more potent than any memory. And now that you've surrendered to me, we can never go back. I won't allow it."

The clench of her thighs were all I needed to ensure she liked it. Her life had spiraled out of control and I wanted to make it my mission to help her regain it. Together, we would be invincible.

"Axel," she gasped, going up on her tip toes as I doubled my efforts and circled my fingers around her clit.

"Don't worry, my sweet candy girl, I am going to make you come until you have given me everything you have to give." I thought I had moved on with my life without her, but it was all a lie. I was possessed by this woman.

She reached behind her and grabbed at my crotch. A movement I allowed only for a moment, as my eyes rolled to the back of my head when she made contact and squeezed my dick through my jeans. For the first time in too long to count, I had an inkling of what I'd missed. But when she tried to fumble her way to getting my zipper undone, I pushed her hand away.

"Not yet." I growled. "This time, we do this my way."

She whined in protest, which I brushed away. The time for protest and complaint had passed. Now it was all about her pleasure and how far I could push her before she broke.

So I stood, grabbed both of her wrists in my hand, and pinned them behind her back. This forced her head down, giving me an even better view of her pink pussy, shining with her juices. Using two fingers I slid through her slit, gathering, before bringing them up to my mouth for another taste.

I seriously could not get enough of her. I was going to mark my fucking calendar for the first day after this case ended as "eat from my candy girl all fucking day" day. I was going to make her come until she passed out and then wake her up and do it all over again. I would have laughed if not for the half naked writhing woman underneath me. I had her pinned and unable to get away, but she was strong, and sitting still waiting for me to fuck her wasn't her style.

I leaned over her back, pinning her arms between us, and placed my mouth right next to her ear. "How bad do you want me inside you?" I whispered darkly, the rough tone of my voice rumbling through my chest.

I didn't wait for her answer. Her pants and whimpers were more than enough reward for me. If she couldn't talk, then I'd done my job well. Now, we were both ready for more. I reached down and unzipped my pants, carefully freeing my cock. Fisting it, I squeezed, willing myself to keep control.

But the gleam of her pussy beckoned me, and I couldn't resist. I slid the head of my cock up and down her hot slit.

"Oh my God, Axel," she cried, her hands flexing and clenching in my grip as she resisted my hold. I only tightened my grip before I slowly fed a scant inch of my dick into her sweet velvety cunt. Her whole body shuddered and the ripple of her around me nearly did me in. I pulled on every ounce of control to keep from driving into her at warp speed.

"You want more?" I teased, knowing full well she was half ready to kill me for this.

"Do it" she breathed between clenched teeth. "Please don't tease me."

There it was. That little plea was enough to have me slowly pushing forward. If I wasn't already half out of my own mind, I'd make her wait. The idea of teasing her mercilessly and watching her unravel in my arms sounded like heaven.

"You're so mean," she complained, her neck straining so she could turn and glare at me.

I chuckled. "You think so?"

Before she could answer I shoved forward, all the way to my balls in one hard thrust. The curse words that came gasping out of her mouth only fed into the pleasure I took from catching her off guard. "Still too sweet for my candy girl?" I asked, taunting her.

"Fuck you," she grunted, trying to push her ass back and take me just a little bit deeper. If the little minx thought she could wrestle me for control, she was about to learn a tough lesson. I rocked onto my toes, angling my cock so that it did indeed slide a little further inside her. The keening moan that followed let me know I'd hit the right spot just like I remembered.

Fucking A. Her pussy was clenching on me and it was enough to pull me under if I wasn't careful. I sank my hand into her hair, grabbed a fistful for leverage, and began fucking her with long, hard strokes.

The words coming from her were no longer coherent, and I smiled as she drifted aimlessly on the highway of pleasure, finally realizing she had no control and let go and enjoy the ride. We had finally reached that point of no return, and I had to admit I loved it as much as she did because I got a front row seat to watching all the stress and anger leach from her body as she reached for the orgasm she wanted more than anything else.

This was the woman I had longed to see. The wild wanton hiding beneath the thick walls of fear she kept erected around her. This was the woman I'd waited for.

"Are you going to come for me, candy girl?" She was on the verge. We both knew it. Asking however, forcing her to acknowledge what I did to her, meant everything to me.

"Oh God yes," she whimpered, her body trying to thrash even harder against mine. Each flex of her back and ass were pulling at me too. I could feel the rise of my orgasm slowly descending from my core, building tighter and angrier as it built.

"Come on my cock," I ordered. "Scream it out. Announce it to the world who's making you come so hard you've lost your mind."

"Axel," she gasped, her body quaking so hard it shook my couch.

"Yes, candy girl. Give me that sweet cum." I barely got that out before she was screaming loud enough to bring the roof down. We weren't in the busy clubhouse, but I didn't doubt that some of my brothers still heard her.

"Mine," I grunted. "Say it."

"Yes, yours."

I closed my eyes as the pleasure of her words washed over me, and the ripples of her orgasm tried to strangle me. We were both thrusting now, our hips frantic and erratic as my punishing thrusts grew harder each time I bottomed out in her pussy. I was half tempted to pull out and maneuver us so that she could take me in her mouth and swallow me down.

My mind briefly grasped the vague concept that I wasn't wearing a condom, causing me to slow. I briefly entertained pulling out and marking her body with my cum, before finally dismissing that.

"I'm not pulling out, candy girl. I'm going to come inside you." I gave her all the warning I could, hoping like fuck she didn't say no. The visceral need to fill her with my seed had already taken root and I couldn't let it go.

"What?!" she gasped, still coming apart in my arms.

"I'm. Not. Pulling. Out." I punctuated each word with a demanding thrust, each of which she greeted with her own.

"Uhm—Oka—" She didn't finish because I'd angled my dick once again and either another orgasm had hit, or I'd found a way to increase the intensity of the one that still had her muscles clutching around me.

My heart melted at the sight of her laid bare with her head thrown back, the woosh of air that came out of her mouth because she couldn't breathe, let alone scream, and the beautiful tears I could just make out from this angle. She'd found the stars, and I was ready to join her.

My hips moved faster, roughly pounding into all that slick heat as my orgasm raced through every vein in my body before exploding as I lost complete control. The power of it sizzled in my blood as I followed through on my promise and filled her with my hot cum.

By the time I came down from that high, I had no idea how much time had passed. I released her hands, but stayed right where I stood, locked tight inside her.

I did lean forward and rest my forehead on her back so I could absorb the little aftershocks still rocketing through her every couple of minutes. I'd never fucked a woman without a condom before. Not even her. She'd only gotten pregnant the first time because we'd gotten really rough and broken the condom.

Never in my life had I even felt that visceral need to make a woman take all of me like that. She'd brought something primal out in me.

"How do you feel?" I asked, half expecting her anger to have returned.

"I think I finally understand that expression 'the little death'. I mean, this isn't the first time you brought me to orgasm, but I swear I don't ever remember it being quite like that."

I bent forward and pressed my face to her skin. "You smell so good. Like sex and candy."

"Is that why you called me candy girl? Because that was new." She smiled weakly.

"Because you taste like candy to me. You are now my new favorite treat of all time."

She laughed and I figured it was time to move so the two of us could get more comfortable. I eased from her body and she slowly came to her feet. I could see the mix of our fluids marking her leg and I decided then I liked seeing her like that. I wasn't sure what had gotten into me, but I could feel a new obsession coming on.

"No condom," I said, figuring we should probably address it.

"No condom," she repeated with a nod of her head.

"And if you get pregnant?"

"I haven't had a period in a while because of the strenuous athletic training I do, so I'm not sure if it's possible. But I guess if it happens, we'll deal with it then."

I nodded, agreeing that it wasn't worth borrowing trouble now for something that hadn't even happened yet. But deep down the idea of a baby with her...made my stomach clench with want. Now that the idea was in there, I had a feeling it wasn't going away. Neither was my desire to fuck her like that again...

Chapter Twenty-One

Axel

SOMEONE WAS POUNDING on my door, and I was going to kill them. I'd woken next to Mandy, after a nice long nap, hard as fucking hell and ready to do something about it when the noise had started.

A glance at the bedside clock read one-thirty pm.

Fuck.

I was late, and there would be hell to pay with JD. We had planned for a club meeting to go over all of the new information Tel and Mandy had managed to gather the night before. Everyone was on edge waiting for a killer to make his next move. The waiting was total bullshit and he was as sick of it as everyone else. We were more than ready to go on the attack.

Only she had kept my mind and body occupied. I

looked down at her curled on her side, a pillow hugged to her chest. It was a miracle the racket at the front door hadn't woken her yet. With more than a little reluctance, I lifted off the bed and fished a pair of pants from the floor.

Our clothes were still in the living room, and while these had been crumpled on the floor for God knows how long, they would have to do.

"What's going on?" she mumbled, either roused from the incessant pounding or my movements on the bed.

"Just someone at the door that I'm going to stab for disturbing us."

She rolled over onto her back and hooked an arm across her face. "It's the middle of the day, isn't it? They're probably waiting on us."

"Probably. Still doesn't excuse this bullshit." I turned toward the door, clenching my fists.

"Wait." She suddenly sat up and from the corner of my eye I got a fucking glorious view of her full tits. If I thought my dick was hard before, that was nothing compared to now. Not with my mouth watering and my whole body quaking with the need to lick those nipples until she begged me to stop.

"I gotta go and set them straight. This is unacceptable." Whoever stood at my door they were effectively cock-blocking me, and I did *not* appreciate it.

"I'll go with you." I turned to catch her scrambling from the bed while simultaneously pulling one of my blankets around her naked body.

"It's a little late for that don't you think?" I tipped my head to indicate the almost modest wrap around her. "I've already seen every inch of you. EVERY inch," I emphasized thinking about having her legs spread wide for me on the bed or her ass cheeks parted in the living room. There wasn't a place I could go in this cabin that wouldn't remind me of today.

She tightened the blanket and shrugged. I guessed that was all the response I was going to get.

"It will only take me a few minutes to get dressed, as soon as I find my clothes…"

I thought about those booty shorts I'd ripped off of her. "Not what you had on earlier. If anyone else sees you in those fucking short shorts, I'll have to gouge their eyeballs out."

She stopped short and turned to look at me. "That was oddly descriptive. And a little creepy under the circumstances. And I didn't mean those. I left my duffel in the bathroom with my regular clothes in it."

"Good," I said, scowling in the direction of the still pounding on my door.

"For God's sake. Why are they pounding like that?"

"I don't fucking know, but it *is* on my last nerve. Get dressed, and after I figure out what the hell is going on, we can talk about what's next."

She opened her mouth like she wanted to say something and then immediately closed it again. Whatever it was she decided it could wait. Good thing. Because I wasn't ready for another argument if that's where she wanted to go. Instead, she headed for the bathroom and

I went for the door. I passed the couch, scooped up her shorts and panties, and shoved them under a pillow until I could retrieve them later.

I didn't care if a single one of my brothers knew what we'd done in here, but that didn't mean I wanted her to be embarrassed by it.

I had to admit I had a fondness for those shorts, as long as I was the only one who got to see her wearing them. I wasn't normally this insane about how any woman dressed, but there was something about her that made me a little bit crazy.

And that was very different from ten years ago. I didn't remember feeling quite the same back then. I guess I'd been more focused on the fun and less on the future. Even after hearing about the baby. I remember feeling very divided over what my future looked like. Then I'd been so focused on becoming a prospect that it had been hard to see anything beyond that.

And if I was honest, I'd been angry as hell when she left, but that had fueled my ambition and motivations with the club for a very long time. If not for the incessant banging driving me fucking mad, I might have tried to work through some of the murky thoughts now plaguing me. But—

"I'm coming." I crossed to the door, my view completely hazed with the need to murder someone. "Stop your fucking pounding before I pound your fucking fa— "

I jerked open the door to find a fucking committee. JD, Tell, and Zook were all standing there looking all grim and shit, with Tel's arm still in mid-air from where he'd been using it to pound the thick wood. Good. I hope his hand was god damned sore from that bullshit.

"About god damned time we've been out here for fucking ever," JD growled.

I smirked. "You could have called."

"We did. For two hours. You didn't answer, and now this can't wait."

I tried to remember where the hell I had left my phone and why I hadn't heard a peep out of it, but I'd been a little busy to keep track of it. I had it in the kitchen... I jerked my head in the direction of the island to find it still sitting there from earlier. Hell.

"Come in," I said gruffly, leaving the door open while I moved to the kitchen to retrieve said phone. Sure enough, even before I got it unlocked I could see the blow up of notifications waiting for me.

"What's so important it can't wait?" I asked absently, holding up my phone for face ID to unlock it.

"What's so god damned important here that you can't answer your phone, or open your god damned door in a timely manner?" I didn't have long to work my way around JD's obvious anger before the reason I'd been unavailable sing-songed her way into the living room, ineffectively hiding the blush tinging her cheeks.

"Afternoon."

All three men turned and stared at her, studying her as if they'd never seen her before.

"Hey," JD responded, uncharacteristically monosyllabic. Tel and Zook followed suit. If they hadn't already guessed why I'd been unreachable before, they were certainly putting the pieces together now.

"Houston called. When you didn't answer your phone or respond to any of his messages, he called me."

Mandy's blush deepened at JD's announcement, which wasn't helped by the insinuating glances he kept throwing in both of our directions. For now, I chose to ignore the tension that caused. There was a reason JD was here, and I wanted to get to the bottom of that. I could see there were several missed calls and voice mails from Houston.

JD didn't have to explain anything about Houston to Mandy. She knew it all. From the three of them growing up together, to him leaving the club for the military, all the way to him getting involved with a crime boss's daughter and the subsequent fallout . Somehow, despite the distance between her and the club, she'd managed to be there for every milestone along the way.

That made me give her a hard look. I still didn't believe in coincidences, which made it difficult for me to believe that she'd landed back in our lives by accident or that the killer in question now wasn't somehow connected to all of us. The back of my neck skipped the itching phase and went to straight up burn. The answer was right in front of our faces.

"And?" I finally asked corralling some of my thoughts and tabling them until after this discussion. Houston obviously had news.

"There might be a secret Mazzeo male heir."

"Excuse me?" My blood had gone past cold and straight to frigid at those words. I'd known no matter who we were dealing with they were a psychopath, but add in those genes as well? This situation had just gone sideways.

"That's impossible," Mandy interjected. "If Frank Mazzeo had any other children, either living or dead, we'd know about it."

He assumed the *we* she referred to was the covert government faction she'd belonged to. On the outset it had appeared that she worked for the FBI, but my perception on that had changed quickly.

"Nothing's impossible," JD replied. "And I think, at some level, we all either knew or suspected that the perfect storm was brewing. Now, it's about to explode."

I had so many questions I didn't know where to start so I started with what I thought was the most obvious. "Why do they think there's a male heir? Izzy never mentioned any siblings whatsoever."

"I don't know why we didn't think to look up the bastard's will. I guess we all just assumed everything had gone to Izzy."

JD shoved a folded-up piece of paper into my hands. "What is it?" I asked as I opened it and read, my eyes going wide as I did.

"It's a copy of Frank Mazzeo's signed, notarized and fully executed will and testament. The lawyer had done his due diligence with Izzy and read this to her in its entirety, but he failed to notify anyone that the named heir had actually come forward.

I read it again, just to make sure I'd understood it correctly.

I, Frank Mazzeo, leave the entirety of my estate to my sole, living male heir. In the event he is no longer living or cannot be located then the entire estate is bequeathed to St. Francis church.

Holy shit.

"I didn't realize he left nothing to Izzy. What an asshole. But who the fuck is this male heir? We don't have a name."

"Keep reading. Specifically, page two." Tel practically vibrated with excitement. Apparently, he'd found something no one else knew.

I kept reading, but my eyes were beginning to glaze over through all of the legalese. I hated this shit. Why did they have to write their documents in a way that guaranteed almost no one without a law degree understood them? What exactly would be wrong with a plain language will? I give so and so this and I give so and so jack. Easy peasy.

It wasn't until I got to the very end, near where the signatures were located when I finally hit the jackpot.

Legal male heir has been located and verified through certified and independent blood typing. See attachment A. Franklin Mazzeo Jr. has come forth and proven to the full extent of the law that he is the sole known male heir to one Franklin Mazzeo and thus this will is now fully executed and filed with the King

County Superior Court blah blah blah. There was more information about dates and places but nothing was as important as the name I had in my hands.

Fucking Frank Jr.

Until I turned the page and saw the grainy picture.

I couldn't make out the face of the man getting into the back seat of a dark sedan, but I didn't need to.

That's when I knew instantly, down to my bones, that he was the man hunting Amanda Turner.

Chapter Twenty-Two

Amanda

SINCE I HAD zero chill and little to no patience, I'd
started to examine the paperwork in Axel's hands while
he read. I didn't have to ask how they'd gotten a copy of
a legally filed court document so fast. I'd witnessed first
hand how good Tel was as a hacker. At this point I
believed there wasn't a computer made that he couldn't
get into.

Yes, I was impressed, but I was also terrified. Cyber
crimes were high on the priority list these days and one
slip up and the MC would be back at the top of the list
when it came to investigations. Domestic terrorism was
at an all-time high, and the government wouldn't hesitate to link their crimes to any potential incidents.

Now this.

My stomach cramped at the idea that a Mazzeo would once again helm the crime syndicate in Seattle, allowing it to continue with barely a blip. It made what I'd been through feel futile. Although if he had his way, I wouldn't live to see it. Apparently, this asshole had made it his personal mission to avenge his father's death. Fucking great.

And if this one was anything like his father...

I shook my head of those morbid thoughts. Now was not the time to dwell on personal feelings. I needed more information.

"What else did you find about him? Where did he come from?" I was prepared to continue but paused long enough for someone to give me something —anything.

Tel's eyes shuttered for a moment. "He's scrubbed clean. I've never seen anything quite like it. Either he's a lily-white newcomer to the crime world—unlikely, since no one would trust anyone that new—or he's got a real pro working for him."

"Any idea who that might be?" Axel asked.

"Who? The cleaner?"

Axel nodded.

"Not yet. So far, I've been unable to find a trace of anyone associated with this name. Only this picture."

"Why does it look so familiar? Have we seen this before?" The perplexed look on Axel's face pulled my attention.

"Good catch. Yeah, we have. Check this out." Tel pulled another picture from his bag of tricks and handed it over. I looked around Axel to get a better look, but this one, I hadn't seen before and had no idea what it related to. Axel, on the other hand, had a good eye for detail. Maybe too good. He never seemed to forget anything.

"Is this what I think it is?" There were two men in the photograph. This one as grainy as the first. How in the hell was this guy avoiding getting his image captured? No one was that good.

"Fuck yeah, we think it is." JD grumbled. "It's hard to tell, one hundred percent, because these images suck ass, but I'm pretty sure that's our coffee hut in the background. The first one that got hit."

"What do you mean hit?" I was out of the loop.

"There was an incident about two weeks ago. Propane tank on our flagship coffee drive-through exploded. We thought it was an accident, until two more went down just like it."

"You own coffee huts?" I don't know why that sounded ridiculous, but it did.

"Sure do." Axel laughed. "One of our old ladies had the idea to add some legitimate revenue to our coffers, and this state's love of coffee is no joke. Each of our huts is a mini cash cow. Well, they were, until three of them were taken down by mysterious accidents."

My mind boggled. "Three of them? And you think this guy had something to do with it?" I nudged the photo still in Axel's hand.

JD shrugged. "It's as good a theory as anything else we've got. We were all involved in bringing down

Mazzeo and his international sex slave ring. If this guy is really Frank's son and out to avenge his father's death, then his list of targets just got a lot longer."

"Shit," Axel exclaimed. "This is bullshit."

"It's the price of doing the business we do. Just means we have to go on the attack instead of sitting back waiting on this fucker to make a move. But I ain't going to lie, we're sitting ducks. He seems to know a lot more about us than we know about him. Our security is good here at the compound, so that's in our favor, but one step off, and that changes."

"What do you want to do?" Axel asked, looking confident that he already knew the answer.

"Take the fight to him, of course. We've still got a line into that new club. Someone there has to know something."

"But you just said leaving the compound wasn't safe. Why the hell would you encroach on his turf until you know more about him?"

JD laughed and the other men followed suit. "No way in hell are we going to sit around and wait to be picked off. He's already put a dent in our income and killed a Fed. He needs to be stopped before this shit escalates."

I wasn't sure it wasn't already too late for that. Getting a head in a box felt pretty damned escalated.

"Maybe that's exactly what he wants. If he can divide the club, he might think that gives him an advantage." I wanted to know a lot more about this syndicate they kept mentioning. But that was the analyst in me talking, not the field agent. I couldn't blame them for wanting to do something. I had the same urge. And it seemed they were going to do what they wanted, no matter what I had to say about it.

So, when in Rome...

"When are we leaving for Seattle?" I asked, already calculating the weapons and ammunition I had brought with me and where I could get more. Because what I had was not enough.

All four men turned and looked at me. "*We* aren't going anywhere. There's crazy, which I'm all for, and then there's asinine. If he's trying to do anything, it's probably to get *you* off of the compound."

I narrowed my eyes at Axel. "If you think I'm going to sit around while you go fight my battle for me, you're an idiot. If anything, *I'm* better trained for this kind of thing."

Axel's eyebrows climbed into his hairline and the scowl on his face turned downright explosive. The other men, they looked away, but there were mumbles I couldn't make out under their breath.

"Oh yeah?" Axel drawled, an aura of calm about him that felt deceptive. "Do you want to put that to the test?"

Since my frustration and anger were as high as his, I was game for whatever. "Sure. What did you have in mind?"

"Axel," JD warned with a pointed look.

"What? She just challenged me. You expect me to let that slide?"

"I don't," I said. "If it's a test you want, I'm more than

happy to give you one. Name your poison. Shooting? Hand to hand combat? Driving?"

Tel snickered. "She's probably a better shot than you are."

"Yeah, but he'd take her easily in hand to hand. She's so tiny."

I tried to ignore the jabs from Tel and Zook, but obviously they were going to fan the flames. And tiny? Really? That's a word no one had ever used to describe me. I was taller than average and with all the training I put myself through, my body had definitely bulked up since high school. Although Zook was a big man. He looked almost like a bald, leather-wrapped giant. From his perspective, everyone probably looked small.

"We don't have time for the two of you to get into a pissing contest. This isn't a competition. This is serious business."

"Never said it wasn't," Axel said without taking his gaze off of mine. "But I can tell you right now, she's not going anywhere until she proves herself."

"Oh shit," Zook groaned. "Even I know those are fighting words."

He was right about that. "I don't have to prove anything. I do what I want." A second after those words left my mouth, I regretted them. I needed to tread a little more carefully. It wouldn't surprise me to find myself locked in some sort of cage 'for my own good'. These men could be barbaric when it came to keeping those they cared about safe.

"Okay, when you two children are done, you let me know. I'm not going to watch."

"I am," Tel blurted out with far too much excitement, while tapping out something on his phone.

"Me too," Zook piped in.

"So, what's it going to be Ms. Kickass? You ready to take me on?"

Maybe he was kidding, and maybe he wasn't. Either way, he'd thrown down a gauntlet I couldn't resist. "I'm still waiting for you to choose." I probably should have done the choosing myself. They were right I probably couldn't take him down in a physical fight. Although I did have a few tricks that would at least give him a run for his money.

"Driving," Tel said. "We'll make it a race."

I looked sideways at him. "In what? I don't exactly see any race cars around here. The trucks?"

A slow smile crossed Tel's face. "Already covered. The guys are on their way with the ATVs."

Axel shook his head. "I don't think that's a great—"

"Perfect." I interrupted. I'd done some training on some 4-wheelers. I could at least handle driving one of those, and I might have a fighting chance. Although shooting would have been fun.

Next time. That thought brought me up short. It wasn't smart to entertain ideas such as that. To suggest that we were now friends or something more would be a mistake. I didn't belong here any more than I belonged at my job. And staying in Sultan was out of the question. Although my options on where to go next were as limited now as they'd been when I'd returned. As soon as this thing with the Mazzeo heir was done, I would have to figure out what came next.

It was time to get back on my own two feet.

Before Axel could complain or say something else to piss me off, the whine of small cycle engines sounded from somewhere in the distance.

"That was fast."

Tel shrugged. "I like to get shit done. Why wait?"

JD was shaking his head as he walked down the front path, seemingly headed in the direction of the clubhouse. But I'd caught the slight smile on his face before he turned away. I didn't know exactly what he was up to, but if I had to guess, I'd say he'd just gotten exactly what he wanted.

However, I didn't have time to analyze any of that because two four-seater side by sides zoomed around the corner and came to a quick halt right in front of the cabin. From the cuts they wore it was obvious they were other members of the club, but these I'd yet to meet.

"Mandy," Zook looked up at me and met my gaze. "I can call you Mandy, right?"

I bit my lip and nodded. The sudden familiarity of these men I barely knew made my chest clench. I hated to admit it but being here with them and getting to work with them was fast becoming a highlight of my year. I glanced over at Axel quickly and found him studying me with an intensity that caught me off guard. What was that about?

"Cool. Mandy, these are our newbies. They just got patched in."

Both men gave me a quick smile and nodded their heads. I knew going from prospect to full member was a big deal and I imagined they both had to be pretty badass to make the cut. And they were both smoking hot. Where the hell were they finding these guys? I didn't remember Sultan as such a hot bed for hotness back in the day.

Maybe it was the beards and tattoos. I'd always had a weakness for both. This thought made me look in Axel's direction once again. He still had that intense stare focused my way, but this time it made my belly swoop and my whole body light up from thinking about all the ways he'd made me come this morning.

Pull it together, Mandy.

If I didn't control my reaction every time I looked at him, I might find myself flung over his shoulder and carried back into bed. That thought made a shiver work down my spine. One could only hope.

Axel stepped closer and I took a step back. He had a freakish way of knowing exactly what was on my mind.

Instead, I smirked at him and said, "You ready to get your ass kicked?"

Chapter Twenty-Three

Amanda

I LAUGHED at the brother who stood next to the driver's side with a helmet in his hand, held in my direction. "Tell me you're not serious."

"As a heart attack," he replied without cracking so much as a smirk. "VP's orders."

I looked over at Axel on the vehicle next to mine and frowned. He was looking over at me with a satisfied smile across his face. A face not covered by a helmet I noticed. Bastard. I wanted to argue but knew to my bones that the effort would be futile. It also wasn't the hill I wanted to die on. I snatched the helmet from Bear's beefy hand and proceeded to put it on my head and fastened the strap.

I was seriously going to enjoy putting him in his place. I'd done well at the Academy, excelling at all my classes, including both the defensive and offensive driving courses.

I just had to keep my focus and watch the terrain as well as Axel's vehicle. We were only doing two laps so I wasn't going to have a lot of extra time to make adjustments.

"We're going to keep this clean, Turner," Axel called from his vehicle. "There's a trail that runs the perimeter of the property, we'll stick to that as much as possible. And no bar banging."

"Bar banging?" I asked a moment before I realized he was talking about the bars on the back of the vehicle. "No bumping, right?"

He laughed. "Sure, Turner. Although in racing we call it banging."

"Whatever. Let's just get this over with. We have a bad guy to catch, and we're burning daylight."

"Patience, grasshopper. I doubt he's going anywhere. He's pretty fixated."

He wasn't wrong, and to be honest, beating him on this makeshift racetrack sounded like a blast. Something that had been in short supply in my life for a very long time. I started my vehicle and put it in gear, waiting for one of the guys to get us started.

Both vehicles rumbled loudly, effectively disguising the sound of my heart, beating out of control, as a rush of adrenalin pumped through my blood. I was ridiculously excited by all of this. I bit my lips to keep my grin from spreading ear to ear. It wouldn't do for them to see me acting like an idiot. I was about to show them what a badass I could be and I needed the look to go with it.

"Ready?" Tel yelled over the roar of the engines.

I held up my hand with a thumbs up and then put my hands back on the steering wheel. My muscles were stretched so taut I thought they might be on the verge of breaking.

"Set," Tel hollered, raising his hands high in the air. As soon as he brought them down it would be on, and I couldn't wait. I shot Axel one last glance, noticing he had put on a helmet at the last minute. Still trying to suppress my laughter, I gave him my best "you're going down" look before looking forward again.

I couldn't remember the last time I'd been this excited. I was trying to remember for sure when Tel's hands came down and my foot automatically pressed down on the gas. The big, knobby tires dug into the ground, sending dust and dirt flying in every direction as we both tore off from the start line.

Axel immediately pulled ahead, throwing more dirt in every direction, including my windshield, temporarily blocking my view.

I grunted in frustration, but powered through, following my instincts and the shape of his vehicle in front of mine that I could still make out.

He obviously had the home team advantage of being familiar with the course, so my goal with the first lap was to stay right on his tail, not lose too much ground, and learn the track for the second lap. Then as soon as I could, and when he least expected it, I would pass him for the win.

It was obvious by the way he drove he wasn't going to go easy on me and that was fine by me. That would only make my win sweeter when it happened.

We whipped the vehicles around curve after curve and jumped them over the jarring hills in a repeated fashion until I could feel every bone rattle in my body and my teeth grind down on each other like they wanted to wear them down. Physically, it took a surprising amount of strength to keep the vehicle under control.

There were a few tight turns that I braked through more than Axel, giving him an opportunity to pull a little farther ahead. But I could see a straightaway coming up and I hoped to gain some ground during that. Whatever it took, I had to win. I would not get left behind on this case just because they didn't think I was good enough.

That whole excuse was BS. I might have wanted to prove something with this race, but I didn't have to. I would leave the compound with or without their permission. An image of them locking me away in some cage popped into my head again. I had no idea why that image haunted me. I'd seen no cage or anything like it to make me believe they might actually do something like that. But they did keep the layout and contents of their clubhouse on the down low. There were many rooms and even levels I'd seen none of thus far.

We slid into the next curve and this time I was able to get farther along before I had to hit the brakes to finish the turn. My heartbeat raced as I ended up right on the bumper of Axel's rig. I could see why they'd told me no bar banging. On that last turn I'd gained the upper hand, but Axel maintained his position in front of me by blocking my ability to pass.

This race wasn't just about speed. Track position and maintaining control were every bit as important as how fast the vehicle drove. We approached the start/finish line of the first lap, and I could see more people had gathered to watch. As we raced by the crowd, I thought I heard some woops and keep goings from the group.

This was it. There was only one more lap, so I had no more than a few minutes to make a play and get my way around Axel. Sliding into another turn, I maintained my speed and started to gain ground. Unfortunately, at the last minute he swerved left, cutting me off and ensuring I had to slow down and stay behind him.

Gah.

Sweat trickled down my back as I strong armed the wheel to keep the vehicle on the track and myself in the race. If this kept up, I was going to lose this whole thing. With my mind going a mile a minute trying to keep up, I didn't see the latest hill until both Axel and I caught air above it.

My heart jumped into my throat and I let out a whoop of excitement as I sailed through the air and then landed with a hard bounce. There was another turn coming up and this might be my last chance to take the lead. I leaned into the start of the curve kicking up a thicker layer of dust in Axel's direction.

Whether my actions caused it or something else had happened, Axel braked sooner than expected entering the turn. Oh my God, this was it. I could see the option to get ahead in front of me. I dive bombed the vehicle underneath him to cut the corner. Unfortunately, he recovered quickly and was this close to taking back the little ground I had gained and was closing the gap I'd created to get by him.

I glanced quickly to the side to look for options. There was only one, and if I wanted to win, I had to take it. I grinned wildly. They could argue later I'd cheated, but sometimes you had to do whatever it takes. I jerked the wheel to the right, bumping hard but quick against his vehicle. It was just enough to make some room.

Yes! I stomped on the gas and squeezed through by what felt like the skin of my teeth. *Oh. My. God. I was in the lead!*

And about to pee my fucking pants I was so excited. Laughter bubbled up from my chest and burst free. What the hell was happening? First mind blowing sex with the man I couldn't stop thinking about and now this?

Who the hell was I and where had the real Amanda Turner gone?

I couldn't see Axel behind me, but I could practically

feel him breathing down my neck. I could also imagine how pissed he was about me giving him a little bump out of the way.

Either way, I strong armed the steering wheel with everything I had, maneuvering myself into the middle of the road to keep him from passing me again. That would also create a lot of extra dust that would make it a little bit harder for him to see and maybe not catch me.

By the time we hit the last straightaway, and I could see the finish line, I caught sight of his vehicle in my peripheral vision. He was already past my back bumper bar thingy and moving up. I could try nudging him again, but I had a feeling if I pushed my luck too hard, I'd end up flipping this thing.

So, I did the only thing I could. I prayed and pushed the gas petal to the floor. The engine screamed. Hell, I screamed. The big tires bounced over the uneven terrain, and by the time we reached the last hill that would launch us over the finish line we were locked in a dead heat.

"Come on, baby!" I screamed as the rig hit air. At this point, I wasn't sure if I cared whether I won or lost anymore. This was the best moment of my life. It tasted like freedom and fun. When I landed with a hard bounce, I stomped on the brakes and skidded to a halt. I ripped the helmet off and threw back my head as the sound of my glee filled the air around me.

It didn't matter that I probably sounded like a cackling witch.

"Holy shit!" I vaguely heard someone exclaim. It was difficult to hear anything with the ringing in my ears and my entire body still vibrating from the rough, but exhilarating ride.

"I think she won."

My heart leapt into my throat. *What?*

Seconds later the vehicle was surrounded by hulking men in black leather cuts and some of their women too. They were all talking at once, but I couldn't hear a word they said. I was in shock. I had to admit, despite my confidence, it sounded crazy. I'd known I could hold my own but beating Axel hadn't been easy.

"Congratulations," Bear said, taking my helmet so I could climb out of the rig. "I don't know how you did that, but I'm impressed."

"Don't be. She cheated." I heard Axel's angry voice behind me and I turned to face him.

"Cheating is a strong word. I did what I had to in order to get the job done. It was harmless. Anyone would have done it."

"She's right about that," Tel interjected. "You banged the hell out of me last week."

Axel glared at his club brother for a moment before both men broke into huge grins. "You're right. No one likes a sore loser. I guess I owe the winner my congratulations."

While I didn't know exactly what that entailed, I did not expect it to be him hauling me against him and fusing his mouth to mine in front of the entire crowd.

Cheers and catcalls erupted and more than a few

"get a rooms" were called out. All I knew was that by the time he released me I wasn't sure my legs were going to hold me up. My lips tingled, my everything else throbbed, and the happiest moment of my life had gotten impossibly better.

Chapter Twenty-Four

Axel

I STOOD in the entry of the clubhouse and watched Mandy be swept away by half the club and their women. Anyone else, and I might have questioned their loyalty. They were clapping her on the back and offering her shots of tequila to celebrate her win.

Bastards.

I smiled, pride filling my chest. She'd done insanely well out there and beat me fair and square. I'd warned her about bar banging for her own safety because I didn't want her hurt, not because it was really cheating. That was all part of that kind of racing. But she'd more than proven she could handle herself.

"Did you let her win?"

I bristled at JD's question. Maybe it wasn't a stretch

for him to question her win, but it annoyed me none-theless. It was one thing for me to underestimate her without cause and a whole other situation for someone else to do it. Her and I had a complicated history that came with a bucket of trust issues. That didn't mean I wanted anyone else to have a problem with her.

"Nope. She got me on that last turn. I don't know where she learned to cut the corners like that, but she is one hell of a driver."

"CIA trains their people well. A test probably wasn't necessary."

I smiled, letting a full grin cross my face. "Maybe not. But it sure was fun, and look at her now. I think she needed this."

"I take it you two have worked through your differences."

My smile faltered. I didn't know about worked out, but we might be headed in the right direction. Maybe.

"Let's just say we've worked out a truce."

JD chuckled and clapped me on the back. "A truce isn't a bad place to start. Relationships are complicated, some more than others."

I looked at my prez and wondered whether he was talking about me, the past, or maybe even his present. If anyone understood complicated it would be him. He had the scars to prove it.

"Complicated is an understatement. Probably more trouble than I need is more like it."

JD's laugh deepened. "The ones worth your time

always are. Just give it some time. I have a hunch there's more to her story than either of us knows."

"What does that mean?" I searched his face for an answer. "If you know something I should, you need to tell me. I can't protect her if I don't know everything up front."

"Then I guess you'll have to ask her. She's the one with the answers you need, not me."

I hated it when he hit me with his cryptic all-knowing bullshit. But I also knew he would only say what he wanted to say, no matter how much he was provoked.

"Go have a drink with your girl," he nudged. "Take a moment to enjoy each other before we all go to hell turning the criminal underworld upside down tomorrow."

"Tomorrow, huh?" I was happy to hear that. I was done waiting on this prick to make a move. I was beyond ready to bury a bullet between his eyes.

"I know what you're thinking." I doubted he did, but I didn't see the point in arguing. "When someone's messing with your woman, all you can think about is how you're going to end it. Just make sure she's okay with what you're thinking, so it doesn't drive the two of you apart. She has been living in a different world for a while now."

I thought about that for a moment. "As far as I can tell, she doesn't live by the rules of her world or ours. She isn't afraid to get dirty, but her loyalty is question-able. I'm not sure that's something I can or should get past." We were both painfully aware of the fact she'd worked with Frank and that association had nearly cost us more than we could afford to pay.

There was also a clear difference between what I wanted to believe, and what might actually be true. Digging into our past might have been necessary, but at what cost?

JD shook his head. "Talk to her, Axel. Find out for yourself what made her do the things she did. There has to be an explanation on her part. There has to be."

"Or this Mazzeo shit-head is just cleaning up the mess his father made in a very final way. If he gets rid of everyone involved, then the slate is clean for the new organization, and he cements his position in the new organization." That seemed the logical answer. Only, I didn't feel that in my gut. This dickwad had taken chances most men in charge did not.

"Worry about it tomorrow. Go congratulate your woman, and have some fun. After tonight, it might be a while before we can relax again. Declaring war on a crime syndicate isn't likely to make us very popular."

I nodded. While I'd heard what he said, my brain had focused on the my woman part and gotten stuck there. Was that really what I wanted? Or what she wanted? JD must have sensed my hesitation so he took that opportunity to walk over to Mandy and give her a congratulatory hug. One of the prospects behind the bar offered them both shots of tequila, which they clinked together and downed in one swallow.

I shook my head. If I wanted to talk to her about us,

I needed to break this up before they got her sloshy drunk. Mandy drunk would probably be lots of fun. But Mandy sober could make clear decisions and understand what it was I had to say.

As I was about to walk that way, Bear crossed my path and blocked my view of Mandy. "What the hell, Bear?" I grumbled, trying to look around his massive bulk. The dude was as big as a standing grizzly and as lethal as one too. Not to mention the long hair and the long beard making him as hairy as one too.

"Sorry," he laughed. "Just thought I'd tell you she's quite a woman you've got there before you haul her off to your cabin for the real party."

"Thanks," I agreed, hesitantly. On one hand she did feel like mine, and she was amazing. But on the other I still couldn't reconcile the fact that she'd worked for the Mazzeo organization. Everything I'd seen the past few days indicated a serious passion for getting the facts she needed and a strong desire for serving justice. Frank had stood for the opposite.

I really wanted to put the past behind us, but that little part of me didn't want to let it go. We all had faults. We all made decisions that others didn't necessarily agree with. So why couldn't I let hers go? Even JD seemed to be over it.

Because you're a stubborn asshole?

There was that. And not a one of us was in a position to judge. There were plenty of black marks on my soul, all done in the name of the club, and they would never see the light of day…

You reap what you sow.

"I hear we're going after the man who's been stalking her. I'm sure you want first dibs, but just know any one of us would take him down. We've got both your backs."

I compressed my lips in a kind of grim smile. While I appreciated his words, they weren't necessary. It was a given in our club that any one of us had the others back. Still, I appreciated him saying the words.

"Thanks, man. I definitely can't wait to get my hands on that asshole. But first, I've got something else I need to do." I'd already turned my focus back to Mandy, still standing at the bar, as each of my brothers stopped by to say a few words to her.

Bear followed my line of sight and started laughing. "I get you. Do what you gotta— "

Suddenly a loud explosion sounded from somewhere on the compound. It was so strong it rocked through the building, rattling the walls and everything inside not nailed down. Glass shattered as bottles and glasses crashed to the floor and pictures fell from the walls.

"What the hell?" In a few seconds the entire clubhouse exploded in chaos as the women screamed and others dove for cover.

"Was that an earthquake?" someone shouted.

"I don't think so," JD responded as he ran towards the door. But Bear and I were closer and we got the jump on the rest of them as we scrambled to get outside to see what was going on.

Bear, as big as he was, moved with lightning speed. He wrenched the door open, and another blast tore through the club, sending him flying through the air before crashing into a table and chairs. My mouth was open in a yell, as smoke and flames filled the doorway. I rushed to Bear's side and felt my heart nearly stop at the sight of him knocked out, a large piece of debris sticking out of his cheek, and his leg at an awkward angle.

"Fuck." I pressed my fingers deep into his neck and felt for a pulse. It took a second, but I finally found it, although it didn't seem particularly strong.

"Is he alive?" JD asked, rushing to my side.

"Yeah, for now. But he needs a doctor."

Out of my peripheral vision I caught Zook running for the entrance with a fire extinguisher in his hand. I glanced around the room and realized with a piercing pain to my chest that Mandy was no longer at the bar.

"What the fuck? Mandy!" I yelled.

"She's—"

I didn't hear whatever else JD said, as I rushed to where I'd last seen her and found her lying on the floor. Her eyes were open, but her pupils looked freakishly large. "Are you okay? Where are you hurt?"

"I'm okay, I think. My head hurts though." She reached up into her thick hair, felt around, and then winced. The pain she triggered forced her hand away from whatever it was, and blood now coated her fingers.

"Jesus Christ. Mandy, baby. Don't fucking move." I

shifted towards her head and crouched lower so I could get a better look. I held my breath until I was able to determine that unlike Bear, she did not have anything sticking out of her head. "Looks like something hit you on the head, or you hit something when you were knocked to the ground."

"But the blood," her voice rose.

"Head wounds are always the worst when it comes to that. Even if they are superficial. But I think we have to assume that you probably have a concussion and will need to get to a hospital."

"No way. That's just the kind of thing he'll be hoping for."

My breath froze in my chest. Of course. That fucker would be looking for a way to get her off the compound. If he couldn't come to her, then he would make her come to him.

"It's okay," I finally said. "We have a doctor who can come to us."

She turned to look at me and met my eyes. "I'm going to assume I don't want to know why that is, right?"

I didn't bother to answer. She wasn't dumb and didn't need me to mansplain anything to her. "Do you think you can sit up?"

"Yeah. I'm sure I'll be fine. But what about everyone else?"

I reached a hand under her back and helped her into a seating position before settling in behind her so I could give her some support.

I glanced around the room, still frantic with chaos, as those who could checked on everyone who might have injuries. Most were now either sitting or standing. While there was soot and smoke cutting some of the visibility, it looked like most were okay. Except Bear. He was still on the floor with several members huddled around him including Cash.

Thank God he was here.

"It's hard to say for sure until I get a full assessment, but I think most everyone is okay."

"Most?" Her gaze bounced wildly around the room before finally landing on the huddle where Bear had landed. "Who is it? Is he dead?"

Fear squeezed my throat when she voiced her concern. I didn't even want to think something like that, let alone repeat it.

"No," I insisted. He was one strong motherfucker. If anyone could pull through it would be him. "He had a pulse when I left him to find you. He was at the door when it exploded."

Her sharp intake of breath hit me square in the chest. I couldn't show it, but I was feeling as freaked out as her. Seeing Bear laid out on the ground—hell, any of our guys on the ground—rocked me to my core. Any one of us could have died.

"We need to help him. Maybe I can—" She tried to push off of me and a second later her body swayed to the side and I caught her before she landed headfirst —again.

"You're not going anywhere. Cash is taking care of

him until the ambulance gets here. He's a paramedic and the best in his field. He's got this."

She slumped back against me, her relief clear. My muscles were tense, but some amount of relief still seeped in as I realized that this could have been so much worse. Whoever had rigged that door to explode had no way of knowing who would open it, and it could have been any one of them laid out on the ground, including Mandy.

Bile rose in my throat at the same time a fresh wave of anger filled me. An attack on our clubhouse would not go unanswered. We were going to—

"Holy Shit. Look!" someone yelled. "The back of the compound is on fire.

Chapter Twenty-Five

Amanda

"WHAT?"

"Where?" Axel and I both spoke at once, but he didn't look nearly as confused as I felt.

The woman who'd announced the news shrugged. "I couldn't tell exactly from the kitchen window, but there's a lot of smoke, and I can see the flames in the distance. It looks like it might be the casino."

Axel's demeanor changed instantly. I wasn't even looking at his face and I could sense it. His muscles had gone rigid and I wasn't even sure he was taking a breath. "The Casino?" I asked.

I wasn't trying to play dumb. The government had had no luck in confirming what kind of business might be running from back there. Based on the traffic and some of the visitors going in an out, we'd made an educated guess. We'd also decided to back off from the Club at that point. Whatever they did back there it involved some big hitters in every facet of business and government.

No one wanted to touch that kind of ticking time bomb.

"Are you okay for a minute if I go and check on this? There might have been people on site."

"Oh my gosh. Yes. Yes. Go. I'll be fine."

He didn't make it two steps before he collided into an angry JD. "What the fuck?"

"I just heard. Do we have confirmation?"

"Not yet," JD growled. "Everyone is either here, or at Turners' for the night. The two handling security out there aren't fucking answering their phones."

"We'll send some guys down there now. They can report."

There was so much anger in both their words, but it was also obvious that it served as a cover for a great amount of fear.

"I don't want anyone in here going near a door. We don't know if any of the others were rigged as well. I'm not losing anyone else tonight."

"Bear?" Axel nearly choked on that one word, and I didn't blame him. I could already feel the press of tears against the back of my eyes at the idea that we'd lost the big man who'd encouraged me just a short while ago at the race. My stomach twisted and I worried I might throw up.

"No," JD offered gruffly. "But Cash is struggling. I can see it. And the place is about to be swarming with Sultan FD and PD any second."

"Thank God the casino was closed tonight. Any other night..."

"Don't even go there. I'm already half blind with rage. If I start thinking about what could have happened, I'm going to fucking kill someone."

It was weird to hear JD talk like this. He'd always seemed so calm and in control. Even now he was barking orders and making sure everyone inside his compound was safe. Only with Axel did he let his guard down and some of his anger out.

"There has got to be a way to get out there." Axel seemed to survey the room as he weighed his options. He was smart and careful. Analytical even. I didn't remember him being like that before. He'd changed a lot.

"What about surveillance?" I asked, pulling myself to my feet on only slightly shaky legs. "Is there surveillance on the building that would give you a view of any of the doors and windows?"

Axel and JD thought about her questions, but it was Axel who turned to her, shaking his head. "Most of the surveillance is on the windows and doors, but the cameras face away from the building not towards it."

"What about the security shack or any of the closer cabins? Do they have cameras that could be used to view the building?"

"I like the way you think," JD said. "Tel, get your ass over here," he bellowed across the room.

Tel wasted no time in following orders. "Yeah?"

"You hurt? Can you operate?"

He nodded. "Yeah, I'm fine. What do you need?" He didn't look exactly fine, but the injuries I could see did look minor.

"I need any security cameras you got on any of the outbuildings that can face this one and give me eyes on our doors or windows. Can you do that?"

He pulled his tablet from his vest pocket and tapped on it with his fingers practically flying. "Uhh... yeah I've got two. Izzy's old cabin, and believe it or not, the one on Axel's cabin has a great view of the kitchen window."

"Well, hell. Show me."

Tel turned his tablet around and we all huddled around it. Sure enough, he'd zoomed in one of the cameras so that it was pointed right at one of the windows. And the image was practically high def in quality. They weren't kidding about how seriously they took their security.

"I don't see anything, do you?" Axel asked JD.

"No. It looks clear. Although that's no guarantee."

"Fuck guarantees. We've got guys out there. I'm going through that window."

"What? No." I grabbed his arm. "We don't know if he's out there or what else he has planned."

I looked at JD for help and he simply narrowed his eyes and ran his fingers along his beard. "She might be right, but we need eyes out there. We can't wait for the FD."

Axel grabbed my shoulders and met my gaze. "It's unlikely he'll make another move in person here. He might have caught us off guard once, but it's not going to happen again. I'm more concerned on how he plans to get to you."

"He could be after you as much as me," I argued. "There's still too much we don't know. We don't even really know what he looks like, which means he could be anyone anywhere."

"Which is why you're going to stay here where the whole club can take your back. Especially when the FD arrives. But this is a small town, remember? Strangers stand out here like a sore thumb."

He was right. Axel had lived here his whole life. It was unlikely anyone lived here that he didn't know at least by sight. The same with JD. "I still don't like it. This could all be a ploy to separate us."

"Don't worry. No one's going to go anywhere alone." JD interjected before turning back to Axel. "Take at least two guys with you." When Axel started to argue, JD stopped him by continuing. "That's not a request. From here on out, no one goes anywhere alone or unarmed, is that clear?"

"Yeah, it is." Axel leaned over, lifted his pant leg, and pulled a gun free from an ankle holster. He checked the safety and then tucked it into the back of his jeans. "I'm set. I'll let you know what the hell is going on in a few minutes."

JD nodded and walked away, going back to check on Bear. My stomach tightened again at the reminder of his severe injuries. I had a bad feeling, and that wasn't good. I'd learned a long time ago to trust my instincts.

"I don't suppose you'd consider taking me with you?" I asked.

"Nope. Not while you likely have a concussion. You need to take it easy until we get a doctor to assess you."

I could have argued that I felt fine, but not only did I not want to waste my breath, it might have been a lie. My head ached, and the accompanying nausea made him likely right about a concussion.

"Then don't get hurt."

He smiled, reaching out to cup my cheek. "You worried about me?"

I was, but that didn't mean I'd say it. "Just hoping to save anyone the hassle of having to go rescue you," I lied.

Axel roared with laughter, and it felt good that in the light of this nightmare that I'd seemingly brought to their doorstep, he could still find a moment of levity.

On that note, he walked away as two other club brothers filed in behind him, and they all disappeared into the kitchen. Tel, who I'd almost forgotten was still standing close by, moved in and motioned for me to look at the tablet.

"We can surveil them from here. At least until they get past the line of trees that surrounds the casino. All the cameras out there are either damaged or cut off. We won't know for sure until Axel lets us know what he finds."

Goosebumps erupted across my skin. That nagging bad feeling intensified.

"I really don't like this. He could be walking into anything."

Tel nodded. "If anyone will be fine, it's him. Axel has at least nine lives, and I don't think he's used up more than a few."

I knew that was supposed to be a joke, but it didn't feel funny. I hated waiting on the sidelines with my hands essentially tied. It was total bullshit.

However, I had no—

"Wait. What the hell is that?"

Chapter Twenty-Six

Axel

WE SPRINTED across the open field in the direction of my cabin, taking no more than a few minutes to get there. There wasn't a lot of cover between the clubhouse and there, and I didn't want us to take any chances if someone was waiting for us.

Plus, I knew that Tel would still be watching us and whoever had set these explosions likely knew that. But once we got into the tree line, we were completely on our own.

Fortunately, the sun was about to dip below the horizon and we could use the shadows for cover as we approached. We reached the tree line without incident but opted to avoid the open pathway we usually traveled.

All three of us were on alert, guns at the ready, expecting the worst. Or so we thought, until the building came into view. Out here, the smoke was uncomfortably thick, and in a few minutes it was going to be tough to breathe easy.

The first thing I saw was a body on the ground. Shit.

Putting on speed, I made it there first and dropped down to check for a pulse. I was so focused on whether or not he was breathing I didn't register right away the mangled condition of Brody, one of our newest prospects.

"Boss." A hand landed on my shoulder right at the moment I realized. He was gone.

Anger and grief welled inside me, warring for control. This wasn't my first experience with this kind of loss, but it had been a while since we'd suffered a direct attack like this.

I surveyed the front of the building, flames licking along the front wall that had a giant hole in the middle. Like the clubhouse, it seemed that this explosion had originated from the front door as well. Only this one was bigger with smoke pouring from every crack, break or hole in the building.

"We need to find him."

"If he's inside the building that's going to be difficult before the FD gets here. It looks like the entire building has been caught up."

I was about to tell him too bad when a small explosion busted one of the front windows. "Help!" A warbled and weak, but clearly feminine cry came from the inside, striking my chest with fear.

"Holy shit!" Rooster, one of the prospects cried. "Someone's in there."

Not someone. One of the women. I jumped up and ran for the building.

"Axel. Wait. You can't go in there. It's too dangerous. Wait for the FD! I can hear the sirens."

I grunted in response as I skidded to a stop close to the open doorway. The flames were out of control and filling the entire space. He was right that I shouldn't go in, but that wasn't going to stop me. No way in hell could we wait and risk that one of our women wouldn't make it. Not when she was clearly still alive.

I was going to have to take a chance at the back door or one of the windows. I raced around to the other side of the building. It was dark now, and a little harder to see back here. I wasn't sure if I could tell whether the doors or windows were rigged. I decided to assume that the door would be, but that the windows were likely safe since we'd had no issue at the clubhouse.

I just needed something to break the glass...

Of course, where was an ax or a hammer when I needed one? I might not have had any tools nor could I see shit in the pitch dark back here, but I did know there were some cast iron tables and chairs out here. Many of the employees used this area for their breaks when they could manage to get away from the busy tables.

By sheer memory I ran in what I thought was the

right direction, practically stumbling into one of the chairs a second later.

Fuck.

I hefted that motherfucker over my head, and using the flames inside the building as my guide, I slammed it into one of the windows, hoping to God whoever was stuck inside wasn't too close and that it wasn't rigged with explosives. The glass shattered, some of it bouncing my way and slicing my skin. I ignored it and fished my arm inside to unlock the window and open it more fully so I could get in without slicing my arms and legs into ribbons.

I could hear the sirens wail as they closed in on the building, but I wasn't about to wait for them. I scrambled through the too small opening and cursed tiny fucking windows. There was no way I was going to get anyone out through this thing, which meant the front or back door were my only other choices.

I pulled my hoodie up over my nose and hoped to fuck it blocked enough of the smoke from my lungs to get this done. I was going to be pissed if I died of smoke inhalation.

"Hello!" I yelled as soon as I was inside. Flames were everywhere, licking up the walls and across the ceiling. Debris had already fallen all over the place, probably from the initial explosion. Which meant the structure was already compromised, and it wouldn't be long before the fire caused the rest of it to collapse.

I was halfway through the building when I saw a

body on the ground, flames licking at her legs. Fuck. Fuck. Fuck.

I looked around the burning room for anything I could use to douse them. When my gaze landed on the partially burned curtains still hanging on the wall, I sprinted to them, yanked them free, and ran back. I grabbed the ends not currently on fire and used them to douse the flames on her legs. It felt like it took forever, but they finally extinguished and I collapsed on my hands and knees, coughing.

My hoodie had dropped from my face, and I could feel the smoke already burning my lungs. It was difficult to take a breath. It was then I noticed the blonde curly hair and realized who I'd found.

Oh no. No. No. No.

My adrenalin spiked and I jumped to my feet. I rolled her over and scooped her into my arms. I wanted so badly to check for a pulse. If she wasn't breathing and didn't make it...

Forcing those thoughts from my head, I stood and tried to assess which way to go. Through the flames at the front door or the somewhat clear path to the back door that could be rigged with explosives. Either way, I was fucked. But if she died... I made the split-second decision to risk the flames. I was pretty sure I could still move fast and we stood a better chance of making it out that way.

"Axel!"

I heard my name but couldn't tell from which direction. I was out of time. I sprinted for the front door, dodging debris and straight through the heart of the fire because there was no clear path.

The heat instantly became unbearable and it felt like I slowed to a crawl. I didn't think we were going to make it. It felt like my entire body was on fire. But somehow, by some miracle I felt a pull at my arms and something heavy wrapped around me seconds before we crashed to the ground.

Suddenly I was surrounded by people and the woman was lifted from my arms. I tried to ask if she was alive, but I couldn't breathe let alone speak. My attempt only resulted in a series of coughs that I couldn't stop, until I started to puke.

"Jesus, man. Are you fucking crazy or do you have some kind of death wish?" I recognized the voice and the face looming above me as that of Mike Brown, one of the long-time volunteers for the Sultan Fire Department.

"Someone had to," I wheezed, finally getting some air in and out of my lungs. "Is she alive?"

"You could have gotten more people killed if you'd collapsed in there. My guys would have had to go in, and that building collapsed seconds after you emerged."

I was going to strangle Mike for his continued bitching. I reached out and grabbed his coat and yanked him down to my level. "I asked if she is alive, motherfucker." I imagined the look in my eyes was as wild as I felt, but I could tell by the look of fear in his, he'd gotten my message.

"Yeah, she's alive. Barely."

"Someone needs to get JD and tell him" Every word out of my mouth felt like glass shards scraping up my throat. Smoke and fire were evil little shits. "I couldn't have been in there for more than a minute or two."

"Eyewitness says you were in there for more like five to seven. You're damned lucky you are still conscious."

I rolled over on my back and stared up at the darkened sky. He had no idea the sheer will I used to get her out of there. Not only for JD's sake, but for Mandy's too. If I had died in there, she would have been really pissed at me. And I would have lost my second shot at the woman I loved.

I let that thought soak in for a moment before I immediately rejected it. Maybe it wasn't the smartest thing, going back in the past. But considering I'd lived more than a decade based on a lie, it deserved my time now.

I liked her a lot back then, and might have been in love, but what the hell did I know about love when I was eight-fucking-teen? I'd been an idiot just like everyone else at that age. One only had to look at Houston to see that. He'd run away, leaving me and the club behind without so much as a by your leave.

And I'd let that butt hurt feeling then control my reaction to what I'd thought was Mandy's betrayal. I scrubbed a hand across my face. She was right about one thing. It was time to stop re-living and re-visiting the past. It was bullshit, but it was over. We were different people, and if I couldn't see her for who she was now, then I was an asshole.

"Axel?"

I heard her frightened voice before I saw her. I tried to sit up to look for her, but Mike's hard grip held me down. "I don't think so, pal. Not until the paramedic is done with you." He no sooner got the word paramedic out than another familiar person filled my vision. This one a redhead I happened to know a little better than Mike.

"Hey, Axel. Long time no see." I might have winced, but I was still too focused on trying to see past this woman to the one I'd heard. When I said nothing, she continued. "I'm going to put this oxygen mask on you, and then I'm going to assess your condition, okay?"

"Mandy?" I tried to yell for her so she'd know I was here. There were a lot of people running around, and people talking everywhere. But my voice came out barely a whisper.

The woman looking down at me pursed her mouth, and I could read the disappointment. "Jeanne. My name is Jeanne."

I closed my eyes against the hurt in her voice. She'd mistaken my attempt to call for Mandy as me forgetting her name. "I didn't forget. But I can hear Mandy calling my name. I need to speak to her."

She smiled, which came out a little more like a smirk. "New girlfriend? I can't say I'm surprised," she said, placing the mask over my face. "Mandy, however, is going to have to wait. I need to make sure you're okay."

I brushed the mask off of my face. "I'll be fine," I said, lifting my head to look around the woman trying to help me.

"Oh my God. There you are." She closed the distance between us and dropped to the ground next to me. "I heard two people came out of the building on fire and I about lost my shit. I knew it was going to be you."

She was confused. "They were exaggerating. I wasn't on fire."

"I beg to differ," Jeanne the paramedic held up my arm where what looked to be burned remnants of my leather jacket fused to the red, raw flesh of my arm. She then placed the mask back over my mouth. "Now, let me do my job and get this bandaged up. It might be a while before we can get you to the hospital."

"I'm not going to the hospital," I said from beneath the mask. Words no one acknowledged.

Mandy ran her fingers through my hair and pressed a kiss to my forehead. "I'm just glad you're all right. He is all right, isn't he?" she asked, turning to Jeanne.

"Probably. He's too stubborn to be anything else." I wanted to shut my eyes against Jeanne's assessment, but I could see Mandy looking back and forth between us like she was trying to figure something out. Yes, I wanted to tell her. It's exactly what it sounds like. I slept with her, okay? I slept with them all. Every woman I could. I was literally the definition of a manwhore, and until now, kind of proud of it.

"Amanda? Amanda Turner is that you?"

My eyes flew open in time to see Mike the firefighter had returned. I groaned. How I'd forgotten we'd all been in school together and he and Amanda had been *friends,* I had no clue.

"Mike?" she asked, blinking up at him.

"Yeah. I can't believe it. I didn't know you were back. When? I mean how?" I rolled my eyes at his fumbling of words.

"It's a long story. But it's only temporary. I'm just visiting."

"Oh," he sounded crestfallen and I wanted to punch his pretty face. "We should get dinner and catch up sometime." When she didn't answer right away, he fumbled some more to cover the awkward silence. "Or just—uhm—coffee. Or Bubba's for drinks. You remember that place, right?"

She laughed. "That I do. And I'm not surprised at all it's still the go to."

I started to lift my mask and tell Mike to back the fuck off, but Jeanne gave me a sharp look and knocked my hand away.

"Uh—hey Mike," she started, a smirk crossing her face. "I think she's already taken."

I'm not going to lie, I think my chest puffed out despite the lack of oxygen in my lungs.

"What?" He sounded as confused as he looked. If I wasn't annoyed, I would have laughed. Mike was harmless. I doubted the nicest guy in town had a chance in hell with a woman like Mandy. She lived on the dark side now like me. Hell, maybe even darker than me. She'd never be happy as a soccer mom, chronicling her life on Instagram because she was bored to death.

Jeanne pointed at me and gave him a look that said, "duh", and a few long seconds later the dawning finally crossed his face.

"Oh."

"We could still catch up," she hesitated, looking as unsure as Mike now. "Sometime."

"Sure. Sure," he said. "Just let me know." When he suddenly turned and walked away without so much as exchanging a phone number, a strangled noise did rumble from my chest. It was meant to be a laugh, but I wasn't quite there yet.

"Don't look so happy," Mandy hissed at me. "We both know this thing between us is temporary."

It was Jeanne's turn to snort a laugh as she wrapped gauze around my arm. Suddenly, the fire in the casino was looking a hell of a lot better than this awkward situation.

"What the hell is going on? Where is she?"

My thoughts were interrupted by JD's arrival. Oh shit.

"Where is who?" Mandy asked.

I yanked my mask off before Jeanne could stop me. "Sasha. She's the one I rescued from the fire."

"Okay. Is she someone's old lady or daughter?"

I shook my head. "He won't admit it, but she's *his*."

And if she didn't make it, I feared what he'd become.

Chapter Twenty~Seven

JD

WHY EVERYONE WAS STANDING AROUND
HOLDING their dicks, when I'd asked a fucking question I didn't understand. Had they not heard me?

"You have two seconds to answer me before I freak
the fuck out," I warned. I'd gotten word she'd been
pulled from the burning building, and I was now operating on a pure adrenaline overload.

"Where is she?" I yelled again.

"If you're talking about the woman from the fire,
she's already been taken to the hospital. We were going
to wait for an airlift, but that was going to take too
long."

One of the paramedics was blabbering on and I just
wanted him to shut up.

"So she's alive?"

The man nodded. He didn't have to say it, but I could see it in his eyes. The word hung in the air without anyone saying it—*barely*.

"JD."

I turned to see Axel laid out on the ground, an oxygen mask in his hand and a female paramedic wrapping up his left forearm. His pants were burned to almost nothing, but the skin there didn't look bad. Mandy was sitting on the ground next to him, her hand gripping one of his, blood still caked in her hair and on her face.

This had turned into a shit show of epic proportions.

"Jesus Christ. What the hell happened?" Everything inside me was screaming to hop on my bike and race to the hospital, but I was responsible for all of these people. I had to get a status report and make sure I had a VP capable of taking charge before I ran off halfcocked.

I took a deep breath and locked down the riot of emotions running roughshod over my nerves. She was alive. I had to remember that and get my head back in the game. Although this was as far from a game as it could possibly be. I'd known how dangerous and deadly this case could be, but I'd never dreamed she'd get pulled in somehow.

Should have fucking fired her ass months ago.

Woulda. Coulda. Shoulda. I hated that fucking feeling.

Axel sat up, but when he tried to push to his feet,

both the paramedic and Mandy protested. "I don't think so. The two of you aren't going anywhere until I say so."

The female paramedic had nice big lady balls. Good for her. She would need them to take care of this crew. "Better listen to the woman," I said, smirking. "I'd hate to see what she'd do to you if you didn't."

Axel grumbled something, but it wasn't clear. I'm sure it was some complaint followed by a few fucks. I'd never met a man who loved that word more than him and that was saying something considering how much we all used it.

The paramedic turned to me then. "Your lady friend is in good hands. The best, actually. They will take her to St Francis, which has the number one burn unit in the country."

I nodded, despite the pit in my stomach growing larger. My lady friend. I wasn't going to touch that with a ten-foot pole. There was also the matter of what she hadn't said in those few words, and I was fully capable of reading through the lines.

"She was inside? Why? She wasn't supposed to be here today."

Axel shrugged. "I couldn't say. She was unconscious when I found her, so you'll have to ask her later. You see the prospect?"

I shook my head, the weight on my shoulders growing heavier. "Not yet. But I heard."

"What about Bear?" Axel asked, looking about as grim as I felt. "He going to pull through?"

"Cash thinks so. They just left for the hospital with Cash in the ambulance with him. No one is going anywhere alone. Got it?"

He nodded, but it was the curious look from the paramedic that caught my attention, reminding me that I needed to pay attention to what I said. The last thing any of us needed was more people getting involved in club business.

"Speaking of ambulances." The paramedic paused from the cleanup work she was doing on Mandy. "I think the two of you should go next and get checked out. Between his smoke inhalation and your possible concussion, you're going to need some attention."

"No!" Mandy reared back, pushing the woman's arm away. "No hospital."

"But—"

"It's okay," I said. "Our club doctor is already on his way. I think he can monitor everyone from here."

The paramedic glared at him, but smartly kept her mouth shut. I wasn't in the mood to argue with her, especially with the PD walking the grounds and asking everyone questions. We had bigger things to worry about than placating a nosy health care worker.

"Look, it's not as if we're not grateful for what you've done. We are. My guys are tough, though, and trying to stick them in a hospital if it's not absolutely necessary isn't going to go well. For anyone."

She still seemed skeptical, but she didn't look ready to fight him. In fact, she looked tired. "I don't think anyone can argue if you have your own private doctor.

As long as he or she is good at their job and not dicking you around. These injuries are no laughing matter."

Under different circumstances I would have laughed my ass off. She didn't mince words or bother with niceties. Efficient and blunt were my two favorite things.

"Don't worry. He's good. Just getting him here from Seattle takes time. We could always use another medical professional on call. You ever do any private work?" I didn't know why I was asking her now. My timing couldn't be worse and I needed to get to the hospital. But I couldn't have the talk I really wanted to have until she finished up.

"I haven't yet. But that doesn't mean I couldn't." She placed what looked like the last bandage on Mandy and started cleaning up the mess she'd made. Gathering her things and loading up the big canvas case she carried. "Sultan isn't exactly a hotbed of paramedic work." She glanced around at the scene. "At least not usually."

I snorted. "You must be new here."

"I am." Her answer was so short it seemed obvious she didn't want to elaborate. That was fine by him. Her personal life was none of his concern. Besides, as soon as Tel got hold of her information, they'd know more about her than her own parents.

"Leave your phone number with the prospect over there, and someone will get in contact with you. If we're a good fit, we'll let you know."

She nodded, giving one last look at both Mandy and Axel. "I recommend you put that oxygen mask back on and keep it on as long as possible. I think it's going to be a while still before we leave."

Axel nodded but made no move to put said mask over his face. Instead, he waited until she was out of earshot and hissed at me, "Why in the hell are we recruiting in the middle of a crisis? Shouldn't you be on your way to the hospital?"

His words bit into my stoic resolve. Sasha wasn't my old lady, and running off to find her now only made me look weak, even if that was exactly what I wanted to do. "Based on what happened tonight, I am of the opinion that recruiting another medical professional to the cause is a smart idea. Especially a local one. Where would we be right now if it was Cash who'd walked into that explosive instead of Bear?"

"Don't give me that bullshit. What are the odds of this kind of thing happening again?"

"Probably not high, but not out of the realm as long as that bastard is still hunting. And my being at the hospital sitting in a waiting room isn't going to change her outcome. I have a hundred other people counting on me to fix this shit, and fix it now."

"We can help," Mandy offered. "This is all my fault. The least I can do is help fix things."

I shook my head. "The only one to blame is the fucker who came on our property and set the explosives." I turned back to Axel. "Finding out how that happened is our top priority. I believe in Tel's thoroughness when it comes to security, and I know damned well this couldn't have just happened."

"What are you saying? You think we have a traitor?"

The idea made my stomach boil with acid. It had been a while since this much anger had threatened to devour me. Memories and sadness yes. But this—this was an entirely different thing. I wanted the man responsible on his fucking knees in front of me.

"It sounds crazy. The loyalty of the brotherhood is everything. But this stinks and stinks bad. And I'm not going to ignore the possibility just because I don't want it to be true."

"That's fair," Axel said, my anger projecting right back at me in his eyes. "But a traitor?" He scrubbed his hands over his face. "I don't even know where to begin."

"I do," Mandy said quietly.

I looked down at her, assessing. I'd known in advance she could be more trouble than she was worth. And yet, my gut had told me this was what Axel needed. That making him see the truth and getting beyond the past would make the club stronger. I was going to be pissed if they proved me wrong.

In the meantime, she was still in danger and we had a killer to catch.

"I guess you would," I finally responded. My words hit her hard, as I'd known they would, but both me *and* Axel needed to remember to keep our guards up. She had secrets. And until this matter was settled, and Axel made his choice, he would use her for what he could while keeping her mostly at arm's length. "What do you need from me?"

It was obvious Axel wanted to say something based

on the glare I received. But he had his face in the mask again thanks to Mandy, which was for the best.

"Tel and I could work on it together. He's good at digging up information and I'm good at putting it together."

I clamped my lips to keep my smirk at bay. She had confidence, I'd give her that. Apparently, you could kick her, but that wouldn't keep her down. She was all about the job. The trick would be keeping all of that focused in the right direction.

"Excuse me, Mr. Monroe. We've got a few questions we need you to answer."

I gave Axel one last look and turned to the police officer standing behind me. I had no intention of telling him shit, but I would make it look like I did. Cooperation always looked good and kept certain people off the club's back when it really came in handy.

"Oka—"

"Hey! Over here!" someone yelled from the interior of the casino. "We've got another body!"

Chapter Twenty-Eight

Mandy

BY THE TIME we made it back to Axel's cabin, we were both dead on our feet. My head throbbed, and he looked ashen.

"Are you sure you don't need to go to the hospital? You don't look well at all."

He shot me one of those "whatever" looks he favored so much and continued inside. "I'll be fine. Thanks to you, I kept that damn mask on for hours. I'm so oxygenated now, I'm going to be farting goddamned fairy dust for a week."

I tried not to laugh. I really did. Despite the joke, he looked annoyed as hell. But the image he'd just painted in my mind couldn't be contained. I didn't know what fairy dust looked like so my mind conjured a giant cartoon troll farting glitter instead.

Laughter bubbled at first, which I kept mostly contained, but the more I thought about glitter coming out of his ass, the more my control slipped until I dropped down on the sofa holding my stomach with tears coming out of my eyes.

"So happy to see you find that so funny."

"Can you blame me? If you're going to put an image like that in my head, there's gonna be laughter."

For a split second, I thought he was going to laugh too. His lips definitely twitched. But it disappeared almost as quickly as it appeared.

"Are you sure *you* don't need the doctor again?"

That question sobered me up. After meeting their on-call doctor, I immediately understood why JD had been recruiting that paramedic during the fire. That man had been a douche with a capital D. "I don't want him touching me again."

Axel looked at me with alarm. "What the fuck does that mean? Did I miss something inappropriate? I'm going to kill that fucker."

I shook my head. "No. No. Nothing like that. Keep your shorts on. Just call it intuition or whatever, but that guy gave me the creeps. I don't think he's a good guy."

"He's a doctor making under the table house calls for an outlaw motorcycle club. He's not."

"Then why use him?"

"I refer you to my previous statement. But if that's not enough, look around, sweetheart. We live out in the sticks where our choices are limited. They don't grow doctors on trees out here. Sometimes we have to go with what we can get. Although I get it. If he wasn't damned good at his job, and even better at keeping secrets, we would have given him the boot a long time ago. He rubs everyone wrong."

"Do you think that's why JD was so interested in that woman earlier?" I started to brush my fingers through my hair and hit a tender spot. I winced, immediately stopping.

"Maybe." He dropped down next to me and pulled me onto his lap. "I don't really care right now. I'm exhausted." He kissed the side of my head not far from where I'd just touched it. "How's the head?"

"It's okay." I was tired too, but I was also wired from all the craziness that had gone down. While the exhilaration from the race was long gone, it had been closely followed by a serious of chaotic events that my mind couldn't stop thinking about. I wanted to put all of them together into a neat little puzzle, so I could file them away where they belonged, but there were too many holes in my information.

"Okay is too vague," he said.

"You should get some sleep," I urged, ignoring his complaint. "I don't need a babysitter."

"That's not what the doc said. He wants me to wake you up every hour through the night to make sure you are okay." He brushed a finger across my cheek in a gesture so tender it made my chest ache. I still wasn't used to attention like this, and I didn't know how to respond. Especially when I liked it a lot more than I should.

"He's just being cautious. I feel fine."

He bent down and pressed his lips against mine. "You do feel fine. Better than fine actually. But I'm still going to wake you every single hour."

I groaned. That did not sound like fun. Especially not for him. "I'll sleep out here and set alarms on my phone. There's no need for you to deal with it. You need a good night's sleep. I can take care of myself."

He rolled us around until suddenly my back was pressed against the cushions and he was on top of me, pressed between my legs. "That's not the point," he said, licking and biting at my neck until I started to squirm. "Sure, you could take care of yourself, but that's not what's going to happen. We're going to take care of each other."

My resolve melted under his clever logic and the sweet seduction of his tongue. All my good intentions of things going back to normal between us disappeared before my eyes. He was pressed between my legs, in just the right spot...

"I'm not sure that's what the paramedic *or* the doctor had in mind when he suggested you could watch over me."

"I disagree," he said as he pushed his body harder against mine. Not just his body. Let's be real, it was his dick he was using against me and I wasn't sure I had a defense for that. Not with the memory of him inside me this morning still fresh in my mind. Although admittedly it seemed like days not hours since I'd been in this position.

Maybe just one more time.

When I left town, I would need all the memories I could get for the long road ahead of me.

"Stop thinking about whatever it is you've got going on in that head. Focus on me. Us. This."

"I am," I cried out as he bumped against my clit with perfect precision. "But we shouldn't be doing this."

"Why the hell not?" He pulled back, but only enough to reach between us and flick the button on my jeans open.

I tried to formulate a good response for that, but he already had my zipper down and his warm fingers were sliding under the edge of my panties. No one on planet Earth could be expected to resist someone like him. It had to be physically impossible. And he was about half a second away from discovering just how affected by him I was.

He inched lower, sliding his long fingers along the seam of my pussy.

"Fuck," he hissed. "You're already so wet. You want this as bad as I do." He took that moisture and rubbed it around my entrance, teasing me mercilessly.

He wasn't lying. Wrong or right, I couldn't deny what he did to me. "That doesn't mean we should be doing this." I grabbed his shoulders and pushed my hips into his hand, practically forcing his finger inside.

"Mandy," he growled as he tunneled as deep as his hand would allow.

I arched my back and held my breath. I could already feel an orgasm building. How he could do that to me so quickly still astounded me. After everything I'd endured, it was a miracle. I'd honestly believed that I would never feel this way again. And yet...I wanted more. So much more.

"You're going to make me come," the words were out before I could stop them.

"Of course I am. And when that one's done, we're going to do it again." He bit gently at my neck. "And again." He dipped lower and bit my breast through my shirt, but still sending a thrill straight through me. "And again."

"Axel." It was the only word I could get out as the pressure in my core wound tighter. He sensed my need as sure as I took another breath, and added a little more pressure on my clit with a flick of his thumb. That was all it took for the world around me to explode.

Everything fell away as splinters of sensation locked my body in a moment of perfect time. I couldn't move, couldn't speak, hell, I couldn't even take a breath. I was suspended in that moment of pure bliss with my nails clenched into his shoulders and the muscles of my core beating my body with pure pleasure.

"Fuck yeah, that's beautiful," he whispered in my ear before moving to capture my mouth. His tongue swept across mine, adding yet another layer of pure beauty to the perfect storm he'd created.

When everything finally broke, I wrenched free from his mouth and let loose with a scream. I was coming so hard I thought everything might break. I didn't even realize he'd moved, or slid my pants down until he thrust inside me.

"Goddamn that's tight as fuck," he groaned, seating himself to the hilt only a second before pulling back out. Over and over he repeated that, until I was mindless and writhing underneath him. He was right it was going to happen again.

"Do it," he commanded on another growl. "Don't try to hold it back. I want your pussy coming on my dick this time."

He grabbed my hair and forced my eyes to meet his. His pupils were so large, making his eyes look black. As if he was the devil himself.

"Come," he ordered. "Now."

I had no defense in the face of such ferocious need. But I also didn't need it. If he was the devil, then I would gladly take a trip to hell with him.

I stopped fighting myself and gave all the control to him. My body shook wildly as that buildup of my core intensified and then exploded. Bigger, stronger, uncontrollable. I held on as tight as I could and rode the sweet, intense, and mind-blowing ride.

"Fuck yes! Goddamn it, Mandy, I fucking love this. Need this!" His words were rough and punctuated by the short jerky movements of his hips as he pounded into me. "I'm never giving this up," he cried out. "Never!" At that, he buried himself one last time and his cock pulsed inside me, bathing me with his release.

I was still in the throes of aftershocks as my mind

tried to comprehend exactly what he'd said, or more importantly what it had meant. Admittedly, now was not the time for me to analyze him or this situation. My brain was on a euphoric high and I wanted to enjoy it for as long as possible.

"Jesus Christ," he gasped. "That was fucking amazing." I would have reveled in those words for days if I could have. His praise meant the world to me.

Unfortunately, he was breathing hard and the sound of his wheezing as he attempted to get air into his lungs alarmed me. "Shit. I knew we shouldn't have done that." I pushed at his chest hard, but he didn't budge. Lying on top of me he was like dead freaking weight.

"Relax. I just need to catch my breath."

I swatted at his arm. "You do NOT get to tell me to relax. Not after you charged into a burning building and nearly got yourself killed." My voice rose a lot higher than I'd meant it to. But I think some of the fear from earlier was leaking through the walls that were crumbling thanks to him. "Let me up! I need to check your oxygen levels." I'd just gone past fear and straight into panic without passing go or collecting my two hundred dollars.

"Mandy." He raised up on his hands and released some of his weight that pressed down on me. "I'm going to be okay. I swear it. I promise you if I'm having any real trouble, I will let you know."

"Then let me up so I can check. I just need that peace of mind."

I could tell he didn't want to move, and I kind of

didn't blame him. Having him inside me again was pretty much the greatest feeling. But the fact it probably came with strings scared the hell out of me, and I needed a little more space to breathe. I'm sure all of that was written on my face and it was pretty much confirmed when his eyes shuttered and he pulled from my body, releasing his weight and a rush of warm liquid on my thighs.

It was then I realized he didn't have a condom on...again.

Son of a bitch.

Chapter Twenty-Nine

Axel

I WAS ON A SERIOUS, fucked-up roll.

I ripped my shirt over my head and quickly used it to clean up as much as I could. It wasn't enough. "Hang on."

At the look of pure horror etched on her face, I quickly disappeared into my bedroom and the adjoining bathroom to grab a towel. I'd made a mess of things and I wasn't referring to the wet spot on my couch. Furniture could be cleaned easy enough. My fucking Mandy without a condom not so much.

I wet the towel with some warm water and avoided looking at myself in the mirror. I knew better than this. But what really seemed wrong was the fact that in a way it didn't bother me at all. If she got pregnant with my kid, I would not be sad. I'd be thrilled.

It was kind of weird to admit that, since my entire adult life had been spent avoiding any kind of attachment at all. I'd made sure that every woman I was with understood that their place in my life was only temporary and if they couldn't deal with that, I scraped them off.

When Mandy had gotten pregnant all those years ago, I had not been ready. My only experience with family up to that point had been a father who liked to beat the shit out of me, and a mother who turned a blind eye. However, my years with the club had taught me different things, including the importance of family, even if it wasn't from blood.

I returned to the living room. Mandy had pulled up her pants and curled onto her side.

"I was coming right back to finish." I held up the towel.

"I figured since we'd already made the mess, it wasn't going to make much difference at this point. I'll just take a shower."

She started to get up and I stopped her. "We should talk."

"No, we really shouldn't. It's been a crazy long day, and I'm exhausted. I think we both need some sleep before we can begin to put any of today's events into perspective."

She was right. We'd been going non-stop for almost

twenty-four hours. Stressing her out more wasn't going to help anything.

"You hungry?"

She shook her head. "Huh-uh. You?"

"I can always eat, but I'm more tired than hungry, so it can wait. Honestly, I'm liable to end up face first in the food."

She gave me a tight smile. Not what I'd been hoping for, but I'd take it—for now.

I grabbed her hand and pulled her up from the couch and into my arms. If nothing else, I needed a kiss. To my surprise, she gave it willingly and kissed me back. It was just the balm I needed for everything we'd been through today.

We proceeded to take turns showering, and by the time I was done, she was already curled on her side of the bed in those damned short shorts and one of my t-shirts. I ignored the twitch of my cock and climbed in beside her.

"I hope you don't mind I decided to sleep in here with you. I just—" she hesitated and I could see the concern in her eyes. "I just want to hear you breathing every time I wake up."

My chest clenched. That was better than any confession of love I could have wrangled out of her. Not that I'd intended to do that.

"You got your alarms set?"

She nodded and I pulled her all the way against me and placed her hand on my chest. "Go to sleep, baby. I'll be right here with you. I promise."

For once in her life, she didn't argue or try to challenge me. She closed her eyes, and within minutes, her breathing evened out and the worry lines on her forehead finally relaxed. Yep, having her here, pressed against me, was the best damned feeling in the world. Finally, she was home.

———

"How is it?" she asked, hovering over the island waiting for my critique.

"Honey, you could have fed me day old cookies for breakfast and I would have been fine. You didn't have to go to this much trouble."

"It's an omelet, Axel, not coq au vin. It wasn't any trouble. And it's not breakfast. We slept through both breakfast and lunch. At best, it's a late dinner."

He glanced down at his cellphone to see it was after 8pm. It was true, they had lost a lot of time. "We obviously needed it. How do you feel?"

"I feel great. Once we got past all those hours of waking me up every five minutes, I slept like a rock."

"Same. My arm's a little sore and my chest feels a little tight, but other than that I feel as good as ever."

She smirked at him. "Actually, that sounds like a lot. Maybe we should take one more night and see how we feel."

I shook my head. "We can't. Text from JD says we're moving out and headed to Seattle tonight. We've got a meeting."

"Is this about that other body that was found in the building."

I hated to admit it, but I wasn't sure. Sleeping through a night and day had lost me a lot of valuable time to follow up.

"I don't know. Probably. As soon as we're done here, I need to get to the clubhouse and get an update."

"I'm going with you." She grabbed her empty plate and carried it over to the sink. I wanted to argue with her, throw the club business card at her, and make sure she never got near anyone dangerous again. But she'd earned the right to be at my side when we went after the Mazzeo fucker. Not to mention, after the escalation to explosive devices, I didn't want her out of my sight.

I finished off my omelet and was about to grab my shit and head to the clubhouse when someone pounded on my door. *Again*.

"This sure is a busy place. Is it always like this?"

"I don't know when the hell this place became Grand fucking Central, but I'm sick of it. Has everyone lost their mind and forgotten how to use this thing?" I held up my phone and waved it in front of my face. "If someone wants to talk to me, they should fucking text me."

I hopped off the barstool and crossed to the door with a snarl and a *fuck you* ready to go for the asshole still pounding on the thick wood.

"What the hell is your problem? You never heard of a—" I wrenched open the door, and everything else I'd been about to spew died on my lips.

"Hey."

"Well, holy shit. Look what the cat dragged in."

"You can't possibly be surprised to see us. You didn't really thing the probability of a Frank clone on the loose wouldn't bring me and Izzy running."

That made total sense, and he was right. I should have seen this coming. I stood back and directed both Houston and his now fiancée Izzy to enter. "To be honest, I hadn't really thought about it. We've been a little busy what with all the death and dismemberment going on."

Izzy winced, and I half regretted my words. It wasn't her fault she had a psychotic brother. She hadn't even known he existed. I just didn't think adding more people to the current mix seemed wise.

"Thanks, fucker." Houston growled.

I shrugged. "Last I checked, it's not my job to baby you." Yes, I was acting like an ass and no, I didn't care.

Since I could practically feel Mandy's disapproval at my back, I turned to her. "You remember Mandy, right?"

Houston stared blankly at her, while Izzy's eyes softened measurably. That was weird.

"Wait." Houston squinted his eyes and scrunched his face. "You don't mean Mandy. That's Kelly."

"Kelly is my middle name, and the one I chose to use professionally, but you might also remember me as Mandy Turner."

Houston's eyes went wide as I hung back and watched all of this go down. Izzy still hadn't said anything and that seemed odd. Houston now looked like he was going to have a heart attack. I guess memory lane would do that to you, if you didn't want to remember certain memories.

Like when you and your best friend fucked the hell out of your girlfriend—together — and what was an awesome night of fun turned into your worst nightmare when your best friend went home to his father killing his mother.

Well, that got dark fast. At least I'd had the foresight not to say any of that out loud.

"No fucking way." Houston moved further into the living room in her direction. "Of course, now that you say that, I don't understand how I didn't see it."

"Someone care to explain it to me? What's happening?" Izzy asked.

"Sure, babe. Agent Kelly Turner aka Amanda Turner is Axel's high school girlfriend."

Well, that was one way he could put it, I guess. He didn't know the rest. He hadn't stuck around long enough to find out that she'd also gotten pregnant and had nearly become my baby momma. And that I'd spent the next ten plus years fucking my way through the female population in an attempt to forget her.

"Ohhh. Really? What a small world." True story that. Tiny. Miniscule. "Although it makes plenty of sense when you think about how you were also the woman the club had been looking for. You're from here." Izzy approached Mandy with her hand outstretched and shook it. "I do remember you in Vegas. It's nice to officially meet you?"

That had come out more like a question than a statement. I understood their hesitation. Mandy's involvement with Frank had nearly gotten Izzy killed and she and Houston weren't likely going to let that go.

Even I was still struggling with it. It just didn't fit with the girl I knew from the past and the woman I'd been getting to know again. She didn't want to talk about what went down with her and Frank and that still bugged me.

It didn't seem quite right that I could be falling for her all over again without knowing more. Did that make me blind? Was our old history together a greater influence than the recent past? There were too many thoughts and questions swirling in my head to deal with this right now.

"Things didn't quite turn out like I'd expected in Vegas," Mandy said quietly. "I was relieved to hear that you recovered quickly."

"Thank you."

"Why are you here? This is the last place *she* should be." I pointed to Izzy, who shot me a dirty look.

"*She* doesn't care what you think. If I have a brother out there and he's going around killing people, I can't stay out of it." Izzy had her hands on her hips and I knew from experience that did not bode well for any of us.

"It's too fucking dangerous," I growled.

"I tried to tell her. In a variety of ways. In the end though, I opted to take control and let this happen.

Otherwise, I was going to wake up to find her gone rogue. This way I control her security."

She rolled her eyes and I had to choke back my laughter. The memory of Izzy shoving a gun in my face popped into my mind. That felt like ages ago now. It wasn't that long ago, actually, but a lot had happened since then.

"JD isn't going to like this."

"You are not wrong about that. He's pissed enough right now to breathe fire. Why the hell do you think we came here?"

I laughed, feeling some of the tightness in my chest their appearance caused loosen. It was nice to see me and the Prez could still see eye-to-eye on some things.

"Have you spoken to him yet? Is he back from the hospital?"

"Yes, he is."

We all turned to the rough voice in the doorway.

"JD." I nodded, deciding that it was getting entirely too crowded in my small cabin. "What's the word?" I was hesitant to ask because if she didn't make it, it was going to be a huge problem. But I preferred to bite the elephant instead of letting it sit in the room and cause problems.

"She's still in ICU in an induced coma. She's suffered third degree burns over a good portion of her body. But we've reached the point where the doctors are hopeful about her recovery. It's just going to be a long road for her."

"Thank God," Izzy said before rushing over to JD to

envelop him in a hug. I wasn't sure he would accept it, but after a few tense seconds in which he stiffened, he wrapped his arms around her and buried his face in her shoulder.

Houston and I exchanged glances and then I looked over at Mandy. Her eyes were wet with unshed tears, and I could only guess that she was thinking about what could have been if I hadn't made it out of that building when I did. I immediately crossed to her and pulled her into my arms. I could feel Houston's gaze drilling into my back, and I knew there would be questions I would have to answer later, but that was his problem not mine.

We all had the autonomy to make our own decisions and this one was mine, whether they liked it or not.

"What about the other one?" I asked. "Do we have an identification yet?

He nodded. I had a feeling his rage was currently on a tight leash, and it wouldn't hold for long. "Apparently, the governor sent his aide ahead of his planned visit last night. It's why she was there when no one should have been."

"Holy fuck."

"The governor?" Mandy asked. "As in the governor, governor?"

"You sound surprised," I said. "I thought the Feds were well aware what went on out here. At least that's what you implied." All heads turned to Mandy and I immediately regretted my words.

"What the hell does that mean?" JD asked.

Good question. And one I wanted to hear again because maybe Maddy hadn't been as forthcoming as she should have been.

"It's not as dire as it sounds," she started. "At least not anymore. There was a task force assigned to the club for a while and they'd been gathering intel. Although, nothing concrete had come to light about any illegal activities. There were a bunch of guesses and hunches, but no one had proven a thing. Until the higher powers suddenly shut it down. That investigative task force is no more."

"And you were a part of it?" JD asked.

She hesitated and that was all the answer he needed before he turned to me. "Did you know about this bullshit?"

"Yes. But if no one is actively investigating there isn't anything to worry about."

"Boy," he seethed, his fists clenching at his side. "That's a decision for me to make, not you." I didn't flinch or move in any way, but I still expecting I was about to get clocked.

"What about the Mazzeo heir? Do you think he's responsible for all of this?" Houston asked, stepping between me and JD and distracting him from whatever he'd been about to do.

"I know he is." He reached into his pocket and pulled out a piece of paper. "This was delivered a few minutes ago. Same courier as before."

I took the note and opened it, my whole body going rock hard with rage in an instant. Motherfucker.

"What does it say? Maddy tried to look over my shoulder.

"It says, 'I'm coming for her next. There's nowhere else to hide.'"

Izzy sucked in a breath.

Houston clutched her hand and squeezed it.

Maddy had gone silent and I searched her face for some sign of what was going through her head. There was none. She'd closed down in a blink. So, I turned to JD.

"What are we going to do about this?" If he said *nothing*, I was going to go berserk and punch something. But once again my president did not let me down.

"We're going hunting. Right now."

Chapter Thirty

Amanda

THERE WAS nothing like an imminent death threat to spur action. Within the hour almost the entire club along with Houston and Izzy were loaded into various vehicles and motorcycles and headed to Seattle.

They all had blood on their mind and the intent to kill. I wasn't sure who had it worse. JD or Axel. They were both blindly moving on a mission with woefully small intel to go on.

Tel and I had put our heads together in the backseat of Axel's truck, and along with information given to us from Izzy we were able to triangulate some possibilities. Her father owned several properties in the greater Seattle area, but only a couple were likely to be the kind of places that her brother might hide.

In the meantime, the governor had gone on his own rampage and he had the SBI raiding every single facility ever associated with Frank Mazzeo. They'd looked the other way for too long, but that didn't mean they didn't know where to look. They absolutely did. So far they'd hit a dozen and whatever was left of the Mazzeo operation was being rounded up and dragged into holding.

"They just hit another one," Tel announced, turning his computer around so the others could see the action the security cameras were capturing in real time.

"Wow. How many does that make now?" Izzy asked.

"Thirteen," I answered.

"I imagine whatever group of criminals make up the new corporation, they have got to be doing some mad scrambling about now."

"That's assuming they didn't know in advance what the Mazzeo kid was up to," Tel said.

"You think they were?" Axel asked.

"Unlikely," I answered. "Men in their position don't generally like to antagonize law enforcement unless they have to. They prefer to keep their business private and out of the limelight. Retaliation against other criminals is one thing, but retaliation against the federal government? That's a reach." I studied the man currently on camera for a moment and smiled, recognizing one of the agents I'd worked closely with before. "They had to know coming directly after the MC casino would cause problems with more than the MC. Provided they knew the clientele you had coming in an out of there of course." Axel stared at me in the rear-view mirror but didn't say anything in response. He didn't have to. That was answer enough. "So, if they'd known, they probably would have taken care of the issue in-house."

Izzy swiveled in her seat and met my gaze. "What does that mean?"

"I think you know."

"Fuck." Axel cursed. "You think they will kill Mazzeo themselves?"

I shrugged. "They aren't going to take all this raiding lying down. They are currently losing loads of money by the minute every time one more business goes down. Even if it's just a setback, they could potentially lose millions. Do you know anyone who just sits back and willingly loses millions?"

"You need to drive faster," Tel said to Axel. "They just hit another. That makes fourteen."

He did as directed, but now that they were in Seattle, traffic was thick and there was only so fast he could go. But they weren't but a few miles from the first waterfront penthouse they wanted to check. Soon they would be within range to hack the building cameras and hoped to gain an extra advantage that way.

"Wait. Hold on," Izzy screeched, pointing in front of her. "JD is pulling over."

I looked through the windshield to indeed see that the line of motorcycles in front of them were all moving onto the shoulder of the road. "What's going on?"

"No idea, but I guess we're about to find out." Axel

swerved across three lanes of traffic and fell back into line behind the rest of the club. "I don't like this. We're sitting ducks out here."

"Agreed," I added, unease working up and down my spine.

"Everyone stay here. I'll see what's going on. Izzy you get behind the wheel just in case. If I signal, I want you to leave. Don't freak out. Don't ask questions. Just drive and get somewhere safe, got it?"

She nodded. "Okay," she said, sliding over to the driver's seat.

Axel shot me one more glance and then he shut the door and walked in the direction of the rest of his club. I didn't like this one bit. If they were trying to pull something and leave us behind...

We all watched out the window as Axel approached JD. It started off innocent enough, but thirty seconds into whatever they were talking about, Axel was gesturing wildly in obvious anger.

"Oh boy, that doesn't look good," Izzy whispered even though we could all hear her in the silent truck.

Tel returned his focus to his computer. "That's par for the course for those two. If they weren't arguing about something I'd be worried."

"That doesn't seem healthy," I mused. "And it sounds exhausting."

"That's one way of looking at it," Tel said, not looking up from whatever he was doing. "But part of Axel's job is to be the devil's advocate. He's supposed to challenge the president. It ensures the best decisions for the club get made."

Surprisingly that made a lot of sense. But the anger vibe I was getting from this distance didn't look like a simple challenge. Axel looked ready to kill.

Izzy turned to me. "I don't know how to say this," she started.

My guard went up as the pained expression on her face led me to believe I wasn't going to like whatever she was about to say. "Just say it. I deserve whatever it is. I hate that my actions put you in danger."

"It's not your fault." I wasn't sure how she could say that, but I decided to keep my mouth shut and let her continue. "I saw you once before Vegas," she whispered, "in my father's office. I didn't put it together right away…it's just—" my blood froze and I started shaking my head. Whatever she was about to say I didn't want to hear it. I didn't want her to be sorry for me—or anything else. She reached forward and squeezed my hand. "What he did to you—what he threatened you with… If I had a little sister to protect, I would have made the same choice. You did what you had to. That's all that matters. I would never hold that against you."

While I could feel the pin prick of tears at the backs of my eyes, I knew from experience that they wouldn't fall. But the pitching of my stomach, that was a different story. I remembered the night she'd witnessed. I'd caught a glance of her horror a moment before she'd fled, followed by a tiny sense of relief that she'd not been caught.

Frank and Marco had been especially creative with their torture that night…but it was the threat against Natalie that had finally broken me. My sister was only sixteen. I couldn't let them get to her.

"I'm glad you understand I had no other choice, but I would have understood if you couldn't accept it."

A slight smile pulled at Izzy's lips as she reached out and gave my hand a quick squeeze. "Bygones," she simply added, and I nodded, grateful that I didn't have to say anymore.

I closed my eyes for a moment and shook the memories from my head before doubling down on my focus for the mission at hand. I returned my attention back to the two men arguing outside, needing something else to occupy my mind.

"What's going on with the Feds?" I asked Tel, while keeping my eyes still on Axel the whole time.

"I think they're going to go for number fifteen. As far as I can tell the governor and the SBI director are not slowing down. They seem hell bent on showing these assholes that they live and work in their city at their leisure, not the other way around."

"At this point there could be some retaliation. The mafia isn't going to just roll over and close their doors."

He nodded. "This could be headed for a bloody standoff. But I'll keep—"

Tel didn't get to finish because Axel returned to the

truck and slammed the door closed a lot harder than necessary. "Mother fucker!"

"What happened?" I had to ask. I couldn't wait for him to calm down. I was too anxious to know what they were planning to do.

"The Corporation wants a meet. They say they're willing to negotiate."

I reared back in surprise. That was the last thing I expected in these circumstances. "Mazzeo?" I asked.

He shook his head. "No. That's the fucking rub. They claim he's acting on his own and they have nothing to do with his actions."

"That's bullshit," Tell swore from the backseat.

"That's exactly what I said. And while JD doesn't disagree, he thinks we need to take the meet."

"Where? When?"

"Now. They don't want to wait."

"They're desperate." I'd stated the obvious, but desperation did not make good bedfellows. They were liable to make a move against the club if they didn't tread carefully. "They may blame the club for all of this."

"I thought that too, and I said as much. We're still going to meet with them at the Punishers clubhouse in Seattle."

More alarm bells clanged in my head. "That's not neutral territory. That's a suicide mission."

"I know and since I don't have time to take you back to the clubhouse, we need to figure out somewhere safe for you to go. The governor offered one of their safehouses."

"Oh hell no! Nope. That is not happening. I'm going to that meeting."

"Me too," Izzy said, holding up her hand the moment she saw Axel about to object. "Don't even waste your breath. We all go or no one goes."

"Izzy, this is club business. You know the deal."

She shrugged. "Go ahead and pull that card. The second you drop us off *somewhere safe,*"—she used air quotes to emphasize those two words—"we'll be out the door on our own mission."

I nodded. "She's right. If the club wants to go play footsies with the mafia without us, then we're going after Mazzeo without you. We already have the information that I need."

The truck got silent when I finally shut my mouth. I watched the muscle in Axel's jaw twitch repeatedly as he clenched the steering wheel so tight, I thought he might break something.

The seconds ticked by as the tension in the cab of the truck grew thicker. I understood his anger *and* his fear, I had the same feelings for him over the idea of him walking into that other club's house no matter how much back up he took with him. They'd given us no time to prepare, and without a plan our odds were not great.

Finally, Axel turned to face both Izzy and me. "I swear to fucking Christ. If either of you ends up kidnapped or worse there is going to be hell to pay. And I don't just mean on their side. My punishment will be swift and extremely painful on all sides of the fucking table, is that clear?"

It took the will of everything I had in me, not to tell him where he could stick his punishment. If it wasn't for the very real fear I read in his eyes, I would have flayed him alive with my anger alone. I didn't know how we were going to get past it, but if he continued to pull that club business line on me I was going to go insane.

I simply nodded, because if I opened my mouth right now, it was a guarantee that he wouldn't like what I had to say. And for the sake of this mission, and its mile wide flaws, we all were going to need level heads before we got there.

He reached under his seat and pulled out a thick black vest, handing it over to me. "Put that on." He then turned to Izzy. "There's one for you under your seat as well. "Put it on and for the love of all that is holy please keep your mouth shut."

I saw the same fire in Izzy's eyes that I felt in my belly. She wasn't the kind of woman who wanted to sit on the sidelines either. But she wasn't stupid. We both knew this was not the hill we wanted to die on.

A moment later, Houston climbed back into the truck, eyed the bulletproof vest his fiancé had on and shook his head. "I told you." That's all he said before Axel pulled the truck back on the road and got back in line with the rest of the MC.

We were all probably headed for certain death, but there was a bit of poetic irony for me, in that we were all going to do it together. I might have had to fight for my position in this truck, but they'd actually cared enough to listen. Not happily of course, but it was a hell of a lot more than I expected.

They were a great team, but it seemed more than that to me now. They were more like a family...

My chest constricted at that thought. My family had abandoned me the moment trouble came knocking. I'd insisted on leaving and drawing the danger away from them because it was the right thing to do. This wasn't their fight. But they'd also let me go without a word.

Axel wanted to stand by my side, and he didn't even realize why it was so important.

Chapter Thirty-One

Axel

AS WE WERE USHERED into the clubhouse, my stomach tightened in an impossible knot. I understood Maddy's objections more than she knew. This whole situation stunk, and I couldn't think of a single reason to go through with it other than it might be the only way we get to the Mazzeo freak.

Since the governor had gone off half-cocked without talking strategy with anyone beforehand, and practically started a war with this mysterious corporation, I had a feeling the entire Seattle criminal underworld was about to explode. We were all on thin ice walking in here.

Of course, we had the building surrounded, but so did they. Tel had hacked into their security the minute we were close enough to pick up the signal. It had taken him about ten minutes, which was about nine minutes more than usual. So these jokers, whoever the hell they were, had bank *and* smarts. Dealing with them directly would not be a walk in the park.

The building they used for their headquarters was old and looked like shit from the outside, with a crumbling brick facade and windows covered in what looked like years of dirt and grime, not to mention wrought iron bars in place on every single one. I mentally knocked those off as possible entry points. However, this part of Seattle was built on top of itself and there were networks of old tunnels running beneath everything. I'd bet everything I had that they had access to those and used them often.

I thought about texting Tel with that information, but didn't bother. He'd been looking up everything about the location when I'd left them. There was no doubt he already knew.

The inside, however, I'd keep track of that and he could record it as we went. My first impression was that it was nothing like the outside. Either the MC or someone else had dropped some cake getting the place newly remodeled. Everything looked state of the art, including the cameras in the corners.

"Nice place," I said, making sure I looked over everything as we were led through to the meet. One of the MC members, the sergeant at arms according to his vest, gave me a sharp look but no one said a word. They just kept moving and we followed.

"I see them," Tel said in my ear. He'd outfitted a club pin with a tiny camera that I wore on my vest and assured me that no one would ever guess what it actually was. But it allowed him to see everything I did and hear whatever he might need to. He'd be digging up answers as any questions, spoken or unspoken, popped up.

"Jesus Christ, these assholes have expensive taste. Clearly, working for the mafia is paying them well. You might be walking into more trouble than we'd planned on. Keep your guard up."

I ignored his stream of conscious thoughts for now and moved closer to JD's side. I didn't need the warning. The hairs were already standing up at the back of my neck. Thank God Mandy and Izzy had agreed to stay outside. It would have been way too suspicious if they'd come in and they likely would not have been allowed inside the meet room. Of course, I would have preferred if they were more than two blocks away. We'd spotted a lot of people on our way in, and probably more that we didn't. They could be as surrounded as us at the moment, and not even know it.

"Relax, Axel. She's fine. I've dropped eyes in every direction. No one is getting near us without plenty of warning."

Mother. Fucker. How did he know?

"My equipment picks up more than sound and sight. I don't take chances that I'll miss anything." Right then I wasn't sure if Tel was brilliant or a fucking maniac. Probably both. I was just really glad he was on our side.

His confidence, however, wasn't enough. Houston and I were well aware that no one had to get close to take any of them out. If this was some kind of trap so Mazzeo could get to her, I didn't believe for a second he would use a sharpshooter to take her out. His interest in all of this was too personal.

No. When he killed the people he considered key, it would be done up close. He was going to try and get her face-to-face. Which meant he and I would be face-to-face instead. Mandy's assessment of his psychotic behavior had been the same.

We were silently ushered into a big conference room with three men already sitting at one end of the table and a whole army of others standing around the perimeter of the room with their weapons in their hands at their sides.

"This is bullshit," I said. "There isn't a goddamned friendly thing about this little get-together." I turned to JD. "Let's get the fuck out of here. Let the Feds deal with them."

JD didn't bat an eye or blink at my rehearsed objection. Instead, he nodded in the direction of the three men. "Gentlemen," he drawled. "Your lapdogs already divested us of weapons, so this,"—he waved around the room—"is overkill. If this meeting has a chance in hell of continuing *and* doing anything useful, they need to stand down. Or we're out of here."

"You seem to be mistaken." One of them muttered, a

deep scowl etched across his face. "You no longer have a choice. You are now here at our will, not your own."

"So that's how you want to play this? Start off with threatening us? Okay go for it. Kill us and see what happens next. If you think the governor is a thorn in your side now, just wait."

One of the men shrugged as if he didn't give one shit about the outcome of all this. "A bullet to his brain will solve all of our problems. It's no big deal to us."

No one was going to fall for that bullshit, otherwise we wouldn't be here.

JD laughed. "You are an even bigger fool than I thought if you believe that."

The man who'd spoken last started to stand, but one of the other men cut him a look that halted him in his tracks. He gave JD a vicious look that made it clear he would be all too happy to kill someone, but he returned to his seat regardless.

Okay then. Now we knew who was in charge. That was easier than I'd expected.

For a few seconds longer we all glared at each other. I was livid and unwilling to hide it, while JD looked, cool, calm, and collected. He was the master of his emotions and as far as these assholes were concerned, he could take them or leave them. Although after what happened to Sasha, I had no doubt any of them were long for this world if they didn't find a way to make this right.

Finally, the man in charge made a noise that sounded a lot like a grunt, and all the men lining the room came to attention and then filed out the door, leaving the three of them and the two of us. We were technically outnumbered, but these stuffed suits probably did nothing other than talk about violence—they couldn't hold a candle to the two of us if their lives depended on it. And it might.

"All of tonight's commotion was completely unnecessary. It serves neither of our interests for the government to employ such tactics against us. I guarantee the end result will impact us all in a negative manner."

"You reap what you sow." JD's recital of our club motto echoed through the spacious room. "You should have thought of that before your man decided to come after us, in our own home. Nothing we've done warrants that. Frank Mazzeo got what he deserved and his son is next."

The one man who'd yet to speak smiled, and it unnerved me. I didn't like the look of any of them, but he, in particular, gave me a bad vibe. If any of them would give us trouble over getting what he wanted, it was going to be him. The others looked tired and frustrated.

"Frank was a stupid fool who let his thirst for more power overrule his imagination."

Finally, something we could all agree on.

"That he was," JD agreed. "A sick bastard, too. And it seems his son didn't fall far from the tree at all."

A slight grunt erupted from the man in charge. "Unfortunately, his death created chaos in the organization and tied up a lot of his assets until we found his rightful heir."

I bristled against the fact that they didn't consider Isabella the one who had all the rights. It was she who'd suffered at his hand and her father's demented partner. It was enough to make me wish we could kill him all over again.

I didn't give one shit about his son's story. Nor did I worry about whether psychos were made or born. He'd killed one of ours. He'd killed the governor's aide, and he'd killed an FBI agent. Three fucking people were dead because of him, and two more in the hospital still fighting for their life.

And those were only the ones we knew about. I had a hunch, as good as this guy was at getting in and out of tight places, that these were not his first kills. And they would not be his last if we didn't put an end to him.

"Not a one of us has any skin in that game. Not even his daughter, who is under our protection by the way, so don't even think about making a move on her, wants anything to do with his assets. She signed away her claim to his entire fortune."

"Not his *entire* fortune, it would seem."

"Is that what this is about? Fuck," JD swore again, letting a little of his anger slip out. "Fine. You want to make this about money, go for it. We're leaving. You want to keep letting that fucker come after us, go for it. The consequences will be on your head and at your fucking front door."

"You seem to think you have all the power here."

"And you seem to think we don't. I have no idea what you were trying to gain by asking us here under false pretenses. It's clear you don't plan on negotiating anything."

"Your club cost us quite a bit in the fallout of Frank's death. That's still playing out. Some retaliation should have been expected."

JD exploded, almost taking me aback. "Then let's go to war, mother fucker. We don't *need* anything from you."

Fine." The oldie in charge sighed. "What is it you want?"

Now we were getting somewhere.

"Just one thing," JD answered. "The Mazzeo heir." All three men looked ready to explode. "And this time, make sure he has whatever is necessary in place to keep your business the way you want it before I kill him. Not because I care, but because you do."

Chapter Thirty-Two

Axel

"YOU AREN'T the least bit worried that they let us walk out so easily? Or that they so easily gave up on Mazzeo?"

"Yes and no," JD said as we made our way back to our vehicles. "They gave him to us because that's what they wanted to do before we ever arrived. He is a thorn in their side. A wild card they can't control who is going to cost them everything if he isn't stopped. Why not use him in an obvious power play that gives them the very thing they want without the responsibility of taking care of it themselves?"

"So, you're okay with them using us like that?" None of this sat well with me. Other than the fact in about twenty minutes I would put a bullet into that fucker's brain.

"They need us to get to Izzy. When Mazzeo dies, she will *again* have to sign away rights. That's all they care about. And at the end of the night, that's what we'll owe them."

"And you think Izzy will just do it? When have you ever known her to just do anything? She isn't stupid."

He shrugged. "That's up to her. If she decides to play it a different way, then we'll figure something out. But it's unlikely. Houston won't want her pulled back into this world or risk her death."

"That's a pretty big fucking gamble, old man."

JD shot me a dirty look. "I'm going to take what I can get today, and worry about the rest tomorrow."

I didn't believe that for a second—

"What the fuck?!"

We'd turned the corner to where Tel, Houston, Maddy and Izzy were waiting, but what we found threatened to send me into cardiac arrest. Two bodies on the ground and several slumped over in the vehicle.

We both ran in that direction, JD stopping to check on the first bodies we passed. Cash and Rip were down, and while I needed to know if they were dead, it was the people in my truck that had my heart ready to explode.

"They're alive, just out cold," I distantly heard JD say as I tore the back door open where I'd left Maddy in what should have been about as safe a place as she could be.

What the—

Her seat was empty.

I couldn't breathe, let alone move. If not for JD opening the front passenger side door and yelling at me to check for a goddamn pulse, I might have crumpled to the ground. My worst fear had come true. She'd been taken.

Reaching across the seat, I shoved my fingers into Tel's neck and immediately felt the strong thump thump of his pulse. "He's alive."

"So are Houston and Izzy. Thank fuck."

"He took her." My mind reeled with fear over what he could have done to her by now while we'd been inside.

JD grabbed my shoulders. "Pull yourself together. We're going to find her. That bastard worked way too hard to get her to just kill her right away. She told you herself what kind of person she thought he was."

I nodded, hoping I could hold onto that for a while until we could figure out where he'd taken her.

"So, what the hell did he do to the rest of them? How are they all alive and relatively unscathed? It doesn't look like there was any kind of fight."

JD nodded. "Looks like they've all been drugged or gassed or something.

"Gas. Jesus Christ. What will he do next?"

"Right? At least they're all not dead."

That definitely was a bright side. Not that any of this felt fucking bright. This asshole was into some dark shit, and I really didn't want to find out what he had planned for her.

"We need to wake them up. Got any ideas?"

"Yeah, but last time I checked I don't carry around smelling salts in a first aid kit."

"Wait. Do you have a first aid kit in here?"

"Yeah." I dug behind the rear seat until I could grab it and pull it out. I handed it over.

He grabbed it and dug through it, but I doubted he was going to find anything. A paramedic I was not, so I didn't bother with much more than what it had come with and refills of the basics like bandages and antiseptic.

"Aha!" He pulled out what looked to me like a nondescript little package, ripped it open and held it up to his nose. "This should work." He crunched up his nose.

"What the fuck is it?"

"Ammonia. Who do you want to wake up first?"

I looked around the cab and noticed the computer still sitting in Tel's lap. "Wake his ass up. He's our best bet at finding her. He's got all the information on the properties that Izzy gave him. Hopefully, he had enough time to narrow them down."

JD shoved the little opened package under his nose, and nothing happened.

"Shit!"

"Give it a second. It's not magic." He waved it around, hopefully activating whatever it was in that scent that would wake up his big brain.

After another thirty seconds or so I was ready to scream. I couldn't shake the idea that we had very little time to find her before it was too late. I was about to dump one of the bottles of water I kept in the floor-board when he finally twitched.

"About fucking time, sunshine. Time to wake the hell up."

Tel moaned. "What the hell happened?"

"I was hoping you'd tell us." JD hauled him up so he was sitting instead of slumped to the side, but his head still lolled out of control.

"I—I'm not sure."

"Well, you'd better think of something because Mandy is missing, and I'm going to go stark raving mad if you can't point us in the right direction. Did you find anything else about those properties Izzy gave you?"

"Yeah. I—uhh—think so."

"Here drink this." JD shoved a bottle of water into his hand and helped him pull it to his mouth. "Try waking Izzy up. Maybe she can add to this conversation," JD suggested.

I practically ran around the front of the truck to her door and yanked it open, catching her before she could fall out. "This is fucking ridiculous. I am going to kill that asshole with my bare hands the second we find him."

"Get in line," JD growled.

If he hurt her...

I couldn't function with that image in my head. Instead, I grabbed the small package from JD and pushed it under Izzy's nose. She moved almost immediately. Whatever they'd been hit with, either she didn't get as much or it didn't have as much of an effect on her.

"Izzy. Open your eyes, beautiful."

"Houston?"

"No. Axel. But he's right here. He's fine."

Her eyes popped open and she blinked several times as if attempting to clear her vision. "Axel?"

"Yep. We just got done with the meeting and found you all in the truck. Can you remember what happened?"

She started coughing and I helped her lean forward to get it out and take a breath or two of fresh air. "There was some kind of gas," she choked out. "It burned."

"Did you see where it came from or who did it?"

She didn't answer right away, and it didn't sound like JD was having any better luck in the backseat. "C'mon, hon. I know you probably don't feel good, but I need any information you can give me. Mandy's been taken. Was it your brother? Did he attack you all?"

She shook her head amidst violent coughs. "No," she managed before another series of coughs tore through her small body.

"It wasn't him," came a rough voice from the backseat. I turned to Tel. "Then what the hell happened? I need to know who has her. We have got to get her back before it's too late."

"It was *her*," he said. "She did this."

I couldn't figure out what the hell he was talking

about. "Her? Her who? Izzy?" That made no fucking sense at all. That asshole may be her brother by blood, but she'd never met him. No way in hell she would help him kidnap Mandy.

"Let's get Houston awake. Maybe between the three of them we can put the puzzle together. They aren't making sense," I agreed. JD propped up Tel, went back around to the driver's side and yanked that door open. "Hand me the ammonia."

I did as told, and then settled Izzy back against the seat. She was still coughing, and until she got control of it, we weren't getting answers.

Like Tel, Houston did not wake easy. By the time he stirred, Izzy finally seemed to have some control. "Is he okay?" she rasped.

"Seems like it. I don't know what you were hit with and what repercussions it might have though."

"This wasn't my brother," she whispered. "At least not directly." She hesitated, looking directly at me when she finally spit it out. "Amanda did this. Said she didn't feel good and had to step outside. There was a canister in her bag." She pointed at the rear floorboard, but it was empty and my mind couldn't comprehend what she was saying. "It filled the cab with gas before we could do anything to stop it."

And now my brain was about to explode. "Mandy? You're sure."

"Yeah," Tel agreed. "I wasn't quick enough to stop her. It happened so fast."

"What about the rest of the guys? Where the hell are

they? You had practically the whole club for this. How did one woman get a jump on all of you?" JD's voice sounded dangerously on edge, resembling the same angry emotions making their way through me.

"We sent them after Mazzeo. She got a call on her phone, said it was her government contact and they had a lead on where he was. We were afraid if we waited, we might miss our opportunity. So, we split them up. Left some of them a block over in case we needed backup here, and the rest to a warehouse in SoDo based on her intel. We had no reason to believe she would lie to us."

My blood boiled as Tel continued to paint the picture. Mandy had used us all along for information until she could hunt the killer on her own.

All her bullshit about working together had been all part of an act. I hadn't even bothered to question her easy cooperation. I'd gotten one taste of her pussy and fell completely into her trap.

While she'd plotted out how she would escape and once again, leave her loved ones behind.

Chapter Thirty-Three

Amanda

AS I APPROACHED THE PENTHOUSE, a shiver worked down my spine. Everything about this place told me I'd made the right decision. I also didn't know how long I had before Axel would find me. Since Izzy had given us the places to look, and Tel had done the research, they were bound to put two and two together and figure out where I'd gone.

Even sooner if the new corporation in charge had confirmed this location.

Of course, coming here without backup might be the dumbest thing I've ever done. But I could see too many things going wrong if the entire club came at this place all at once. This guy wasn't stupid, he'd know long before anyone made it inside.

Not to mention, everyone wanted a piece of him now, and he was mine. From the moment that head had been delivered to my door. Either I'd kill him or he'd kill me. It was that simple.

I reached into my bag of tricks and pulled out the extra weapons I'd brought with me and strapped them to my body. Two guns and a knife suddenly felt like not enough, but they would have to do. These were the obvious necessities, but likely not the ones to do the trick.

I was counting on the fact that while he'd see me coming, he would also underestimate me.

I looked down at my phone and confirmed that the security system was still disabled. Tel wasn't the only one who knew his way around a computer. My tablet had been more than enough to gain access. All that was left was for me to get through the front door and—

I'd barely gotten my lock picking tools out of my tactical vest when the front door popped open and a female computer voice welcomed me like this was a god damned video game. I winced, knowing this was going about as I'd expected but still wishing it could be different.

I would have preferred a quick in and out without any messy games. The last thing I needed was for this to get dragged out and Axel and gang show up here looking for their pound of flesh. I'd had enough with the casualties and the blood shed on their behalf. This was my fight, not theirs and I didn't want anyone else hurt because of me.

At the same time, part of me knew the mistake I'd made coming here on my own. Axel would never forgive or forget. And while that was part of the plan, it still hurt.

I slowly made my way through the penthouse, having studied the building schematics before entering, I had a solid knowledge of the layout.

"You might as well step out of the shadows. I know you're here. I've actually been waiting."

I blew out a hard breath as his voice, strong and deep, snaked down my spine. It sounded so familiar. Deciding there was no point in pretending, I stepped with my gun drawn and pointed in front of me into the dining room where he was waiting.

"Well, that's rude. You don't see me brandishing a weapon at your face. Were you not welcomed into my home?"

I jolted at the sight of the ghost I'd been cyber chasing for days. "Anthony?" I asked, unable to hold back my shock. I'd imagined a lot of different scenarios over how this would go, and who he might be, but this was not a man I'd expected to find.

He chuckled. "You sound so surprised."

I was. I'd honestly been expecting a faceless, nameless stranger. Not someone I'd seen every day for months. "You're Frank's son?"

The smile on his face faltered and I got a look at the darkness that lurked underneath the beautiful exterior. "Again with the surprise. Are you trying to insult me? What? Do you think I'm not good enough to be his bastard son because I did his shit work for years? Or because he treated me like nothing more than the hired help my entire life?"

"I—I just didn't know. I thought you were…" I let my words trail off because what I'd been about to say didn't matter. Anthony had been witness to every little thing Frank had put me through. He knew all my dirty little secrets. Because of that, and the kindness he'd occasionally shown, I'd thought we'd shared a kinship. He'd taken care of me more than once. How could he be the cold-blooded killer? It just didn't register.

"What? Come on, Kelly, speak up. Or should I call you Amanda? You seem to have a bit of an identity problem these days, don't you?"

That was the least of my problems. I hadn't seen this coming. Frank's son was his own personal security guard? Although I guess it made sense. It kept him close. Which meant he'd spent years absorbing everything about the business and taking over wouldn't be that hard. He'd also experienced every fucked up twisted thing Frank did in living color. That would probably twist anyone into a monster.

"Does it really matter what you call me?" I asked.

"I suppose not. Either way, you won't leave this room alive. It's time for me to tie up all the loose ends that Frank left behind and that includes you. Your intimate knowledge of his business is unacceptable."

"That doesn't make sense. You know Frank never told me anything important. I couldn't even get enough information for a solid arrest. And I tried, despite all the shit he pulled on me."

He leaned forward and placed his elbows on the dining table. "Which, I suppose is why you resorted to manipulating that little motorcycle club into killing him."

"Can you blame me?" I regretted that question as soon as I said it. Antagonizing him wasn't going to help the situation. Swaying him to my side at this point seemed futile.

"It was ballsy, I'll give you that." He hesitated, his expression turning hate filled again. "But you took away the one thing I'd waited my entire life for."

Oh my God if this was all because this idiot had daddy issues I was going to throw up. Join the fucking club, dude.

"Really? Because from where I'm standing all I can see is that you were handed the keys to the kingdom. You don't have anything to complain about."

"Then sit down and let me explain it to you in words you can understand."

"No thanks, I'd rather stand."

He slammed his fist down on the table and yelled, "Do as you're told, and sit the fuck down." Before I could tell him to fuck off, a young woman with tears streaming down her face appeared in the doorway to my left. I barely spared her a glance until a sick smile crossed Anthony's face. "Sit down and hand over your gun to *Natalie* here, or I'll kill her."

I jerked, looking again at the woman who had appeared from nowhere.

"Nat," I whispered, the horror finally taking hold. Everything I'd worked so hard to prevent unfolding before my eyes.

"Yes, now you see why you should do as you're told." I looked back to Anthony and he indicated a small remote-looking device in his hand. It was then I noticed what she wore. My seventeen-year-old sister had on a black vest made up of explosives.

Fuck. Fuck. Fuck.

I should have anticipated something like this. Frank had a fondness for hurting women and it made sense that his son did too. And as a witness to all of Frank's crimes, he knew exactly what to do to get to me. Apparently, the son had been influenced in all kinds of sick ways by his father.

"I'm not going to ask again," he said, rubbing his finger lightly over the button in his hand.

"Okay," I said, releasing my tight grip on my gun and twisting it in my hand so it was no longer pointed at him. I took the seat farthest from his at the opposite end of the table and when Natalie approached, I handed her my gun.

"Nat," I whispered, her tears threatening to shatter me.

"The one at your ankle as well," he smirked.

I squeezed my eyes shut, unsurprised. We both knew no trained agent would enter a situation like this without some kind of backup, even if that only came in the form of secondary weapons. I lifted my jeans and pulled the smaller of the two guns I carried and handed it over as well.

He sighed. "Now the knife. Stop trying to play games. I don't have the patience or the time." I couldn't take my eyes off the remote in his hand or the way he kept fondling it. It was as if there was a burning itch for him to push it. I wasn't particularly concerned about my life, but Nat was terrified and I had to do something —fast. I couldn't leave her to him and his vices. If they were half as bad as his father's she would wish she were dead.

"Time?" I questioned.

"Of course. Your friends will be here soon and we need to be ready. Although I have to admit, this trap was far too easy to lay. You all fell into it like little marionettes. While I don't think they can cause me any real problems, one can't be too careful."

Now it was my turn to be horrified. I'd counted on my life being at risk, not all of theirs. Or hers. I didn't dare give her another glance. I wouldn't put it past him to push that button just so I could watch her explode into tiny pieces.

"Then why wait?"

He frowned at me across the table. "Are you not enjoying my game?" Since I refused to give him the satisfaction of an answer, he stood and walked towards me. "You still haven't given me your knife. Take it out now and slide it to me on the table." His finger rubbed along that button again and Natalie's tears got louder.

I reached into my vest and pulled the knife I'd shoved in there earlier out by the blade. I fondled it much like he did that damned button and contemplated for about two seconds what would happen if I threw it at his throat.

I could kill him almost instantly from this distance, but there was no guarantee he couldn't press that button first.

"You'd like to sink that blade into me, wouldn't you? How satisfying would it be right now to feel the knife push through my flesh and into my heart? Do you think you could do it before I killed your precious Natalie? Would you like to find out?" He smiled, a sickening twist of his face that left me no option but to cooperate —for now. He likely planned to kill us both, but nothing was over until it was over.

I pushed the knife across the table, and it stopped halfway. We could both still reach it, but neither of us made a move for it. He stared down at me and laughed and I closed my eyes in the face of it. Somehow looking at him and waiting for what came next made it all worse. The sickening betrayal, the memories of the past, it all mixed together in a toxic mess that threatened my very sanity.

That was my second mistake. My first not seeing that he would find a way to get to me no matter how prepared I'd been.

Before I could react, he pounced, grabbing the knife and swiping it across first one bared wrist and then my other. He moved faster than I'd imagined possible and when I brought up my other hand to fight back, he grabbed it and manacled it to the table, as well as the other while the knife clattered to the ground.

Natalie's screams filled the room.

"Shut up and come here, little girl," he ordered her. She shook her head, her fear making her shake, although her screams turned to whimpers. "Come here or I will press that fucking button and be done with you. If you aren't useful then I don't need you. Now get your sweet ass over here."

She was shaking so violently now I wasn't even sure if she could function. "Leave her alone. I won't fight you. Just let her go and I'll do whatever you want." I looked down at the wrist he'd already cut to see he had not missed his mark. He'd sliced vertically across my vein and deep enough to be a problem. I'd be lucky if I had ten minutes to figure this shit out before it was too late.

"Oh for fuck's sake. Just bring me the fucking rope," he ordered.

She stared at him like a deer caught in headlights. Frozen. Unable to move. But she had to or this was all going to end now.

"Natalie, look at me!" I spoke sharply, hoping I could get her to focus. When she turned her head and caught my gaze, I breathed a sigh of relief. "Do what he says. Whatever it is. You do it, okay?" She slowly nodded, but I wasn't sure she comprehended much beyond the fear seizing her. "Trust me. Now go get the rope."

She disappeared through the doorway and returned thirty seconds later with the rope in hand. Obviously, he'd lain his trap in a variety of ways and methodically prepared for my arrival.

I'd been wrong and I should have seen it. He'd stood by and watched Frank do the vile things he was so infamous for. He might have been a bystander then, but that was over now. If given half the chance I believed he would live up to his father's reputation and more. Left unchecked, Anthony could become even more psychotic than his father.

"Tie her arms to the chair," he ordered. "Hurry."

I looked up at him to find him breathing heavy. Heavier than he should have been. My heart hitched. I wasn't ready to count my chickens yet, but there was still hope.

Natalie walked closer, and after a brief hesitation did as she was told. When she was done, he released my wrists and finished tying off the rope. It wasn't tight enough on my arms to staunch the blood flow by much, but the knots were not going to budge.

He pulled an old-fashioned handkerchief out of his jacket pocket and proceeded to wipe my blood from where it had splashed on his face. He wiped his hands as well and I prayed to God that wouldn't ruin my plan.

He returned to his seat and plopped down, looking worn out from our scuffle. "You're strong, I'll give you that. But not strong enough. You still made my job too easy by coming here."

"What choice did you give me? I didn't want to see anyone else die."

He laughed. "You sound so weak. No wonder the FBI or CIA, or whichever one you really worked for, burned you. If, at the first sign of violence you give in, you are worthless."

While his words did have the effect of rubbing salt in my wounds, I easily ignored them. I had much bigger problems. Namely that damned trigger he had in his hand and the fact that any moment he would realize what I'd done.

I had to get my hands on that remote.

Because he didn't know it yet, but he was already dead.

Chapter Thirty-Four

Axel

LESS THAN AN HOUR LATER, I pulled my truck to the curb and put it in park. "Is this it?" I glanced up at the low-rise building that sat on the Seattle waterfront overlooking the sound. Using the information from Izzy and Tel's hacking skills we'd tracked Mandy to this building.

"Yeah. That's the one. I'm already connected to her tablet. Let me see if I can turn on the audio from it and pick up anything." Tel's fingers flew across his keyboard as he worked his usual magic. I had to admit we'd gotten so reliant on his skills, I hoped that we never had to go without them. "A few more adjustments."

Muffled talking suddenly filled the cab. I strained to understand any of it. "Is that the best we can do?"

"I'm afraid so. She's probably got the damned thing in her bag and is too far away from it to pick up anything clear."

"Okay," I said, my gut tightening as I continued to work on picking something up. "At least we know she's in there."

A rap on my window had me rolling it down to talk to JD. "She's in there, but we can't get ears. We're going to have to go in blind."

He shrugged. "Won't be the first time, probably not the last. What about security?"

"I'm going to have to come with you for that. I can't do it from here."

JD nodded. "All right then, let's get it done."

"We're going too," Houston announced and I gave him and Izzy both a side eye.

"Too risky."

"That's for us to decide, not you. We don't need permission."

I wasn't in the mood to argue with Izzy or Houston. My anger had reached the boiling point a while ago and I only had two things on my mind. Finishing the job so I never had to deal with a Turner again, because this was the last fucking job our club would take from him or his family, and punishing Amanda for her bullshit.

"You're sure you want to do this?" JD asked. "We have more than enough firepower if you want to hang back."

I didn't deign to give him a response to that asinine idea. I simply hopped out of the truck and headed towards the building. I was going in right fucking now.

The building entrance was easy enough. The door had already been disabled and no guard was in sight. Courtesy of Mandy, I guessed.

"Let me guess," I said. "Top floor?"

"Yes. But you should take the stairs, not the elevator. I think this building is one of those where the top floor has a private elevator that opens into the residence."

"Where do the stairs go?"

Tel turned his tablet around to show us the map. "Looks like the kitchen. Probably a safe bet they're not cooking a meal together."

I had no response. Nor did I want to think about what exactly was happening inside. She'd chosen to put her life at unnecessary risk and go in ALONE.

"We should expect they'll be waiting on us," JD said in a low voice as we moved up the building. People rich enough to live in this building don't leave it open like this for anyone off the street to stroll in. This is the equivalent of a fucking welcome mat.

I agreed. But whether this was a trap or not, it didn't matter. They were outnumbered at least three to one. We had the tactical advantage here and this was likely our only shot at getting them both.

That nagging sensation at the back of my mind returned. It was having a lot of difficulty processing the contradicting facts about Mandy. While I could admit that I had a certain bias when it came to her, I wasn't that dumb.

Working with Frank had put others in danger, and yet here, she'd gone out of her way, and at her own peril, to keep others safe. Which still didn't take away that feeling that she'd been playing me all along.

Although it all could have been one elaborate lie. That was her job.

We reached the top floor and waited for Tel to work his magic. The keypad meant there were too many combinations for manual manipulation and unless we wanted to blast our way in and announce our arrival, we were going to have to wait and let the brother do his thing.

I grabbed the phone he'd transferred her audio to and held it up to my ear. I still couldn't make out the words, but something had changed. "What is that?" I questioned, straining to identify the new sound.

JD leaned over me and listened as well. "What the hell? Is that—?" He pushed closer. "Is someone crying?"

A chill swept over me. That's exactly what it sounded like. And not gentle cries other. Someone was straight up sobbing. The sound was almost palpable.

"Tel, you've got ten seconds before I bust this door down."

"Fuck you," he muttered. I've got three of the four numbers. Just give me a minute."

"We don't have that long." I had a hunch if he didn't get in there now, someone was going to be dead.

The device in Tel's hand beeped. "Got it." He unhooked his equipment and then typed in the door code. The light turned green and the sound of a bolt on the move greeted my ears. Fuck yes. I wanted to kiss Tel for his genius. I tightened my hand around the gun I was carrying and opened the door.

Immediately, we were hit with voices and the now clear feminine sobbing. Fear washed over me. They were in the next room, and I was almost afraid to discover what we would find.

JD used his hands to signal our forward movement, and together we moved to the mouth of what was probably a dining room. With a final breath and a nod, we stepped into the room together our guns raised and hopefully ready for anything.

I was wrong.

I was not ready for the gruesome scene before me. It wasn't like I hadn't seen worse. Mandy had had a fucking severed head in a box. But this...

It took every ounce of control I had not to rush to Mandy's side and stop the flow of blood oozing from her wrists. Only the shake of her head kept me frozen in place. There was stark fear in her eyes, and until I figured out why, I was going to measure my steps.

While JD picked up on her cues as well, somebody had not gotten the message to Izzy, who opened her mouth before anyone could stop her.

"Anthony?"

The giant of a man turned to face us. "Isabella?"

We should have made our move then, while he'd

been momentarily confused, but by the time we realized exactly how dangerous the situation was, it was too late.

"Don't move another inch," he said, spittle flying from his mouth. Sweat coated his face and neck and something about him didn't look right at all. He held up his hand and instead of the surrender I thought he might be going for, he indicated a tiny device he held in his right hand.

That was also the moment the sobbing that had ceased began again and twice as hard. I looked for the source, twisting to see around the man blocking my view and I sucked in a sharp breath.

Jesus Fucking Christ. There was a young girl standing there, and she had enough C4 strapped to her chest to take out this entire apartment and everyone in it.

"You have got to be fucking kidding me."

The man smiled. "Hmm. You're late. For a while there I didn't think you were going to make it to the party." He laughed. "Look, Amanda. It's your new fuck buddy and his little club."

"Anthony. What are you doing?" Izzy asked, moving as far forward as she could with Houston and us blocking her path.

"Izzy, stay back," JD warned, his voice sharp and full of command.

"You aren't supposed to be here," the big man — Anthony—answered, his expression suddenly serious instead of mocking. "You should leave now. If you hurry you can make it out before it's too late."

I didn't like the sound of that, but I did agree she should leave. "Houston, take her," I growled. "Now!"

He didn't wait to decide. From my peripheral vision I saw him grab her around the waist and haul her against him.

"Stop!" she screamed. "That's Anthony. He was my bodyguard. There has to be some mistake. He's not my brother."

"The only mistake is you consorting with these assholes. You deserved better than this. Now. Get. The. Fuck. Out," he roared.

I watched his hand carefully, hoping in his fit of rage that he didn't accidentally press that trigger button. For half a second my heart stopped when his finger slipped just missing the tiny button.

I didn't bother sparing a glance at JD. I knew he'd seen it too. I raised my gun and took the shot.

The bullet pierced his skull right between his eyes, and for a second, he stared at us almost as if he hadn't been just eliminated. Another second, and he dropped to his knees, and I dove for his hand and the device still loosely clutched in his fist.

"You fucking idiot," Mandy screamed. She was thrashing against the chair, trying to break free.

"Someone tell me it's okay to take this thing out of his hand," I yelled.

"No!" both Tel and Mandy yelled. I froze.

"Is there any pressure on the button?" Tel asked, running over to my side.

"I don't know. I can't tell. You said don't touch him."

"It doesn't matter. We can't take a chance." She looked over at Tel. "You have to get that vest off of her first. Please."

Tel nodded and ran over to the young girl still sobbing uncontrollably. "Calm down. Please. I'm going to get you free. But I can't do anything with you shaking like this."

She grabbed at his hand, her tears flowing freely down her face. It was hard to tell exactly what she looked like with her face and eyes swollen from all the crying, but there was something about her that looked vaguely familiar.

JD crossed to Maddy. "We need a first aid kit."

"I'm fine," Mandy snarled. "Just help her. Dear God, please. Help her." Her words slurred at the end and it was the first real indication besides the blood flowing from her wrists that she was definitely *not* okay.

"You're ice cold," JD observed.

She shook her head and tried to jerk away from him, but her movements were slow and her head lolled to the side.

"Fuck. She just passed out."

"Someone needs to call 911." It was going to kill me not to move if someone didn't do something.

JD looked at me sharply. "And what the hell do you

think happens if the Seattle PD walks in here? She'll be dead before they can even assemble a bomb team."

"You can't just let her die. She's here because of me." The young girl's cries ceased, her face creased with a different worry now. But it was her words that stuck in my mind.

"She's not going to die," JD reassured her, but I doubted he could say that for certain. There was a shit ton of blood pooling around her chair.

"I've got it." Tel announced, lifting the vest slowly away from the girl's body.

"Get everyone out," I ordered. "I'm not releasing his hand until everyone else is clear."

"Tel," JD called. "Put that vest in a tub if you can find one. Hurry." He had already untied Maddy's arms and was lifting her into his arms. "As soon as we get outside, we'll call 911."

"Hurry," I whispered. Unsure whether I was more worried about the explosives going off or whether or not Mandy was going to make it. If I was honest, that wasn't true. I needed her to live. For me—US.

And so I could make sure she understood that going in ALONE was not an acceptable thing to do, and that it was high time for her to show some damned trust.

Tel returned to the room and grabbed the young girl's hand. "It's done. Let's go." She nodded and followed him out.

"Don't get dead," JD warned me.

"There's a first aid kit in the truck. Save her."

He nodded. "I'll ping your phone with the all clear and then you get the hell out as fast as you can."

I nodded because no more words were needed. As he disappeared through the doorway, I realized that my life didn't matter. It was her. It was always going to be her.

No matter what she'd done in the past.

Chapter Thirty-Five

Amanda

SOMETIMES WAKING UP SUCKED.

When it was inside of a hospital even worse. I tried to lift my arm, to wipe the sleep grit from my eyes and found bandages and tubes in my way.

"Hey, you're back. It's about time."

I turned my head to see Axel leaning over my opposite side and nearly whimpered in relief. He was alive. The last thing I remembered was him falling on top of a dead man, trying to rescue my—

Panic seized me. "Where's Nat? Is she okay?" My throat was dry and the words came out rougher than I'd meant them to.

"She's fine. Traumatized but healthy. I didn't recognize her at first. Not until she told me who she was."

"He used her to control me. Just like Frank, he knew my weaknesses more than I did." I could feel the burn of tears at the back of my eyes as an onslaught of memories shoved their way to the forefront of my mind.

"What does that mean?" he asked, confusion bringing his eyebrows together.

"It doesn't matter. It's ancient history."

"Bullshit. You're in the hospital, where you almost died. That's about as current as it gets."

I looked up at him. "It would have been okay if I did. All that mattered was getting rid of Frank's son and saving Natalie."

"That's not an answer. Natalie told us Anthony AKA Frank Jr. used her to get to you. But what does that have to do with Frank Sr.? Is that why you helped him? And how did he even know about her? Tel says your family records were scrubbed clean. The internet says you have no siblings at all."

"I did that after Frank's death. I never wanted anyone to find Nat again. But of course, Anthony already knew about her. He was there to witness —everything."

I could see all the confusion on his face. He wasn't going to let this go, but I didn't want to think about it anymore, let alone talk about it. It was over. The damage was done. "Can I see her?"

He frowned. "She's already gone. They kept her here for psychological evaluation for forty-eight hours and then her mom checked her out. I don't know where they went from there."

I held back another sob at the loss. Even five minutes with her alone would have been nice. I could have said goodbye. "How long have I been out?"

"Almost three full days."

"And Frank Jr.?"

"He's definitely dead. I shot him."

Oh yeah. I rubbed my head as the memories continued to file in.

"You almost got us all killed."

"We were all doomed the moment we entered that little house of horrors. I took the only shot we had to get out."

I guess I couldn't disagree with that. Anthony had only been moments away from realizing that he'd been poisoned when he grabbed my knife. His body's reaction would have been violent, but he might have remained lucid enough to press that button or worse. But like Axel, I'd been out of options. It had been my only choice.

"What now?" I don't know why I bothered asking. No matter what he said, I wasn't going to like the answer. I'd burned my bridges with Axel and the club. No one would ever trust me again.

"I've still got a lot of questions," he said slowly, taking a seat back in the chair next to my bed like he was settling in. "We need to talk about you going rogue in the middle of an operation and almost getting yourself killed, and why you didn't tell me about what really happened with you and Frank Sr."

What little bit of hope I'd felt at finding Axel at my bedside, withered. "I did what I had to."

"Bullshit," he exploded. "We had a fucking plan, and my entire club at our backs. You putting your life at risk was an idiotic move. You almost died."

"Screw you. Working alone is what I do. If you can't understand that…" I clamped my mouth shut before anything else truly hateful came out.

"So what you're saying is that you didn't trust me." He dropped that bomb without hesitation and my stomach sank in its wake.

I don't know why I expected him to understand. I'd known going in that if I went through with my plan, he would never forgive me. Saving my sister in Vegas had nearly cost him his friends so we were always going to be on shaky ground.

"I don't think there's anything else to say." I wanted him to go. Looking at him hurt too much. We'd dredged up all the old memories and then I'd piled on new ones to make things worse. At least I didn't have to worry about anyone else coming after me. I just had to live with my mistakes and find a new life. "You should probably go."

"That's really how you want this to go?"

I didn't respond. I doubted I could answer that question if I tried. How I wanted things to go was irrelevant at this point. Without trust, we were headed toward a disaster no matter which road we took.

He sat and stared at me for a minute more, looking like he was waiting for me to say something else that might change the outcome between us. But I couldn't. Or I wouldn't.

I had a lot to process and I was too tired to fight anymore.

Finally, he stood to leave. "You have no idea how badly I'd like to shake some sense into you right now. You could have trusted me with everything. If you had, you might not have ended up like this. This is bullshit, Amanda."

His return to my full name instead of the nickname he favored hit me hard. I'd not realized how much it had meant until just then.

I started to say something—anything that might change his mind—and nearly choked on a sob. Instead, I watched him walk out with neither of us saying another word. He might have been right, but I guess we'd never know...

———

Two weeks, one day, four hours, and six minutes. That's how long it had been since Axel had walked out of my hospital room. And there had been countless times I'd started to go after him. And every time I refused to go through with it. I knew what it would take to convince him I could be trusted, but I still couldn't bring myself to bare my soul in that way.

One good thing had come of this mess though. I

now had a new job and a place to live that had jack squat to do with my douchebag father. It wasn't exactly glamorous, and the pay was shit, but it kept me busy and with a roof over my head until I could figure out what I wanted to do with the rest of my life.

My affiliation with the government was officially dead. I'd gotten the paperwork via courier just the day before. How they'd found me, living practically off the grid, I didn't know. Probably better if I didn't anyway. I had to let it go and work on putting it behind me.

I'd heard no word from anyone about the aftermath at Mazzeo's penthouse, and I figured the best I could do was be grateful I'd been left out of it. Not that I hadn't considered digging into the official reports. However, the last thing I wanted to risk was getting caught. Even by the MC. Tel would know if someone went looking, and I didn't want to take that chance.

"Hey, Mandy, you ready?"

I looked up at Brianna and smiled. "Yep, I'm coming now." I finished making a coffee to go, grabbed my cleaning gear and headed outside to jump in her car. Brianna was my new co-worker, and since I didn't have the funds for a car yet, she picked me up every day for our shift cleaning cabins for a company that managed hundreds of vacation rentals in the area.

Firefighter Mike had visited me in the hospital and since he was the only person who seemed eager to talk to me, we'd struck up a friendship. When I told him I needed a place to live and a job to go with it, he mentioned his mother was always looking for help. The vacation rental business in the cascade mountains was thriving, but getting people to do the work keeping them clean was a real pain in the ass. She also had a basement she liked to rent out and it had recently been vacated by the last tenants.

I'd jumped at the chance, no questions asked. It was probably a little too close to Sultan for comfort, but I liked being here. Not every memory was bad, and spending time all over the mountain every day had brightened my outlook.

"You going to go with us to Bubba's tonight?" Brianna asked while we sat eating our lunch on the back deck of one of the cabins we cleaned. The view of the snowcapped mountain across the river couldn't be beat. One of these days I was going to buy one of these cabins. Not this one, though. It reminded me of him.

"Nah," I said, shaking my head and taking another bite of my sandwich.

"You say that every time."

I shrugged. "Going to a bar is not my thing."

"I think you'll change your mind one of these days." I doubted that. Especially when it came to Bubba's. Not that there were any other bar choices this far out of Seattle. But I'd drive into the city before I went to the local biker bar. If there was one place I knew I was definitely NOT wanted, it was there.

I stood, anxious to change the subject before she really got going. "I'm going back to work." I gathered my trash and stuffed it into my bag.

"Okay," she said, standing to gather her things as

well. "But this conversation isn't over."

I shook my head, disappearing around the corner, to dump my belongings in the car so I didn't forget them. I came up short when I found someone standing at the end of the deck.

Not just someone. JD.

"What the hell?" I said, clutching my chest. "You scared the hell out of me."

"You should take your friend up on her invitation."

I scrunched my face up at him in confusion until I realized what he meant. "You think I should go to Bubba's? Why?"

"Why not?" he asked, taking a step in my direction. I took a step back. I hadn't seen the MC president since the night everything went to hell. I had no idea what he would say to me, but I was pretty sure it wouldn't be nice.

"I should stay clear of the bikers that hang out there, don't you think?"

He laughed. "If you really intended to keep away you would have left town."

Shit. "Is that what this is about? You've come to warn me that I need to leave town?" Figures, as soon as I get a little settled, another man in my life wanted to cause trouble for me. Although was I really settled? Having a job and a roof over my head didn't really mean much. Not yet.

"You make a lot of shit assumptions for a smart woman." He took a few steps closer and this time I stood my ground. It was bad enough that Brianna was probably going to hear every word of this conversation, I didn't need to make it easy. "I came to see if you were ready to get your head out of your ass. Well, that ain't the only reason I came here." He lifted a big wrench into view from where he'd been holding it behind his back. "Apparently, there's a water pipe issue out here."

I looked left and then right, trying to make sense of what he said. "Since when does the MC take care of plumbing?"

"Since we bought a shit ton of these mountain cabins to use as vacation rentals. Haven't you heard that real estate is one of the best investments you can make for your future?"

My mouth dropped open as I stood staring at the OG badass biker, who I knew for a fact spent more time hunting down killers and kidnap victims than he did turning a wrench to fix some plumbing.

"Aren't fixing things what the prospects are for?"

He lifted his shoulder. "Yep. I could give a shit about this kind of work. But I happened to notice something very interesting on our video camera out here this morning and decided to check it out for myself and kill two birds with one stone."

I rolled my eyes. "I'm beginning to think there isn't much of anything that happens out here that you don't know about. You've certainly got your fingers in all the pies."

He smirked, a devilish look that I imagined had women around the state dropping their panties when he deigned to use it. The fact he was probably pushing fifty did nothing to detract from that. Other than a little gray hair at his temples and scattered through his full beard, he looked much younger. It was only the look in his eyes that might scare women away. He'd lived hard, and as President of the MC he took the full brunt of what came their way.

"I like pies," he said simply. "I also like women who don't bust my balls when I show up unannounced. Especially ones who are hoping for good reviews on their services." I was too shocked for words until he winked, letting me off the hook. "Relax, I didn't come here to critique your questionable cleaning skills."

"Thanks," I frowned. "I think."

"In most cases it's good to be wary. Especially since I came here to set you straight."

"Well, at least the awkward small talk is finally over." I bit my lips to hide my smile. I don't know what it was about him, but I liked James Dean Monroe. Even if he did have a mother who'd named him unkindly. Despite that, and his reputation as a real hard ass, I got a sense of fairness about him that seemed incongruent with his badass biker image.

"You going to stop sassing me long enough for me to say what I came here to say? There really is a water leak I need to contend with." He shook the wrench to emphasize his point.

"Okaaay." I crossed my arms over my chest and braced myself for the worst.

"Jesus. I'm not going to hit you. Don't be so paranoid."

I blinked up at him, a smart retort hovering on my tongue. But his expression had turned equal parts badass and teddy bear, and it was just the right combination to soften me. I dropped my arms and rolled my shoulders. "Just say it, then."

"You should have told him the truth when I sent him to you. He needed to hear it then, and he needs to hear it now."

I scoffed. "I doubt that. He hates me."

"If you believe that, then you're not as smart as I thought you were."

"What exactly is it that you think I should tell him? He already knows the truth about our baby." Well, that was technically true if we were talking about the past. Of course, that had nothing to do with the point I was trying to make. "You all know that I only did what I did with Frank to save my sister. Should I have handled that differently? Maybe. Would I do it differently if it happened again? Probably not. And that's just something I have to live with. It's who I am."

His lips twitched, and for half a second, I thought he was going to smile. He didn't.

"Yes, it's clear you're not a team player. At least not yet. And you're as stubborn as he is. He knows deep down that what the government did to you wasn't called for. But he isn't trusting his gut because he doesn't know why. Put a little faith in him and tell him the truth about Frank. It's all he needs. It's all *you* need."

My body jerked, my gaze flying back to his. What was he saying? That he knew? I nearly shook my head.

No. No. No. That wasn't possible. I'd planned to take that brief part of my life to my grave. That was not the kind of picture I wanted in my head, let alone anyone else's. I was about to tell him as much when he shook his head, disappointment written on his face.

"I could tell him for you, but that would make it harder for him to accept. He'll take it better if he thinks that everyone who knows, besides you, is dead. Anything else might eat him alive."

The pit in my stomach grew heavy. Why couldn't any of this just go away? The answer to every problem did not have to be to talk it out. I was a firm believer in adapt and overcome. Or in other words, let the shit go. "But why? Why isn't the fact I did what I had to do to get a job done good enough?"

He shook his head solemnly. "Because that's just not how this works. Relationships are built on trust, and for some people, trusting is hard."

I could see he was serious and didn't want to let it go. I for one, however, was tired of talking about it. That said. I didn't want to just dismiss what JD said without at least giving it some thought. He deserved that much, considering what I'd put his club through.

"I'll take it under advisement," I finally said.

He barked out a laugh and shook his head. "Okay, little girl. You do that. Now I guess I'd better see about that leak. Don't make me regret not sending out a prospect to do this dirty work."

I stood straight and mock saluted him. "Yes, sir."

He shook his head and walked past me, grumbling

something about a smartass under his breath. I didn't quite catch the words, but I got the gist.

I went back to work because we were due at the next cabin in less than an hour. In true JD fashion he did whatever he did and disappeared as silently as he'd arrived. And for the next several hours I thought of nothing but what he'd had to say until we finished our shift.

It was quiet on the ride back because we were both tired, and I still couldn't get out of my head. But by the time Brianna pulled onto the gravel road that led to my place, I'd made up my mind.

"You still want me to go with you to Bubba's tonight?"

Brianna's head jerked my way in surprise. "Oh my God. Are you serious?"

"As a heart attack." I laughed, hoping it didn't come across too awkward. I'd made up my mind and made a deal with myself. I'd go to the biker bar tonight and if he was there, then I'd do it.

"About freaking time. How about we swing by at seven-thirty to pick you up? We can all eat dinner there too."

"Okay," I said, wondering who she meant by *we* as I closed the door and then headed inside. Either way, I doubted my stomach would be in any condition to eat by then since the nervous energy right now already had me feeling like I wanted to throw up.

But a deal was a deal, even when I made it with myself.

Chapter Thirty-Six

Axel

She's here. At Bubba's.

I stared down at the text I'd just received from Cash and considered texting back to ask him who. Although we both knew I didn't need the clarification. What the hell was she doing, showing up there?

Since I was already almost there to meet several guys from the MC for a beer and the game, I had to decide quick whether I was going or not. I hadn't seen her since I walked away from her in the hospital, and I wasn't sure how I was going to handle our reunion.

Her refusal to acknowledge her mistake in going after a killer alone, had pissed me off. But her refusal to even talk to me about it or the operation in Vegas led me down a pretty dark path.

Without any hard facts, I had nothing to believe but

the worst. And yet... That fucking nagging in my gut hadn't gone away. I just couldn't reconcile the woman from my past with the woman in the present. And the fact that she'd stayed in town and taken a cleaning job, well that just made no damned sense.

There were a lot better uses for her skills than cleaning a bunch of cabins for the tourists...

I turned onto Main Street, and the sign for Bubba's loomed. I thought I had a choice, but before I could make it, my bike turned into the parking lot and came to a stop next to all the others lined up out front. Annoyed that my subconscious knew better than me, I climbed off my bike and stomped my way inside.

Fine. I was going to take her sudden decision to show up in our bar as a sign that she was ready to talk. It was about damn time. I closed the door behind me and stood there for a moment until my eyes adjusted to the darkened interior. After that, it took me all of two seconds to locate her. She was sitting at the bar, her back to the door, and all alone.

My entire body clenched at seeing her there. It had been almost twelve years since I'd seen her in here, and time fell away as if it had never passed. The desire to call her to me, like I'd done so many times before, flooded into me. She would always turn to look at me, tilting her head so that her long hair fell across her shoulder, her glossed lips widening in a seductive smile.

This time, she didn't move. Her blonde hair hung loose and straight down her back, making me want to walk up to her and grab a fistful of it so I could tug her in my direction until our gazes met so I could steal a kiss from her before I demanded that she talk to me.

Fuck. She was like kryptonite to me. I was drawn to her no matter how dangerous it might be.

A sharp whistle from the back drew my attention and I looked over to find Cash and the other guys waiting in our usual spot. I lifted my chin in a nod, but did not make my way back to them. They were going to have to wait because I had other business to attend to first.

Instead, I crossed to the bar and took the seat next to hers. I didn't say anything right away and after a couple of minutes of silence the bartender came over and asked if I wanted my usual. I nodded and he grabbed a bottle of whiskey and poured two fingers into a glass and then slid it in front of me.

He then asked her if she wanted more water, and she shook her head no. I looked at her curiously, thinking it odd that she didn't have some fancy chick drink in front of her.

The silence stretched awkwardly between us, until it was clear she had no intention of saying anything.

"I'm surprised to see you here," I said, feeling some of the hope I'd let in begin to deflate. If she wasn't going to talk we were going to get exactly nowhere.

She toyed with her empty glass, tilting it back and forth in front of her until I was ready to growl in frustration.

"I'm surprised I came here," she finally admitted, still moving that glass nervously back and forth.

"I heard you were still in town."

Her gaze shot to mine. "You did?"

I nodded, surprised by her surprise. "It's a small town, remember? It's impossible to keep secrets or for someone not to notice your comings *and* your goings."

"It sounds creepy, not charming, when you put it like that."

"I don't think I've ever promised charming anything, that's not my style. Although creepy was not my intent either."

A small smile cracked her lips, and I chose to take that as a positive sign.

"I've kept secrets," she whispered, so low I almost didn't hear her.

"Then I guess some of us are better at keeping them than others." I took a small sip of my whiskey and let the familiar burn make its way into my system. At this rate, I had a feeling this was going to be a more than one glass night.

"You might be right."

When she didn't elaborate or make any other comment I wanted to reach over and pull her to me. What was it going to take to get past those damned walls? She'd obviously come here to say something, but this reluctance was pissing me off again.

"What are you really doing here, Mandy?" My question came out gruff and unfriendly despite my intention to go for some patience. "Are you trying to drive me fucking mad?"

"Well, I actually came here with some work friends. But they hooked up with some guys from the club and left me here. I was about to leave and go home."

"Really? You came here? To our bar, where you knew I'd be, and you're just going to leave?"

She turned to face me, her cheeks now pink with anger. "What do you want from me, Axel? You already made it clear that we have trust issues, so why bother? For a second, I got weak and thought maybe... but then I chickened out. Is that what you wanted to hear?"

"And yet you still came. So you must have had something to say. So stop being a little girl and say it." I was taunting her now, but I couldn't seem to help myself.

"I came here because I'm an idiot. Are you happy now?" Her voice rose and I could see she was getting wound up now. Good. Maybe now we could make some progress. "For weeks, I've been going through the motions. I can't go anywhere or do anything without people looking at me weird because of these." She held up her arms and pointed to the small bandages still attached to her wrists. "I'm pretty sure everyone thinks I tried to kill myself."

"Then why not set them straight?"

"I don't like people knowing things about me. Especially if it's bad. I don't need or want their pity. They don't know me. Some might think they do, just because I grew up here, but they don't. I'm not a part of this community. But they sure as shit assume the worst. It might even be safe to say they hate me."

I looked around the room, taking notice that no one at all was paying attention to us. Her paranoia aside, everyone else had their own thing going on.

"So then don't tell them. Why would you *or* I give a fuck about what anyone else thinks? We aren't talking about them, Mandy. No one else is here. It's just you and me and your precious secrets."

"That's another thing!" She leaned over the bar and closer to me. "What fucking secrets? You act like what I did for a living and what went down with it was a big mystery when we both know damn well that you and your club have access to every little detail."

I frowned. "I like that you have that much faith in us, but we aren't all-knowing. Well, maybe JD is because he can be creepy like that."

She laughed, nodding her head. "Yeah, he can." I had a feeling there was a story that went with that look. However, JD was not my concern at the moment. We needed to stay focused.

"I can make an educated guess about what happened with you, I can even piece together some details from everything that went down to take it beyond a guess. But that's not the same as hearing it from the horse's mouth."

She scrunched her face at me. "Did you just call me a horse?"

I laughed, surprised that could happen under these

circumstances. "I guess I did, although that's hardly the point."

She sighed. "What's the point, Axel? I could tell you I went undercover, that I got discovered and subsequently tortured and then blackmailed into helping them. You've seen the scars and you know about my sister. Stop bitching about my secrets already when we both know whether I spell it out or not, it's not going to change anything."

The air around me was suddenly sucked from the room as I pictured every little thing she'd just described. All the signs had been there. Right in front of my face if I'd stopped blaming her long enough to see them.

She'd suffered as much as anyone and then gotten screwed over by the government as her reward.

It was my turn to sigh. I might be an idiot, but she still didn't fully understand either. "It's about trust, Mandy. Do you really not get that yet? Your lack of it fucking hurts. You got hurt because you didn't let us have your back and didn't think twice about it." I paused, taking a much needed beat before I continued, "I'm am sorry though. I should have never walked away from you until we hashed this out. But I'd spent three days not sleeping much in a hospital chair waiting for you to wake up. Three days where I let my imagination and less than positive thoughts get the better of me."

She seemed to think about that a second before her

head shot back up. "You were there the whole time? No one told me that."

"Yeah, I was. I knew Frank Jr. was dead. I put the bullet in him myself, but I still had to stay. Someone had to watch over you and it needed to be me."

I watched her face soften, and thank fuck it did. This bitterness and anger festering between us was driving me to the brink of insanity.

"I don't know what to say. In the moment all I could think about was that endangering you and your friends again was unacceptable. I just wanted to fix it. As for Vegas, I can see in hindsight that I should have just explained about Natalie and what that cost me. But I just..."

I reached over and placed my hand over hers. Her fingers were ice cold. "Just what? Tell me what goes on in that beautiful mind of yours. That's all I want. Just let me in."

"I don't need your pity. I'm not a victim." The sharpness in her tone had returned. I could understand that.

"I know you're not. The woman I love is a strong, capable badass woman. But if we're going to be together it has to be as a team. No more secrets. No more leaving me behind because you think it's for the best. I don't need to be protected."

"I never wanted to help Frank. Never. I hated him. He did everything in his power to break me but I never gave in. Only, I underestimated how far he would go when he didn't get his way. He found Natalie and threatened to do to her what he'd done to me. I had no other choice--I gave in. I hated myself for that almost as much as I was grateful that Natalie was alive and well. Good people lost their lives so I could save one. I didn't blame you for hating me. You almost lost your friends because of me and my choices."

"Anger and hate are not the same, although sometimes we get them confused."

I stared down at her for an eternity waiting for a sign. She didn't quite accept it yet, but she was mine. And possession is nine-tenths of the law and I had no intention of ever letting her go again.

I wanted to grab her hand and pull her close. The pain and guilt evident in her words were tearing me apart. If Frank was still alive I would enjoy taking him apart piece by piece, making him hurt until he begged for my mercy right before I put a bullet in his brain.

"Wait." She narrowed her eyes. "Did you say you love me? As in present, not the past?"

A wide smile crept across my face. "You caught that, huh?" I shook my head at the bad way I'd just blurted that out instead of being more thoughtful with something so important. Especially in the middle of her confession. "Yeah. I fell in love with you a long time ago, candy girl. Then a lot of shit went down and that love got twisted in a bad way. But I realize now it never went away. It just got lost in all the lies and my bad attitude." I laced my fingers with hers and brought them to my mouth for a soft kiss. "I'm so sorry, Mandy. I never should have believed that bullshit story your father fed me back then. I should have known it wasn't true. I am not making an excuse for my behavior, because there is none."

"My father is a skilled liar. He could convince anyone of anything. It's why he gets away with so much. Which I can't say a whole lot about, because my CIA training taught me to be one too. I don't blame anyone for not believing me when the facts looked real bad. My actions didn't compute. And I definitely owe Tel, Izzy, and Houston an apology for gassing them. I do actually feel really bad about that. I didn't want to be responsible for any more of your friends getting hurt, but I can see that leaving was a huge mistake."

I kissed her hand again. "No one ever blamed you for what happened that night at the compound. Frank Jr. was hellbent on getting his revenge and willing to kill anyone who got in his way."

"Exactly!" The tired frown on her face didn't sit well with me.

"And as for Tel, Izzy, and Houston. Don't worry about them," I smiled with wicked intent. "We all agreed that I could handle your punishment for that stunt."

"Punishment, huh?" She looked a little amused and a tad bit worried, not to mention oddly relieved.

I shrugged. "Mostly, it's bygones. But I'm never going to pass up an opportunity to get *my* hands on you."

Her sudden sigh of relief eased some of the tension in my chest. I had missed her more than I thought possible over the last two weeks.

"I don't think you need an excuse for that," she whispered, the breathless sound going right to my dick.

"Hey man, you gonna come watch the game or what?"

I turned and glared at Cash for interrupting. He had the absolute worst timing. "Or what. I'll catch the high-lights on the news."

Cash looked between us, a knowing grin suddenly splitting his face. "I'm just kidding," he snickered. "I only came up here for another round of beers and decided to mess with you. I wish you could see your face."

"Then fuck off. I'm trying to make up with my girl, so I can get laid."

"Axel," Mandy hissed, her cheeks turning pink.

Cash was walking away, laughing, and I was having a hard time holding mine in. It was probably time to cut bait and run before I said anything else that she could take the wrong way.

"C'mon, candy girl. I think it's time the two of us got out of here." I stood, started to pull her off her chair, thought better of it, and scooped her into my arms instead. "We need a fresh start and this time, I'm not taking any chances that you might try to get away."

Epilogue

Amanda

Two weeks later

I'd been lying awake for almost an hour, and I couldn't stay still any longer. I thought I could wait for the sun to come up, but that just wasn't going to happen.

I turned to face Axel and studied his beautiful face. The angles of his cheekbones, the length of his inky lashes. He looked so different when he slept. It was also one of the rare times he looked at peace. Awake, he was my own personal fireball. Always on the go, always ready to join a fight, and always ready to fuck.

I giggled. Making love might have been a more ladylike way to think about it, but it didn't fit him at all.

And somehow, he'd managed to turn me into an insatiable sex-crazed fiend right along with him.

But I think part of that had something to do with his surprise. I just hoped he would be as happy about it as I was. We'd talked briefly about it weeks ago, but nothing had come up since and now his evil plan had come true. I rubbed my still-flat belly and imagined a little black leather-wearing baby rolling around inside there.

Yes, I was acting like a giddy fool, but I didn't care. I was finally *happy,* despite all the insane twists and turns my life had taken. And we were long overdue.

I placed my hand on his thigh and slid it up to encircle his hard cock. I loved that contrast of warm, velvety skin over steel. I wasn't surprised to find him in that state since it was pretty much a given all the time with him. Although he enjoyed blaming that on me.

"What are you doing?" he asked, cracking open one eye. "I thought we were sleeping."

"Uhm, I would think that would be obvious." I laughed, squeezing him harder the way he liked it.

His hand shot out and grabbed at my nipple, which he rolled gently between his fingers. "Don't get me wrong, I love eery second I am inside you and am not going to turn down any opportunity to do so, but I thought you were exhausted?

"I was. But I guess now I'm not."

He glanced at the clock on the bedside table, and then eyed me warily. "It's only been about three hours since the last time I gave you a couple of orgasms."

I frowned and gave him a little pout. "That sounds like a complaint. Are you turning me down?"

"Fuck no." He leaned forward and sucked the nipple he'd been playing with into his mouth.

I immediately threw my head back and moaned from the pleasure of it. He thrashed my skin with his tongue, and I squirmed from the sensation that somehow felt like he was between my legs as well as at my breast. By the time he broke free, I was breathless and desperate for more.

He smiled. "Well, come on then. Show me what you've got." At that he rolled to his back lifting me so that I settled on top of him with his hardness pressed between my thighs.

"That sounds like a dare." I licked and bit at one of his nipples, then pushed at his chest until I was sitting on top of him with my legs straddling his hips.

He grinned. "Oh, it definitely is. Since you woke me up this time, I think it's only fair."

It was my turn to grin, which I quickly followed by licking my lips. My man was a literal genius when it came to oral sex, but I hadn't had much of an opportunity to develop mine.

"So let me get this right," I teased as I trailed my fingers down his chest and the hard wall of abs that were a serious thing of beauty. "You're just going to lay there, and let me do whatever I want?" My fingers reached the head of his cock and his muscles jumped when I lightly scratched my nails across his super sensitive skin.

"There is no just about it," he growled, the sound sending a shiver of need racing down my spine. "But, yes you can have your way with me—for now."

I should have laughed. It was obvious he was trying to keep this light, for a change, but the heat building between my legs and the clenching in my core were no laughing matter. My hand shifted between us as I bent forward to capture his nipple into my mouth.

When he sucked in sharply, I nearly lost my mind. My muscles quivered with need. I was never going to get enough. It would take a lifetime, and even that might not be enough.

"I love you, Axel," I breathed the words I'd kept under guard for years, not even admitting they still existed to myself. It was barely a whisper as I stared into the intensity of his eyes. "Since I was sixteen my heart has ached for this—for you. It's never going to stop."

I'd thought having to face him with what Frank had done to me would be the hardest moment of my life, but I was wrong. This moment. This laying myself bare even knowing how he felt about me left more vulnerable than I'd ever been in my life. Because nothing mattered more to me than his love and the love I already had for our child.

"Mandy," he whispered, the sound of my name causing me to shiver as it coasted across my skin. I didn't wait for his words. Since we'd made up at Bubba's he'd told me many times how he felt and showed me even more. Lifting onto my knees I kissed a trail from one nipple to the other and then down the center of his chest and across the planes of his abs.

It felt so great to worship his body for once. Eager to watch him fall apart, I cupped his heavy balls and encircled his cock with my other. The rough moan that rumbled through his chest encouraged me even more as the world and all thoughts not about him disappeared. At first I only dragged my hair across his flesh, but with my mouth watering and need riding up my spine there was only so much I could stand to drag this out.

I leaned forward and licked across his tip, collecting the pre cum on my tongue. The flavor of him exploded in my mouth. A little salty, a little spice, and a whole lot of my man. There was nothing to compare it to, because there was nothing like him in the world. And definitely nothing like this. Axel had an incredible cock, and I'd miscalculated how hard it would be not to just fall on top of him and ride this thing of beauty like a possessed wild woman.

"Is there some reason in particular you are smiling like that?" he asked. "You look like you're up to something."

"Looks don't lie," I said a second before I inhaled him, taking him as far back in my throat as I could get. Which probably wasn't that far, because he was thick. As in THICK. But I was giving it my best shot, and based on the way he suddenly grabbed my hair and cursed up a damned storm, I had to guess I was doing okay.

Spurred on by the tingle at my scalp and the

desperate way he held me, I began to move up and down his shaft, making sure to drag my tongue right along with me. I tried to use my fingers at the base to pump as well, but at this angle, my movements were kind of limited. And to say the intense pressure building between my thighs was a distraction was a massive understatement.

I swore, the moment he touched me, I was going to go off like a rocket.

"Fuck. That's so good. Make sure you get it good and wet so when I fuck you hard, you'll be able to take the whole thing on every thrust." I almost laughed. At the rate moisture was gathering, that was definitely not going to be a problem.

I doubled down on my efforts, my fingers and tongue working as hard as they could. When he swelled against my tongue and more of that salty precum landed in my mouth, I thought he might be close.

But one minute I was sucking him, and the next I was being lifted across his chest until his cock found its way to my entrance.

"Hey!" I complained.

"I know, baby. But seeing you like this. It's already driving me crazy. And I want to be inside you when I get off." His fingers were still threaded through my hair as he held me perfectly still above him. "Coming inside you. There's just nothing like it."

"It's potent," I agreed, almost spilling my secret.

"Kiss me quick, before you start riding my dick. I

have a feeling once you get started there's going to be no holding back." He was right about that.

I stretched forward, he pressed his mouth to mine, and followed that up with a sweep of his tongue with just the right amount of pressure to make me want to swoon. He didn't seem to do anything half hearted and I fell head first into the most magnificent kiss of my life. I loved him so much, it was all I could think.

By the time we broke apart, my lips tingled and my head swam. "No fair," I whispered. "I thought I was going to be in control."

"Candy girl, you're about to ride my dick with me underneath you. That's pretty in control."

I laughed as a heady feeling bubbled up in my chest. It was only when his hands cupped my ass and squeezed, causing me to gasp, that I resumed a normal-ish train of thought. If normal was me thinking it was time to get fucked. In a very good way. I slid backwards and rubbed him through my folds and closer to my entrance.

His hiss of pleasure swept through me, carrying me into a new river of desire, making it impossible to wait any longer. If he tried to stop me now and wait, I was going to get my gun.

Slowly, I sank down the entire length of his cock until our bodies met and he felt impossibly deep. "Oh my God," I groaned, biting my lip. I watched his eyes as we stayed there for a moment so I could adjust to him stretching me before he squeezed my ass once again and urged me back up.

"You're so fucking wet, I just glide right in. Do you have any idea how fucking good that feels?"

"Uhh, yeah," I panted, trying to catch my breath before I lifted from him again.

"Harder this time, baby," he whispered. "Just do it."

I lifted one more time until barely his tip stayed inside, I hovered there a moment until his hands went to my hips and grabbed them tight. I was seriously about to go out of my mind.

"Ready," he asked. "Let's do this one together. Three—"

I didn't wait for his count. I plunged down as hard as I could, taking all of him in one sweet moment of friction that nearly shot me into the stratosphere. The little explosions along my nerve endings made me scream with ecstasy.

"Holy fuck," he breathed through clenched teeth. His eyes were wide open and fastened on mine, but they looked as dazed and confused as I felt. How could it be even better than just a few hours ago. He'd given me multiple orgasms and nearly made me pass out. And now this...

I definitely wanted more of this.

"Look at your gorgeous tits." He leaned forward and bit one of my nipples a little harder than usual, making me squeal. "They're fucking sensitive. You don't even want to know what kind of ideas that gives me."

Since I could well imagine, I moved again to distract him. Which I don't think worked because he let go of my ass and used his fingers to twist and torment my nipples which were already a little sore. However, that sweet bite of pain added a little something extra along with the drag of his cock across my clit as I rocked back and forth, and before I knew it...

"I can feel your little pussy rippling around me." He wrapped his arms around me and pulled me to his chest, for the most part taking over. "Are you going to come for me?" he asked, taking me a little harder and a lot faster than I'd managed.

I was, but I couldn't manage words. All I could do was moan into his throat as the myriad of sensations took over my body. I was going to detonate, any second, from all the pressure inside me.

"Come on baby, ride my cock. Show it who's boss." I tried to laugh, but only managed a grunt as we moved in tandem, rubbing my clit across the steel length of his cock while he made sure each thrust went as deep as possible.

But when he shifted his hips one more time and slid deep at a slightly different angle, well, that did me in. I screamed from the intensity of the pleasure, my eyes squeezing tight, and my mind fracturing into a million shards of light behind my lids.

My muscles screwed so tight on him, I could barely breathe, as my entire body throbbed and pulsated from head to toe. Even my toenails tingled. I was paralyzed in pleasure, and all I could do was feel all of it. The wet heat between our bodies made our skin stick together, the sensation of being so full my muscles couldn't contract the way they wanted to, and the wild thump of my heart in my chest feeling like it might burst from happiness.

"Fuuucccckkkk!"

I wasn't sure if that meant he had joined me in this out-of-control firestorm because my brain refused to register much of anything. Even my ability to think or speak seemed frozen.

By the time I finally came down from the most mind-blowing experience of my life, I found Axel chuckling below me.

"Why are you laughing?" I asked through my pants.

"I don't even fucking know. I'm so confused and elated and fucking lucky. I don't know what you did, but holy shit. What the hell just happened?"

I smiled wide through the sound of our harsh breaths and his ramblings. It was true. I couldn't remember ever experiencing anything quite like that. I'd woken from a dead sleep and a really good dream.

And I'd been horny to the extreme. Maybe the dream...

"Oh my God," I said, a fit of giggles coming over me. They caught fire and I couldn't stop until I had tears streaming from my eyes.

"Okay, it probably wasn't that funny," he said, wiping the hair off my face and hopefully ignoring the mess I'd made of my face with all the tears.

"That's only because you don't get it. Not yet."

He arched an eyebrow at me. "Care to enlighten me?"

I took a deep breath. Okay, I guess I was really going

to do this. It was time to let the cat out of the bag and hope for the best.

"Pregnant women sometimes get really horny from all the extra hormones. It's something I read about online." I stared down at him, waiting for his reaction.

It took an extra second or two, but then his eyes widened. "Come again? Are you saying that you're pregnant and that means you need more sex?"

I nodded, biting my lips to contain the grin threatening to bust loose. "Yes. I took the test as soon as I woke up. It's in the bathroom."

"Well, fuck me," he said, a huge grin spreading across his face. "You're pregnant. And you're sure?"

My smile faltered a fraction at his question as I pushed up from his chest straddling his waist where we were still connected. "Well, as sure as I can be with a home pregnancy test. I'll have to make an appointment with a doctor to confirm it. But considering we haven't been using any protection, it's not exactly surprising."

He raked his eyes up and down my body, another smile creeping over him. "Pregnant and horny. I feel like I just hit the fucking jackpot. I need a shower and some food before I can be ready to go again. Do you think you can wait that long?"

I swatted at him as he rolled us and trapped me underneath him. "Don't be an asshole."

He laughed at my assessment. "I'm your asshole, candy girl." He pressed his mouth to mine and then trailed his lips down my neck. When he hit a sensitive spot, I couldn't hold back my giggle.

"I thought we were going to take a shower?"

"I said I was going to take a shower. I rather like the mess you are right now."

I wrinkled up my nose. "But I've got—"

He swooped down and caught my mouth in a powerful kiss once again. His lips were soft and rigid while his tongue almost demanding as it swept in and tangled with mine.

"Me all over you," he growled. "I like marking you like that."

My stomach fluttered at his words and the near feral look in his eyes. I didn't know what I was supposed to say to that. I probably shouldn't like that he said it.

"Uhm, Axel?"

"Yeah, candy girl?" he asked, his lips hovering just above mine.

"How long, again?"

His laughter filled the room and as he slipped from my body, I managed to hold back my complaint—barely. He didn't realize it yet, but he was going to be very busy—forever.

———

One week later

Axel

Someone was pounding on my door, and I was going to kill them. Each slam of a fist against the wood sliced into my head as I dragged myself out of bed.

"Who is it?" Mandy asked.

"Go back to sleep, baby. I'll take care of it," I murmured in her hair as I gave her a quick kiss. She needed the rest. Our visit to the doctor the day before had indeed confirmed the pregnancy, and since then I'd been worried about her.

She ignored me and slid from the other side of the bed, reaching for the t-shirt I'd thrown on the floor just a few hours ago when I'd stripped her naked. She'd said pregnancy hormones made her horny so what was my excuse? Since telling me about the baby, I'd spent every waking moment possible getting inside her.

"What are you doing?"

"I'm getting dressed. What does it look like?"

I frowned, shaking my head. "You need your rest."

"So do you. So let's go see who's at the door and deal with it so we can come back to bed." I shook my head again, realizing changing her mind was going to take too long and whoever was at the door wasn't letting up.

I don't know what I had to do to get some damned privacy back around here.

I left her in the bedroom, stomped to the front door, and yanked it open. "Do I really have to keep reminding you all to use a fucking phone and text before…"

My voice trailed off, the words dying out when I saw it was JD at the door with a half empty bottle of whiskey dangling from his fingertips.

"Heeeyyy," he slurred, that one word sounding like it came out through gravel in a blender.

"Shit."

Mandy looked over my shoulder. "I'll start some coffee."

I nodded at her briefly before turning back towards my very drunk president. "Hey, JD. What's going on?" I stepped back so he could enter.

"Been at the hospital all day visiting Bear and Sasha." The anguish in his words was so thick it sounded like they'd been ripped from his throat.

"I thought they were both making progress." Seeing JD like this worried me. Not that I hadn't seen him rip-roaring drunk before, but this was different. He looked devastated.

"Bear's doing pretty good, but Sasha..." His words trailed off as he looked away and across the compound into the dark copse of trees nearby.

"Come in inside," Mandy said quietly, slipping under my arm to take JD's hand. He looked torn, but he didn't rip his hand from hers and I took that as decent sign.

I stepped back while she led him in. I didn't think I'd ever seen him quite like this. Not even after Malia's death. And Houston's dad, accidentally shooting the love of their lives, had been a pretty horrific time. Especially for the club.

JD seemed to momentarily come into the moment and got one look at what Mandy was wearing and stopped in his tracks, forcing Mandy to stop too.

"Were you sleeping?" He was used to me and my insane sleep schedule. For as long as I could remember I never slept for more than a few hours at a time and I was always available for JD night or day.

"Yeah," she admitted. "But we can sleep later. I want to hear about Bear and Sasha. I've been thinking about them a lot and meaning to get to the hospital to visit them."

"Bear would probably like that. You really seemed to impress him the day of the race. Sasha though—" His face darkened, and I could see whatever was troubling him the most centered around her. I'd known this day would come. Not that she would be almost killed, but that he would eventually realize she meant something to him and that it would throw him into chaos. I only wish the circumstances were better so I could enjoy it more.

"Is she not doing well?"

"She won't allow me in her room. But I have a doctor on payroll who keeps me apprised of her condition. I'm not sure if he's telling me the whole story or not though. He says she should pull through, but that her injuries are extensive. That if she makes it then she has months of healing and skin grafts or something ahead of her."

That pit in my stomach that appeared anytime I thought of finding her in that building, her clothing already on fire, grew about ten times at the news. "I should have gotten there soo—"

"No!" JD roared. "That is not why I came here. You are at no fault." He turned to Amanda too, where her face looked a little ashen as well. "Or you! Listen up, because I do not want to repeat myself. The only fucker or fuckers responsible are either dead or sneaking around this club pretending to be loyal. Neither of you is to blame." He turned back to me. "You saved her life. By all rights, she should have ended up in the morgue right alongside the governor's aide, and would have, if not for you. Got it?"

I nodded and Mandy followed suit. Although I sure as fuck didn't feel like some kind of savior. I should have spent a little more time investigating this bullshit instead of worrying about whether Mandy could be trusted.

"Wait?" My brain finally seemed to catch up with all of his words. "You still think we have a traitor in our midst?"

Anger flashed in his eyes a second before they narrowed. "It sure as fuck seems like it. Tel is adamant that no one outside the club could have gotten through his security to plant those goddamned explosives. And while I'm not naive and I know nothing is fool-proof in this world, I've got a bad feeling in my gut that won't go away. I'm missing something important and I intend to figure out what or who it is."

The idea of investigating my own club brothers made my stomach twist. Loyalty is everything here and each one of us knew that. A traitor? Fuck, my blood was already boiling just thinking it might be possible.

"How are you going to figure out who it is?" Mandy asked. I looked over at her and could already see the gears of her beautiful, complex mind working on the problem.

"That's why I came here. I want you to work with Tel to figure it out. Just the four of us will know what's going on behind the scenes until we figure this shit out."

"Uhm—"

He shook his head. "I know you aren't about to tell me you already have a job. You have skills I need for this, and I pay a hell of a lot better than a cleaning company can."

She looked up at me and I could see the excitement in her eyes. She wanted the job. Her entire body practically vibrated with it as she fidgeted moving, from foot to foot from thinking about it. Part of me wanted to say no. She was pregnant and the last place she needed to be was in danger. I also knew that I couldn't tell her what to do. That would be a sure fire way to not only get my ass kicked, but for her to tell me to fuck off.

"I was going to say I'd committed to cleaning cabins. But it's not the job I care about. It's the fact that Mike went out of his way to get me the job and a place to live. His mom took me in no questions asked and I know how hard it's been for her to keep employees."

"Mike? Who the hell is Mike?" I asked, my eyes narrowing that I'd heard nothing about this Mike before now.

"Firefighter Mike. Remember from the night of the explosion? He found out I was in the hospital and he visited me."

"Well, Mike can fu—" I stopped short at the head signal JD gave me that was his way of saying, shut the hell up. When Mandy's hands hit her hips I knew I'd been about to go too far. "We can talk about it later."

My jaw clenched, but I let it go.

JD shook his head. "Give her whatever notice makes you feel okay with it, I don't care. This isn't a situation we are likely to resolve in a couple of days. If someone is fucking us over they have been hiding it well. The job isn't going to be a cake walk."

Mandy raised her brow and I barely bit back my bark of laughter. Prez knew just the words to light her fire. He was playing her like a damned musical instrument.

She looked over at me and I nodded. She would have my full support in whatever choice she made. At least if she worked on the compound, I could make sure she took care of herself and her and Tel slaving behind a computer screen would not be as physically taxing as her scrubbing toilets and her traipsing up and down the mountains. I'd assign a prospect to her after Tel and I dug through their backgrounds again. No prospect had access to compound security and wouldn't likely be our traitor, but with her, I couldn't be too careful.

"I'm going to need at least three weeks."

"Done. Come to the clubhouse tomorrow for lunch. We'll go over the details. Then, if you and Tel want to work on anything in your off time, you can."

"That sounds great," she said, her smile growing wide.

"You probably shouldn't be putting in too many

hours," I started before she cut me a sharp look. I raised my hands in surrender, taking a step back.

"Is there something going on I should know about?" JD seemed confused as he looked between the two of us.

I stepped around him so I could pull my woman into my arms. I stepped behind her, winding my arms around her waist and resting my palms on her stomach. God, I couldn't wait to see her belly grow with our child. It was going to be the most beautiful thing in the world.

"Are you saying—"

She nodded her head. I couldn't see her smile, but I could practically feel her beaming.

"Well, shit. That's fucking great news. Does this mean you two finally settled things between you?"

"Yes," I said.

"Probably not," she disagreed.

Now it was mine turn to shake my head and laugh. "We're going to get married soon."

"What?" She whipped around to look at me. "No, we're not. You didn't even ask me yet."

JD started laughing. "I think on that note, I'm going to head home."

"Wait. I was going to make you coffee. I want to hear more."

"I don't need coffee. I need Gatorade, aspirin, and some sleep. I'm too old for this shit."

"You're not old" Mandy insisted.

"Either way. I just came to give you a heads up on

Bear since it's going to be a while before he can return to work. You'll need to adjust the schedule, and we need to get one of our contractors on board for the rebuild. I want to be back open for business as soon as possible."

"Agreed. I'll get to work on it first thing in the morning."

JD nodded and turned toward the door. "I figured you would." He sounded more tired than drunk now. "Take care of that baby and its momma. They are the most important thing you'll ever do in this life." With that, he disappeared through the door and I made a mental note to go to the hospital and see if I could talk to Sasha. Not being able to see her was going to eat him alive.

"You think he's okay?" Mandy whispered after the door closed behind JD.

"He's been through worse. He'll figure it out —eventually."

"I hope you're right." She turned and pressed her face to my chest. I gripped her tight and plastered her body to mine. This right here. It was the best damned feeling in the world.

"I love you, candy girl."

"I love you too," she hesitated. "Daddy." A deep laugh rumbled through my chest. Fuck, but she was so it for me. Her head popped up and her gaze met mine. "But…We are so not getting married."

"Yeah, we are." I swatted her ass and then scooped her into my arms and carried her back to bed where I dropped her on the mattress and dove after her. "You'll see."

Turns out…

I was right.

Thanks for reading Cruel Savior. Would you like to see more of Axel and Mandy? Not only will they be with the rest of the club in the next book, *Scorched King* (available for preorder now) but you can **sign up for my newsletter on my website at emgayle.com/ newsletter to receive a bonus epilogue.**

Also by E.M. Gayle

CONTEMPORARY ROMANCE

Mafia Mayhem Duet Series:

MERCILESS SINNER

SINNER TAKES ALL

WICKED BEAST

WILLING BEAUTY

BROKEN SAINT

FALLEN ANGEL

Outlaw Justice Series:

SAVAGE PROTECTOR

RECKLESS PAWN

RUTHLESS REDEMPTION

Sins of Wrath MC:

CRUEL SAVIOR

SCORCHED KING

VICIOUS DEFENDER

Purgatory Masters Series:

TUCKER'S FALL

LEVI'S ULTIMATUM

MASON'S RULE

GABE'S OBSESSION

GABE'S RECKONING

Purgatory Club:

ROPED

WATCH ME

TEASED

BURN

BOTTOMS UP

HOLD ME CLOSE

Pleasure Playground Series:

PLAY WITH ME

POWER PLAY

Single Title:

TAMING BEAUTY

WICKED CHRISTMAS EVE

Books Writing As Eliza Gayle

Southern Shifters Series:

DIRTY SEXY FURRY

MATE NIGHT

ALPHA KNOWS BEST

BAD KITTY

BE WERE

SHIFTIN' DIRTY

BEAR NAKED TRUTH

ALPHA BEAST

ONE CRAZY WOLF

Enigma Shifters:

DRAGON MATED

WOLF BAITED

BEARLY DATED

WOLF TEMPTED

Devils Point Wolves:

WILD

WICKED

WANTED

FERAL

FIERCE

FURY

Single titles:

VAMPIRE AWAKENING

WITCH AND WERE

Printed in Great Britain
by Amazon